P9-CMA-997

Skinny
DIPPING
With
MURDER

Skinny DIPPING With MURDER

Auralee Wallace

St. Martin's Paperbacks

This is a work of fiction. All of the characters, organizations, and events portrayed in this novel are either products of the author's imagination or are used fictitiously.

SKINNY DIPPING WITH MURDER

Copyright © 2016 by Auralee Wallace.

For information address St. Martin's Press, 175 Fifth Avenue, New York, NY 10010.

ISBN: 978-1-250-07777-6

Printed in the United States of America

St. Martin's Paperbacks edition / March 2016

St. Martin's Paperbacks are published by St. Martin's Press, 175 Fifth Avenue, New York, NY 10010.

10 9 8 7 6 5 4 3 2 1

To Hector and Andrea

Acknowledgments

First, I would like to express my gratitude to Holly Ingraham at St. Martin's Paperbacks and to my agent, Natalie Lakosil, for making a home for Erica Bloom. Thanks to my parents, friends, and extended family for their day-to-day support—with a special shout-out to my sister for her social media gusto and to Christine for taking the time to turn her ever-watchful eye in my manuscript's direction. I would also like to send my undying gratitude to Andrea. After all, nothing much happens without Andrea—she's the one who coaxes me out from under the bed when it all seems too much. And finally, to my husband and three children, you always have my deepest love and appreciation. You guys are the best.

Chapter One

Any minute now.

Any minute I'd hear the distant hum of my mother's boat. I glanced at my watch as the dock swayed gently beneath my feet. Now if I could just believe that, maybe the vein in my forehead would stop throbbing.

I scanned the distant shoreline. Home. Otter Lake, in New Hampshire, "Live Free or Die." Camp country. Our town had everything the postcards promised. Long docks stretching into the water. Nights with a billion stars. Rustic cabins nestled into pines. Summers were spent on the lake and winters on the snowmobile trail. Paradise for some fourteen hundred citizens. For me? Well, let's just say Freud would have had his hands full helping me figure that one out.

The walk from the bus stop had taken less than ten minutes, but it had left me drenched with gritty sweat. Even though the lowering sun was dragging the day into late afternoon, it was still stinking hot. I stood at the edge of the dock, staring longingly at the water. Sure, it smelled faintly of rotting fish and lake muck, but it had to be cooler than the heavy air.

Summer at the lake. Happy words, right? Cicadas buzzing. Midnight swims. Crackling campfires. So that had to be excitement I felt in my belly . . . yeah, butterflies just barfing with excitement.

The sun forced me down to sit on the edge of my suitcase, and I counted fifteen minutes tick by on my watch. I thought again about my cell, but I already knew it was a lost cause. The battery had died about six hours back.

I should have seen this coming.

My mother. Summer Bloom. A woman who loved me with a passion that could only be described as delusional. A woman who raised motherhood to a level of mythic proportions. And a woman who could never seem to remember I was sitting somewhere at the end of a dock waiting for her.

In her defense, details were not her thing. She'd leave herself sitting on a dock too.

At first glance, it would probably surprise a lot of people to know that my mother had an instinct for business, but it was the truth. Women from all across the world flocked to my mother's island retreat, Earth, Moon, and Stars, to get in touch with their inner goddesses, and it was all because of her authenticity. In fact, my mother's inner goddess was so robust, I'm pretty sure she'd absorbed mine in utero like some parasitic twin.

I gathered the hair slicked against my neck and twisted it into a ponytail. The view of the distant trees rippled in the heat as my eyes stayed focused on the spot from which my mother's boat should emerge.

Back when I was a teenager, this was the type of thing that really would have bothered me, but I was an adult now. So what if it had been almost eight years since I'd been home, and it took about twelve hours of traveling for me to get to this very spot? This was part of the *being home* experience . . . and it wasn't like I was stranded.

I looked over the edge of the platform to the canoe knocking lazily against the stakes of the dock. Normally, my mom paid Red, Otter Lake's local electrician, whose hair hadn't seen red in about thirty years, to cart the retreat's guests back and forth in his pontoon. Red liked to keep busy, and even though he wasn't much for small talk, he probably would have done the job for free. My mother left the canoe for the times when Red wasn't available. That's the type of place Otter Lake was. I suppose someone could have stolen it. But why?

I sighed heavily, hot breath streaming through my lips.

I could do this.

I just needed to see my mom, do the one mysterious favor that apparently only I could do to save her business, stay off the lake radar, and get the hell back to Chicago.

That's right.

Mysterious favor.

Not many sane people would travel across the country without knowing the reason why. But those people probably didn't have recurring nightmares of their mothers practicing Wiccan rituals in their one-bedroom apartments because said mother got booted off the island . . . literally.

Then I heard it.

A motor humming in the distance.

I jumped up from the suitcase, ignoring the sweat dripping down the backs of my calves.

She had remembered. This was a good sign. Maybe things had changed. A lot of time had passed.

A second or two later, my stomach sank as I watched a slick boat bounce its way across the lake, chrome finishings glinting in the sunlight.

Not my mother.

Things at the lake definitely had changed. Nobody I used to know could afford that kind of boat.

Slowly three hazy figures came into view.

No.

It couldn't be.

It just couldn't.

I was a good person.

"Hey!" a voice shouted. "Boobsie Bloom!"

I closed my eyes.

This *was* happening.

"Hey guys," I called back, squinting underneath the hand I had shielding my eyes. Yup, a little thicker all over, but it was definitely them.

The three fluffateers. Actually the first part of that name was another f-word—their choice—but it was best not to think too deeply on that.

Any hope I had that things around the lake had changed faded before the vision of grubby baseball hats and tank tops drooped over fledgling beer bellies.

"We heard you were back, and just in time for the Raspberry Social."

That was Tommy, leader of the three and Grady Forrester's cousin.

Who's Grady? Only the guy every girl was in love with back in high school, myself unfortunately included. He was beautiful back then. Cartoon-prince beautiful—not the kind who likes glass slippers and balls, but the kind who's a bit of a jerk, and a starburst dings off his teeth every time he smiles. Yup, everyone in Otter Lake had at least one story of a near miss with a moose, and all the single females? Well, they'd all had at least one head-on collision with Grady Forrester. Mine had been nearly fatal . . . metaphorically speaking. Tommy looked a lot like

Grady, but was nowhere near as good-looking. I could only imagine that must have stung a little.

"Yup, here I am," I said, struggling to keep my voice neutral, adult.

A loud belch blared in response.

Dickie. Less evil than Tommy, but more perverted.

"This calls for a beer! Here's to Boobsie Bloom being back in town." All three cracked open a can and chugged in unison. I'd like to say I was shocked by the drinking and boating, but I'm not that good of an actress.

"Thanks, guys. That's, uh, real sweet, but should I be calling you in?"

Dickie slapped his beer over the right side of his chest. "Nonalcoholic. Swear to God."

The vein in my forehead throbbed again.

"Right." I bent slightly at the waist and grabbed the handle of my suitcase. "Well, it was great seeing you guys, but—"

"Erica Bloom, where are your manners? We were just catching up. The eight-year anniversary of that fateful night is almost here. It can't go by unnoticed." Tommy smiled and elbowed his minions. "Men, let's take a moment to remember that special night from so many years ago and pay it the respect it deserves." All three whipped off their hats and held them to their chests.

I was trying to hide the fact that they were getting to me. I really was. But they knew. I might as well have had steam coming out of my ears. And when I saw the amused glint in Tommy's eyes, I also knew I couldn't stop what was coming next.

"Look out, boys! She's going to blow!"

And there it was.

The nightmare chant of my childhood.

I had almost forgotten.

I'm not going to say I left home and completely rein-
vented myself . . . but I left home and completely rein-
vented myself. And then within minutes of being back, all
my hard work was gone. I swear, you bite one kid on the
shoulder in the first grade after he calls your mom a space
cadet, and suddenly your anger becomes legendary. And
yes, that one kid was Tommy.

I pointed at him and laughed halfheartedly. "Good
memory, Tommy. That's me. Watch out. I might blow." I
caught myself giving some warning jazz hands.

God, make it stop.

All three laughed, shooting looks of admiration back
and forth.

No. No. This was not happening. I was not the Erica
Bloom of all those years ago. I would not be baited by
beer-swilling man-boys who'd left their best years back in
high school. I was a calm, confident woman—who needed
to end this conversation now.

"Aw, don't look so sad, Bloom. We're messing with
you," Tommy said, putting on a pouty smile. "In fact, if
we had known all of that business at the social would
make you leave, well, we might not have done it." He
paused for a second then slapped the other two on the
shoulders. "Who am I kidding? We totally would have
done it."

My face burned hotter. "You know that's not why I left,
right, Tommy? I—" I caught myself just as that slow Grady
smile slid, once again, across Tommy's face.

That settled it.

It didn't matter that I could feel blood pulsing behind
my eyeballs. I was better than this. I would not let these
guys faze me.

"You know what, Tommy?" I said, inhaling hot air
through my nose. "It was pretty funny."

"What? That's it?" Tommy looked at me sideways, smiled, and turned his bare shoulder toward me before chomping his teeth together.

I'll admit it. Things could have gone badly for me in that moment. I saw myself launching off the end of the dock. I saw me clotheslining Tommy into the water. I saw me going to jail for his semiaccidental drowning. And yet, it still seemed worth it. But then I heard, "I like your hair, Erica."

Harry.

Sweet, sweet Harry.

The third fluffateer. He was the nicest of the three and had always been taken with a nice head of hair—especially his own. It was probably a good thing that his parents hadn't been the ones to choose the name Dickie.

"The dark brown goes really well with your blue eyes," he said, cocking his head. Unlike the other two with their baseball caps, he wore a fishing hat covered with lures. "And the bangs and ponytail? They are *so* happy. Totally happy. Happy hair." He chuckled to himself.

Harry. Always so sweet . . . and so high.

I was just about to say thank you when Dickie jumped in.

"No, I liked that bleached-blond thing you used to do," he said. "You could have done porn with that hair." He had the face of a man who had given this some thought.

Suddenly I realized I was knee-deep in water yanking at the rope that tethered the canoe to the dock. Hmm, I didn't remember leaving the dock. Great, now I was experiencing stress-induced blackouts.

"Okay, guys. It's been great catching up, but you must have stuff to do?"

All three stared back at me blankly.

"Jobs?"

Nothing.

"Children? I mean, all of that unprotected . . ."

Silence.

"Never mind. Okay, well, my mom's expecting me, so . . ."

"We'll give you a ride, won't we, boys?" Tommy said, slapping the other two with the back of his hands. They nodded like puppets.

"That's sweet. Great boat by the way. But you know, I've been gone so long. I miss canoeing. Not much of that in Chicago. You understand."

"Sure. Sure," Tommy replied, nodding. "But before we go, you're coming to the social, right?"

I tried to smile, but I probably just managed to look nauseous.

"No, nope, no. I'm only staying the week. I have to be back at work before then." That was a total lie. I had about three months of vacation days saved up. I was a stenographer back in Chicago, and for the most part, I liked it. Life made sense in court. Stupid people got punished in court. Stupid people who weren't me.

"Well, if you change your mind . . ."

A paper airplane shot out of Tommy's hand. The point hit me right between the eyes before I could bat it away. I tried to ignore the sound of high fives as I unfolded the yellow sheet of paper.

All the particulars of the social glared back at me in bold type, but my eyes zoomed in on the cartoon character hastily drawn on the bottom left-hand corner. It was a beaver posed as a pinup model wearing a raspberry-print bikini and a knit hat.

I could feel even more blood rushing to my face.

"We worked really hard on it," Dickie said.

Tommy nodded. "It looks like you. Don't you think?"

I barely managed a weak laugh.

"You sure you don't want a ride?" Harry asked. "You don't look so good."

"No, I'm great. Super, in fact. Just super."

"Well then, later, Boobsie," Tommy said.

The boat's engine roared to life, and Tommy's *up to no good* smile slid back across his face. My brain hooked on some memories and tried to pull them into focus in time, but they didn't quite make it. Before I could duck, the boat fishtailed away, sending a fabulous spray of water smack into my face.

Forty-five minutes later, I guided the canoe alongside the dock leading up to the retreat.

I rested the paddle across my thighs as I took in the view. Tiger lilies framed logs dug into the hill forming steps leading up to the main house. Cedars and pines gave shade to the steep slopes on either side. Little had been done to the property or the cabins since it was built in the fifties, so it gave off a sleepy sense of nature mixed with nostalgia. I had watched hundreds of female visitors stand at the bottom of those steps and, within seconds, their shoulders would drop and smiles would spread wide across their faces. For me, it was a little different. As a kid, I swear every time I climbed those steps, someone in the forest was whispering, *chi chi chi ah ah ah.*

I quickly pulled the canoe onto the shore and grabbed my suitcase. I then hustled over to the stairs. The sooner I got there, the sooner I could leave.

At the top, I dropped my suitcase to wipe the sweat from my face.

The main lodge stood a couple hundred feet away. The same faded gravel path ran right up to the roughly hewn front steps, and the same overgrown hydrangeas still nestled up against the sturdy wraparound porch, softening the heavy feel of lumber.

So cute. So forest-friendly. So terrifying.

Behind the lodge, twelve cabins dotted the woods. As far as I knew, only five were in working order. And by working order, I mean didn't leak. None of the cabins had electricity or plumbing. Just beds, curtains, and the sweet smell of cedar. More pebbled paths led from each cabin to a communal washroom outfitted with three composting toilets and three showers connected to tanks filled with sun-warmed water. When I was twelve, I made a vow never to use those toilets, not even in an emergency. A dock spider crawling into your sandal will do that.

I rolled the handle of my suitcase in my palm.

Eight years.

I was going to see my mom for the first time in eight years.

The sun made its final dip below the horizon behind me, cooling my clothes damp with sweat.

It wasn't like I didn't talk to her. She called me every other day at least.

And I never meant for it to be eight years, but all that time had just kind of built up. My mom would have come to visit me, but travel wasn't exactly her thing. Airplanes were filled with radiation, apparently. Buses, toxic fumes. And after much debate, she reluctantly agreed that hitchhiking probably wasn't the best option. Truth be told, I think maybe we were playing a game of chicken. I didn't want to come back to Otter Lake, and my mother really, really did want me to come back to Otter Lake—and for more than just a visit. We both had been holding out to see who would crack first. Guess that had been me. As I watched the first few bats swoop and dip around the roof of the lodge, loads of *what ifs* began to jostle around in my head. What if she looked different? Really different? What if she had aged? I mean, of course she must have aged, but I was not at all comfortable with that idea.

A light clicked on, illuminating one of the big windows of the lodge. I took a few steps closer.

A figure walked across the room.

There she was.

Her hair was a lighter shade of brown than mine but never could be thought of as mousy. There was too much of it for that. Tonight she had it parted down the middle with two barrettes on either side holding back the waves from her face. We shared the same color eyes, but hers were large and round, giving her the look of someone who was perpetually innocent and slightly startled.

I exhaled slowly in relief. She looked exactly as I had left her—a bewildered, misplaced flower child who had found the fountain of youth in veganism and yoga.

A sudden rustling in the hydrangeas snapped me out of my thoughts. A pair of glowing eyes flashed menacingly at me from beneath the heart-shaped leaves.

"Oh, you can't be serious," I muttered to no one.

An enormously fat, orange and white cat shuffled out from beneath the branches.

We stared at one another.

I broke first.

"How are you not dead?"

The cat hissed back at me then turned with the gravitational pull of a medium-sized planet and made his way toward the porch.

Caesar was the closest thing I had to a sibling . . . a sibling I never wanted and would have happily drowned at birth given half a chance. I sighed. Years back I had added Caesar to the list of things I would not discuss with my mother. Also on that list were the quality of my bowel movements and the importance of the female orgasm.

The main door swung open.

"There you are!" My mother rushed through the threshold, arms flung wide.

I couldn't stop the smile from erupting on my face. "Are you talking to me or the cat?"

My mother's eyes darted about the porch until they landed on the fur-leviathan mounting the final stair. "Caesar, how did you get outside? You know you aren't supposed to be out here after dark."

The giant beast rubbed against my mom's leg, nearly toppling her.

"I know. You're a good boy."

Caesar croaked at her in return. He always had sounded like a fifty-year-old with a bad smoking habit.

"Still here, Mom."

"Erica," my mother said, gliding down the steps in her flowing sundress. "My wonderful girl." Then I was in her arms, face smothered by her masses of hair.

"Hi," I said through the thick aroma of lemon grass, mint, and mom.

She rocked me back and forth. "I sensed you coming. Just now when I was doing my evening gratitude prayer."

Suddenly a new voice called out. "Hah! Too bad she didn't sense you on the dock!"

I looked over to a dark spot on the porch to spy the women I knew were there.

"Oh, no," my mother said, leaning back and covering her mouth with the tips of her fingers. "The dock!"

"Hi, Kit Kat," I called out to the darkness. "Hi, Tweety." I could barely make out their white permed curls shuddering with laughter.

Kit Kat and Tweety were identical twins, who had to

be in their early seventies by now. They lived in the only other cottage on our almost thirty-acre island and were built like wrestlers. They smoked, drank, and lived by the belief that if you didn't have to kill it, why would you want to eat it? They also found everything my mother did hilarious. They never got tired of it. One of my earliest memories is an image of the two of them rocking with laughter, arms crossed over their bellies.

"Let me look at you." My mom's eyes moved over my face, taking in every inch. The eight-year punch of guilt got me in the stomach. "You look tired."

"It was a long trip."

"Well, come inside. I've got a new blend of tea that will fix you right up. Your room is exactly the same."

She led me by the arm toward the steps.

"That sounds great, but I thought we could have a little chat first."

My mother turned to me, eyebrows lifted. "About what?"

"About why I'm here . . . exactly."

Chapter Two

"You have got to be kidding me."

"I don't understand why you're so upset." My mother always used a baby voice when she thought she was in trouble, but now its pitch was reaching a level of innocence that even a newborn couldn't live up to.

I half growled, half sighed. "You don't understand why I'm upset. You don't understand why I'm upset?" I hadn't realized how tightly I was gripping my mug until Tweety leaned across the harvest table and splashed a shot of gin from her flask into it. "Well, Mom, let me help you understand. For starters, insurance fraud is illegal."

"Fraud? Who said anything about fraud?"

"You did. Just now," I said, leaning in and jabbing my finger on the table. "Mom. I'm a stenographer. I've seen people go away twenty years for less."

"I'm sure you're exaggerating. And Erica, honey, I hope you don't get this upset over every little thing. It isn't good for you. Let's take a break and do some stretches." She grabbed her ankle and pulled her leg to the sky. "Or a swim! When's the last time you skinny-dipped?"

"Mom, put your leg down. You know I hate it when you stretch in the middle of a conversation. And, no, I don't want to go skinny-dipping with you." Both Tweety and Kit Kat started snorting from across the table. I shot them death glares.

"Baby. I didn't know what else to do. Marla left without giving me any notice. How was I to know the insurance group required me to have a licensed mental health professional to supervise *every* therapy session?"

"Um, because it's your business to know."

"I don't think I like your tone." Her hand flew to her chest to cover her heart while she leaned forward. "And this is not a business. This is the jour—"

"—ney of your life. I know. I know." I thunked my forehead against the surface of the table then rocked my head from side to side. It wasn't lost on me that I was an almost twenty-seven-year-old acting like a child, but I couldn't seem to stop my behavior any more than my mom could stop hers. "I'm not a licensed professional, Mom."

"What's that, sweetheart?"

I flung my head back up. "I am not a licensed professional."

"You took that psychology course. I remember."

Don't scream. Don't scream. You look like the crazy one if you scream.

"One course. Online," I said carefully, jaw tight. "I'm pretty sure that's not going to satisfy your insurance company."

"Well, you're smart enough to be a psychologist."

I threw my hands in the air and shook them. "That's not the same thi—"

"And don't worry," she said, shaking her head, mounds of hair quavering about her face. "I've already told them all about you."

I pressed my lips together then pulled them apart with a loud smacking sound. "You told them I'm a stenographer?"

"I told them you worked for the Justice Department."

I paused a beat before answering. "They think I'm a court-appointed psychologist, don't they?"

"Well," my mother said, smoothing her fingertips over her forehead, "I'm a bit clairvoyant, but I'm no psychic."

Laughter puffed out of the geriatric twins' lips.

"Great. That's just great, Mom."

"You're overreacting. It's only for a week. Two at most. I already have a great list of potential replacements. It will be fine."

"One week. I'm staying one week. And if the whole thing is just one big lie, why do I even need to be here? Why not just pretend I'm here?"

"Well, you are my daughter. I miss you, and I wanted to see you," she replied, giving me puppy-dog eyes.

"No." I pointed a finger at her. "Don't do that."

"And," she said, drawing the word out. "We'll have witnesses to prove you were here if they ask."

"That . . . that makes a frightening amount of sense." I rubbed my forehead with one hand and took a long drag of the gin-filled tea from the mug I held in the other. I then exhaled noisily through my mouth.

She smiled sweetly.

"I'm not saying I'm going to do this," I said, ignoring the part of my brain that was screaming in protest, "but I suppose you're not a big concern to the insurance company." I wasn't sure where I was going with this, but the guilt was pushing me to at least explore the idea. "I mean, it's not like they're going to take the time to send someone out here to check up on us."

"Well—"

"Mom!"

"Erica, the agent I was speaking to was so friendly," she said quickly. "And she's going through a tough time. Recently divorced. So I thought it might be nice for her to come to this week's retreat." She fanned out her hands as though reading an invisible marquee. "I'm calling it, 'We hath mo' healing for the woman scorned.'"

Pinpoints of light exploded at the back of my eyes. I looked over at Kit Kat and Tweety. They both shook with silent laughter, arms folded across their bellies. I took a second to silently wish hernias on the two of them.

"Erica, honey, are you okay? You seem really stressed."

Noisy guffaws finally sprang out from the twins' mouths.

"You know, I am a little stressed." I slammed both hands on the table and pushed my chair back. "I think I'm going to go to bed."

"Okay, honey."

I walked toward the darkened hallway ignoring my mom's whispered voice asking, "Do you think she's mad?"

I didn't exactly dream that night. It was more like I was trapped in a dark room with a tinny soundtrack of old women laughing. At some point that laughter turned into the caw of a blue jay, and I knew I was awake.

I blinked open my eyes to find Caesar staring at me from the floor.

That was new.

Our entire lives, Caesar and I had fought over this bed. A few times when I was younger, I slept on the living room couch because he wouldn't move, and I liked the skin on my arms too much to make him. He would never give up this easily.

"Wait a minute," I said, throwing my feet over the side

of the mattress to the floor. "You're too fat to get on the bed, aren't you?"

He said nothing, but I knew by the look in his beady little cat eyes that he was imagining eating my entrails.

"You should see a vet about that."

I padded barefoot down the hall to the kitchen in my tank top and boxers. I froze in the doorway, staring at the wooden cupboards, as the first horrible realization of the day hit me.

Coffee.

My mother didn't drink coffee. Wouldn't even allow the guests to have it. She said caffeine stunted the free expression of emotion. I couldn't help but agree. It certainly stopped me from wanting to murder people first thing in the morning.

How could I have forgotten?

I moved to the sink and brushed aside the gauzy curtain hanging above to look in the direction of the twins' place. I was tempted to walk over, but they were probably still laughing, and it was wrong to beat on the elderly.

I would not be defeated so easily.

I launched myself toward the cupboards. I didn't have much chance of finding any dairy or meat, at least not until the guests arrived. She made some exceptions for them. But vegan or not, my mother still liked her food.

Bingo!

Muffins.

I grabbed one of the greasy mounds of walnut pieces, carob chips, and rice flour and shoved it into my mouth. I then closed my eyes, allowing the flavor to sink in.

The taste of vegan goddess muffin put a lot of things into perspective for me.

Okay, last night had thrown me for a loop, but I could still maybe turn this thing around. First, I needed to call the insurance company. I mean, my mother—insurance fraud schemes aside—was a good client. She always paid on time. At least, I thought she did. My brow furrowed. Okay, well, I might not play that angle, but surely there had to be some wiggle room in the policy—like sessions she could do without a licensed professional.

Yeah, I thought, taking another bite. Or if worse came to worst, she would just have to cancel the next couple of retreats until she found someone. I wasn't going to lose my job over this, or, worse yet, go to jail. My jaw froze mid-chew. Oh my God! What if they put me in a cell with my mother! They wouldn't do that, would they? No. They couldn't. I slowly resumed my chewing. Either way, I wasn't going to take the chance.

I popped the last hunk of muffin into my mouth and slapped my hands together over the sink, brushing off the crumbs.

I turned and leaned my lower back against the counter's edge. More settled, I allowed my eyes to drift around the kitchen to really see it for the first time since I had been back.

Not much had changed here either.

The same dried herbs and flowers hung from the ceiling. The same patterned china from my childhood looked back at me from behind the glass of the buffet. And the same sad cuckoo bird was still flopped over his perch sticking out from the broken clock hung on the wall.

There were, however, a lot of new tins and glass pots huddled on the counter to my right. Homemade beauty lotions and creams. I picked up one labeled *Facial,* twisted off the lid, and gave it a smell. Hmm, pepperminty. I scooped out a big glob and smeared it over my face.

Yeah. This could still work out, I thought while rubbing the lotion over my cheeks. So I ran into the three fluffateers.

I had handled it. So my mom was still an irresponsible wing nut. Had I really expected anything less? I could do this thing. I wasn't the same Erica who blew up over every little bump in the road. I was a mature adult.

Suddenly my cheeks felt very hot. I grabbed a tea towel off the counter and began wiping my face.

My mom was right about one thing though. All this stress wasn't good for me. I needed to start looking on the bright side of my situation. Caesar, for example, was now too fat to kill me in my sleep. That was good. Also, the guilt I had over not visiting was resetting itself to zero. That was excellent. Plus, I did need a break from working all the time. Maybe this would get me out of my rut. Maybe when I got back home, I would do things a little differently. Like maybe I could return the smile that cute assistant district attorney was always giving me. Yeah. Everything was all right. In fact, it was all good.

Except for my face. My face was getting hotter.

I leaned over the sink to splash cold water over my cheeks when I spotted, through the window, a police officer coming up over the stairs leading to the lake.

I froze, face dripping.

Why on earth would a police officer be visiting the retreat first thing in the morning?

My heart sped up a beat while the word *Fraud!* flashed in my head.

Wait, what did I have to be afraid of? Our insurance fraud scheme hadn't even gotten off the ground.

The officer took long strides up the last few steps. His sheriff's hat covered his face, but he cut a pretty nice form in that uniform. I absentmindedly wiped the water from my face as I watched him walk up the path to the lodge. He looked even better close up. Hey! Maybe a stripper cop got shipwrecked on our island. That might make this trip more interesting.

I smoothed my hair back, ignoring its oily feel. I probably looked terrible. The thought occurred to me that I should go and try to do something with myself before he got to the door, but it was too hard to look away. When he got halfway up the path, his head slowly began to tilt up. I found myself nodding. Yup, let's get a look at that fac—

No. No. NO!

Grady Forrester!

This could not be happening.

Grady wasn't a cop! Grady was a lifeguard at the Wakatinga State Park . . . eight years ago.

Okay, so he probably wasn't still a lifeguard. But he couldn't be a cop! In what universe was that fair? No. Just no. Grady was a scamp. A Dennis the Menace. Grady was one of those guys who was hot in high school, who was then supposed to amount to pretty much nothing, so that all the girls he wronged back in the day could look him up online and feel better about themselves.

Grady was not a cop!

Except he was a cop . . . and he was walking up the front steps to the lodge.

He turned his head in my direction.

I hit the floor.

Okay, time for fast thinking. I checked my reflection in the door of the oven. My hair straggled down in oily strips—I never did get to shower after last night's surprise criminal summit—and while it was hard to really be sure, it looked as though my cheeks were on fire.

Again, this could not be happening.

I had imagined running into Grady hundreds, maybe

thousands of times. And in every single one of those day-dreams, I looked fabulous—like *airbrushed within an inch of my life* fabulous. Answering the door was not an option.

I heard my mother's voice call from the front foyer.

"Sheriff," she said. "What brings you out here?"

Ohmygod. Ohmygod. Ohmygod.

I couldn't make out what Grady said in return, but I did hear footsteps land in the front hall.

I needed to get out of here.

I frantically looked around the kitchen, hoping a door-way that didn't lead right past the front hall would appear. No such luck.

I looked at the window.

No, I wasn't *that* desperate.

"Erica, honey. Can you come to the door? Someone is here to see you."

Oh, I was *that* desperate.

I jumped onto the counter, hiked up the window, and dove through headfirst.

I braced my fall with my hands, but apparently my bi-cep curls were not enough to stop my cheek from scrap-ing against the wood beams.

No time for pain.

I popped back up and took a few furtive, ninja-type glances around my surroundings.

I wasn't safe here.

I scampered toward the side of the lodge. Just as I turned the corner, I heard the front door open.

"Erica?"

I jumped off the porch and hobbled barefoot over pine-cones for the cover of the trees. *This could work,* I thought, ignoring a red squirrel chattering angrily at me. I'd tell my mom I went for an early-morning swim. It sounded like something I'd do, or at least something someone would do.

No problem.

I looked over my shoulder. I could still see the lodge, which meant they could still see me if they turned the corner.

I needed to go farther into the bush.

I pushed back thin tree branches to make my way into the denser part of the forest. Mosquitoes and black flies took the opportunity to swarm en masse. After a minute or two, I had to stop. I needed to get my bearings. My heart hammered in my chest as I tried to still my breath. That's when I noticed the small clearing up ahead.

Huh. There wasn't supposed to be anything there.

And something about it looked . . . off.

Wait! The old well.

My mother always worried I'd somehow fall into it as a kid—it was only partially filled—so she made me stay away from this part of the forest. But even though I wasn't familiar with the spot, something about it still seemed wrong.

Tree branches, snapped in odd places, hung in a circle around where I thought the opening must be. I brushed aside any concerns, and I pushed my way toward it. The branches were too crowded anywhere else to be comfortable, so weird or not, the clearing seemed like my best bet for a hideout until Grady left.

I gingerly stepped closer, watching where I placed my feet. The last thing I needed was to step on a rusty nail and die of tetanus, but then again, that was probably the last thing most people needed.

As I got closer, I could see that the cover of the well was gone. Wait, not gone, smashed through.

Could a tree branch do that?

Maybe, if the wood had rotted through.

Unease rippled down my body. I couldn't put my finger

on any one thing, but something about this whole scene didn't just look wrong, it *felt* wrong.

Then I saw it.

A man's running shoe lying on the ground right by the edge of the abandoned well.

A new running shoe.

I crept closer. I wanted to be able to look into the well without getting too close. I didn't know how secure the ground was around it.

I stopped a few feet back and stretched up on my tip-toes. I still couldn't see all the way down.

Frick.

I got to my hands and knees and edged close enough to the well to plant my palms on the old stone opening.

I closed my eyes, and I took a long deep breath.

On some level, I knew . . . I just knew I was going to see something bad.

And as it turned out, I was right.

Crumpled at the bottom of the well, face half visible, lay Dickie Morrison . . . dead . . . impaled by a weenie skewer.

Chapter Three

"So tell me again what happened to your face?"

I stared at the thick-bodied, redheaded cop in front of me, trying to figure out if she was serious.

"I had an allergic reaction to some homemade face cream."

She scratched the back of her scalp with her pen. "Right. Right. You said that. But what about the scrape?" She whipped the pen back around to point at my cheek.

I fought the urge to duck. "Rhonda, do you really think I had something to do with . . . this?"

"I'll decide what I think when I think it."

I sighed and leaned back against a tall pine tree. Never in a million years could I have imagined this scenario. Back in high school, Grady and Rhonda could have tied each other for the title "Least Likely to Go into Law Enforcement." Rhonda had always been a little intense. I once witnessed her punch a tree repeatedly with her bare fists when it stopped the other team's ball from going out in a pickup volleyball game. Another year, she painted her face for school every day of the Stanley Cup playoffs. The principal finally made her stop after she pantsed a kid for wearing the other team's jersey.

That being said, I had always liked Rhonda . . . we were both part of the outcast club. I just never imagined her as a cop, especially not as a cop questioning me about the death of Dickie Morrison.

"Now, according to your statement Ms. . . . I'm sorry Ms.?"

"Rhonda, you know my name."

"It's for the record," she whispered conspiratorially.

I looked around. Nobody was within at least forty feet of us.

"Erica. Erica Bloom."

"Ms. Bloom. Right. Got it. Now according to your statement, Ms. Bloom, the victim was impaled by a . . ."

"Weenie skewer."

"Right. A weenie skewer. Are you sure?"

I nodded.

"Interesting."

I pushed myself off the tree. "Rhonda, what is going on here? Isn't this an accident? I mean I saw Dickie yesterday afternoon, and he was already drinking. He said it was nonalcoholic, but I knew I should have called the . . . well, you guys. So I'm kind of assuming he tripped and fell after having a few too many."

"So you saw the victim yesterday afternoon?" she asked knowingly, pen hovering over her notepad. "How would you describe your relationship with the victim?"

"Nonexistent."

"Really . . . interesting."

"Rhonda, you know I haven't lived in Otter Lake for a really long time."

"I know," she said, resuming her whisper. "We should totally catch up over beers at the Salty Dawg."

My mouth fell open, but no words came out. I stole a brief look over to Grady. As luck would have it, he was looking at me, the barest of grins on his face.

I still hadn't actually talked to him. Granted, there may have been some incoherent screaming and frantic pointing on my part as I ran from the well back to the lodge. But he then went into the trees to check it out, and before I knew it, what looked like every law enforcement official from here to three lakes over had swarmed the retreat . . . which amounted to about eight people.

An officer handed Grady a coffee, breaking our eye contact.

Wasn't that always the way. People just did things for Grady. He never even had to ask. They probably just made him sheriff so he'd smile for the press release.

Rhonda asked me something. I nodded without looking at her.

He looked even better, manlier.

And here I was, looking like I had just lost a cage match with a balsam fir.

"Ah, Ms. Bloom?"

I redirected my gaze back to Rhonda.

"You said that you have no relationship with Dickie Morrison?"

I nodded again.

"Are you aware of the Otter Lake Raspberry Social?" She handed me a folded piece of paper. I opened it. Another flyer.

"I—" The strangest noise came out of Rhonda's mouth, cutting me off. I paused, then asked, "Did you just make the *duhn duhn* sound from *Law and Order*?"

"No," Rhonda said, scoffing. Her face flushed the color of her hair. "Focus. You're in enough trouble already, young lady."

"We're the same age, Rhonda."

"In years," she shot back. "Now answer the question."

I took a moment to roll my jaw, loosening the muscles. "Yes, I am aware of the Otter Lake Raspberry Social."

"Are you aware that eight years ago, a bizarre incident took place involving one . . ." She stopped to flip through her notes. "Erica Bloom, that's you. And one . . ." She began flipping again. "Dickie Morrison . . . among others . . . and Otter Lake's beloved Betsy? God rest her soul."

"Okay, for the record, I am so over what happened at the social. Really, it wasn't that bad. It—"

Her eyes widened. "Well, it certainly wasn't good."

"Rhonda, I like you a lot, and I really would like to meet up for beers, but I think you should know, I'm about to take that notepad and shove it—"

She put a hand up to my face, cutting me off. "Boy, some things never change," she muttered, looking up at me from underneath her eyebrows. She clicked her pen. "Upon questioning, witness displayed an unusual degree of hostility."

"You're going to write that? I . . . I was just kidding!"

"Erica, I have to do my job. I haven't forgotten what you did for me, but—"

I scrunched my face. "What I did for you?"

"Remember when the Three Fu—" She stopped herself and rolled her eyes. "Guys made lime Jell-O in my canoe that fall? When we got that cold snap? Filled it all the way up?"

"Yeah, but—"

She held up a hand. "I was so stunned. I couldn't do anything, and they were taking pictures of my reaction?"

I paused a moment while the memory came into view. "Oh, yeah."

"You remember what you did?" she asked.

"I threw Tommy's camera in the lake." I smiled. It had been a good throw too.

"Yeah, you did. So I haven't forgotten." She straightened her shoulders abruptly. "But I'll still take you down."

Grady suddenly called out Rhonda's name and waved her over.

"That will be all for now, Ms. Bloom." She snapped her notebook shut and turned toward the group of officers chatting with Grady.

"Great."

She swiveled back toward me, big smile on her face. "Don't forget. Beers at the Dawg. Any night this week." She quickly jabbed a thumbs-up into the air before turning again and walking away.

I thumped the back of my skull against the tree and looked up through the branches at the baby-blue sky. I had brought this on myself. That's what was going on here. If I had visited more often, the craziness would have been spread out. Instead, the universe was giving it to me all in one shot.

An angry yell yanked me out of my pity party. I watched a woman emerge at the top of the stairs from the lake and run full-out toward the lodge. Grady moved like a flash to intercept her, grabbing her gently, but firmly, by the arms. A few words were exchanged, then she pushed Grady hard on the chest with both hands.

It took me a second to place her.

Laurie Day.

Laurie did most of the cooking for the retreat, so it wasn't surprising she was here. It also wasn't surprising that she was upset. Laurie and Dickie had dated back in high school . . . if you could call it that. Laurie dated Dickie, and Dickie did whatever and whomever he wanted. It was funny too, because Laurie wasn't exactly a shrinking violet—she never let anyone so much as look at her sideways—but when it came to Dickie, she always let him get away with murder. Judging by her current state, I could only guess they had still been dating.

The awfulness of the situation suddenly hit me.

I mean, it wasn't like Dickie was some great guy, and I would be hard-pressed to say I even liked him, but nobody deserved to die that way. And I had a bad feeling the mental snapshot of his dead body wouldn't be leaving me anytime soon.

"Erica!"

I looked over to my mom waving at me from the lodge's porch. I walked toward her, eyes still on Laurie, now being led to a picnic table by Rhonda. Hopefully, this would be cleared up soon. Intake was today. Nothing said *peaceful retreat* like a bunch of police officers and yellow tape, and my mom's business already felt precarious enough.

As I picked my way over the uneven ground, still barefoot, the masochist in me couldn't help but take one more look at Grady. Again, as luck would have it, he was looking at me. Our eyes met, and he gave me a brief nod then looked away.

A nod. So that's how things stood. Well, okay then.

Lost in the moment, I didn't notice the tree root that was about to collide with my foot . . . until it collided with my foot. I pitched forward—but recovered quickly. *Maybe so quickly,* I thought, *that no one noticed.* I glanced over my shoulder. There stood Grady chuckling, shaking his head.

Well, that proved it.

You really can go home again.

Five hours later, a swarm of divorcees descended on the retreat. Thankfully, the police had left about an hour prior, and the crime scene tape was far enough into the bushes that I doubted anyone would spot it.

I always had found intake days funny, in the same way it must be funny to be an obgyn. Within minutes of meeting a complete stranger, I would know some of the most intimate parts of her being . . . whether I wanted to or not. My guess was that most guests had already worn out every friend, relative, and casual acquaintance with their stories and were ready to pounce on the first available pair of fresh ears. Today that pair belonged to me.

"Twenty-eight years I was married to that bastard."

I slowly raised my clipboard a little higher in front of my face to create some space between me and the woman standing before me. "Twenty-eight years! Can you believe it?" A hard swoop of black bangs shuddered over her one eye. "You've got a nice place here, by the way. And now he's dating a twenty-two-year-old! Twenty-two!"

I didn't say anything.

I didn't have to.

"She worked for me. Can you believe that? Cupcake apprentice. Fabulous at icing." She swatted a heavily manicured hand at the sheet of hair. "It will be easier to find a new husband than a baker who can ice like that. I should get a younger one too. Husband, I mean. One who can perform without the little blue pill. You know?"

I stared blankly back at her then said, "I just found a dead body."

The woman's highly glossed lips froze.

Uh-oh. Did I say that out loud?

"I'm sorry Ms. . . . Ms.?"

"Franelli. Maria Franelli," she replied, pinning me with her heavily shadowed eyes.

"I was making a joke . . . you know . . . all the cheating

bastards should be dead." I shook my head a little too frantically. "It's not really funny in hindsight."

Maria Franelli gave me a look in return that spoke to
her suspicions regarding my sanity. "Anyway, I hope you
people can help me; otherwise I'll show him my twenty-
two. You know what I mean?"

I nodded again, made a phantom check on my clipboard, and looked around her to the next in line. I needed to
get through these women as quickly as possible. I thought
I could act normally, but apparently, my brain had decided
finding a dead body was traumaworthy after all. I wasn't
much of a crier, but I could maybe give it a shot. Or better
yet, maybe Kit Kat and Tweety left some gin.

The next woman stepped forward wearing a short-
sleeved cardigan with pearl buttons and pleated shorts.
"Hello, my name is Susan Anderson, and I have cried every
day for the last six months."

I pressed my lips together and gave her my best sad-
eyebrows nod.

"He's not worth it, you know? I know he's not worth it,"
she continued, pausing to blow her nose with gusto. "I have
a full life. I have my bookstore and my cats. Would you
like to see a picture?" she asked, reaching for the purse
lying against her hip. Something in my face stilled her
hand. "No? Okay. And yet every time I think about him,
I just start to . . . I just can't . . ."

I pulled out one of the three minipacks of tissues from
my back pocket and passed it to her.

"Thank you," she said, looking at me with her big wet
eyes. "It's just—"

Before she could finish, I gave her the sad-eyebrows
nod again, put my hand on her shoulder, and ever so gently
pushed her in the direction of the others. I didn't feel good

about it, but who knew what would come out of my mouth next.

I raised my eyes to the next in line.

"Hello, my name is Lydia Morgan. I'm here for the retreat."

I gave the woman before me a good once-over. No tears. No trembling bottom lip. Clothes conspicuously free of cat hair. In fact, she looked quite normal in her outdoorsy little T-shirt and khaki shorts.

"You must be Erica," she said, extending her hand. "Your mother has told me all about you."

Confusion quickly gave way. I took her hand. "You must be from the insurance company?"

"That's right. I'm so sorry for the inconvenience it must have caused for you to drop everything to help your mom jump through our silly hoops," she said with a friendly smile.

"Actually, I was hoping to talk to you about that." I did my best to return the smile. "You see—"

"I know. I know. It seems ridiculous. But policy is policy."

"Right. Policy. I had a few questions—"

"Oh, sure, no problem. But there's no need to worry." She laid her hand on my arm. "I love your mom. You know, I'm not normally the type of woman who goes to nature retreats to get in touch with her inner . . . whatever, but your mom. She's so . . . so . . . authentic. And honest."

I allowed myself a brief glare over to my mother. She had Maria Franelli's face cupped in her hands, so she could peer intently into her eyes with her overly large ones. "Yeah, that's my mom. Superhonest." I gripped my pen to stop my fingers from pinching the bridge of my nose.

"And I'm not sure if she told you, but I just got out of a

twenty-five-year marriage. He had been lying to me the entire time." Suddenly her voice jumped an octave. "Secret family in Reno. It's ridiculous to say. Secret family in Reno!" Her hands fluttered above her head, but she caught them quickly and brought them back down to her sides. Her calm smile returned to her face. "That's why I bonded so quickly with your mother. There's not enough honesty in the world."

"There certainly is not."

Why don't you visit more often? my mom says. *You never come home to see me,* she says.

My eyes scanned the room. My mother had moved on from Maria Franelli and was gliding around the room, her arms waving dramatically underneath her filmy white caftan. She didn't even have the decency to look the slightest bit stressed.

"You know what his excuse was?" Lydia said, bringing me back to the conversation. "I'm too boring. He lies to me for twenty-five years because I'm boring! You know, I don't think I could take one more person lying to me."

"Of course you couldn't," I said to my clipboard, trying not to audibly grind my teeth.

"I'm sorry?"

"Oh, I mean, that's completely understandable."

My mother floated in our direction, sweeping up Lydia into a hug. "Welcome! Welcome! You must be Lydia," she said. "Why don't you start showing everyone to their cabins, Erica? I'll take care of this one."

I took a deep breath and forced another smile to my face. "Well, actually, I was hoping to have a talk with Lydia. You know, go over the finer parts of your policy," I said, lightly gripping Lydia's elbow.

"Nonsense!" My mother wrapped her arm tightly around Lydia's shoulder. "She's here for healing."

I further snaked my arm around Lydia's. "And for truth. We were just talking about the importance of—"

"I don't remember the last time I felt so popular," Lydia said, smiling. "But Erica, I know you doctor types are such sticklers for details, but really, there's nothing to worry about."

Doctor? Oh, right, I had forgotten I was a doctor. Funny that.

"See, Erica? Nothing to worry about. Now why don't you start showing the other guests their cabins," my mother said, leading Lydia away. "I'm always telling her to relax. For a psychologist you'd think she'd know better."

A sudden rumbling filled my ears from behind. I turned to see a group of ladies, huddled over Caesar, stroking his massive body. His deafening purrs reverberated over the floorboards. He flicked me a lazy look of contempt.

"Oh, shut up, Caesar," I mumbled.

Multiple heads snapped up in unison, mouths making round Os of horror.

"Right." I clapped my hands together. "Who wants to see their cabin?"

I spent the rest of the evening at the campfire meet and greet listening to horrible ex-husband stories and fighting off flashbacks of Dickie's dead body. Afterward I went to bed, fell straight asleep, and didn't have a single dream worth remembering.

In the morning, I hustled out of bed and out the door before anyone could spot me. The retreat always kicked off with a nature hike, so my psychological expertise wouldn't be required, and I desperately needed to talk to someone sane. I ran down the retreat steps, jumped into my mom's aging boat, and headed out across the lake.

Early-morning mist hovered low over the water, but

the already too hot sun promised to burn it off in short order.

As I glided over the glassy surface, I felt my shoulders relax.

Despite all of the craziness residing in Otter Lake, I couldn't deny its beauty. At just over a thousand acres, most people would consider it a mid-sized lake—nothing special—but for those who lived here, it was just right. I leaned with the boat as I curved its body around a familiar finger of land stretching out into the water.

I also couldn't deny there was something calming about the fact that not much ever seemed to change here. The cottages kept their original charm. The forests still bulged green. And the people never seemed to move.

Yup, everything was exactly how I left it . . . except . . . except for the gigantic raspberry now towering over the town pavilion like Godzilla over Tokyo.

I slowed the boat.

I couldn't let my jaw drag that low and steer at the same time.

Yup, it really was a giant raspberry.

My eyes tracked over the enormous red construction with the happy cartoon face.

What the hell was that thing?

Obviously it had something to do with the social, but while this particular town festival had always been important to the people of Otter Lake, it wasn't radiation-monster-raspberry important.

I spent a few minutes digesting the enormity of the berry before I drove on.

Minutes later I pulled the boat up to Freddie's dock. Freddie had been my best friend back in the day . . . actually, come to think of it, he probably still was my closest friend, and his cottage, if you could call it that, was the nicest on the lake. When we were kids, Freddie lived there with a team of rotating nannies while his parents, originally from Hong Kong, jet-setted around the globe as real estate speculators.

He opened his door wearing a purple headscarf and a blousy pirate shirt tucked into billowing, multicolored skirts.

Yup, given how things were going that seemed about right.

"Well, look who the beaver dragged in," he said, making room for me to step inside.

I closed my eyes to enjoy the cool air of Freddie's air-conditioning before I said, "Huh."

"What?" Freddie asked.

"It's funny. When I was walking up the path to your house I thought I knew what my first question would be, but now I've changed my mind."

"What was your first question?"

"Why is there a giant raspberry threatening to destroy Otter Lake?"

He nodded. "Now what's your first question?"

"Why are you dressed like Captain Hook's wife?"

It had been eight years since I'd seen Freddie too, but we still texted every now and then. The great thing about Freddie, though, was that I always felt comfortable around him. Time didn't matter.

He waved me in with an arm covered in bangles. "Come in. I'm working."

"As what? A circus performer?" I asked, following the swishing skirts down the bamboo hallway. "That can't be right. Circus performers leave their houses. Actually, I don't think they even have houses."

"Oh, don't worry. I haven't given up my career as Otter Lake's one homosexual hermit," he replied, leading me to the office which I knew contained an enormous desk that faced the lake. "And you look good, by the way. I like the bangs and ponytail thing. Oh, and I'm not in the circus. Well, not really."

"Then what are you in?"

"Follow me, and all shall be revealed." He rustled farther down the hall, swirling his fingers in the air, leading me along. "And the berry? That's Candace's doing. She tries so hard, that girl, but on that one, she may have missed the mark. Gotta love her for trying though."

"Who's Candace?"

"Where do I even begin?" he said with a sigh. "A lot has changed since you were last home, Erica. Candace is the PR person working for the developer who would like to turn Otter Lake into a luxury cottage site for the rich and famous. She's nice. You'd like her." He smiled at me over his shoulder. "I even like her, which is surprising given that I'm days away from tying myself to a tree at the construction site. I mean, I'm Otter Lake's rich people. We don't need more. I don't like the idea of competing with other socialites."

I frowned. "Why is it when people say 'you'd like her,' I automatically don't like that person?"

"Because you've got people issues," he said with implied obviousness. "Anyway, they've been focusing on snapping up properties by Hunter's Corners—you know, for the sunset value. In fact, they've already started to build on Ackerman's old property, but everyone's pretty worried that they have plans for the entire lake. In fact, rumor has it surveyors were sizing up Snake Island the other day, so you guys may not be the only island dwellers anymore. They'll probably have to change the name though," he added, crinkling his brow in thought. "Didn't your mother tell you any of this?"

"Nope. She's on her own island in every sense."

He nodded. "Anyway, the raspberry is the developer's way of reassuring the fine citizens of Otter Lake that change is good."

Once in the office, Freddie spun his slightly hefty form, and lowered himself into the chair in front of the computer. He typed a few keys then announced, "I'm back, my pretties. Let Madame Freddie reveal all the secrets of the universe to you."

I plunked myself on the corner of the computer desk and leaned over to see what was happening.

"Stay out of the frame," Freddie hissed from behind a ringed hand. "You'll ruin the mystique."

"Maybe I should come back later."

"Don't even think about it. You are going to tell me all about Dickie. I can't believe you discovered his . . . well . . . his body," he whispered, turning down the corners of his mouth and widening his eyes in exaggerated horror. "This will only take a second."

"You can reveal all the secrets of the universe in a second?"

"Watch me."

I scooted back on the desk. From my angle, I could see at least one person was chatting with Freddie, but I couldn't make out the type.

"I told you he'd do it again," Freddie said, shaking his head. "No. No. Now you listen to Madame Freddie. Once a cheater, always a cheater. I can see his energy, love." Freddie stopped talking, closed his eyes and placed his fingertips on his forehead. "I can see it, and it's spreading . . . spreading and sputtering like a dirty ol' shower head."

He cracked an eye open to read the screen.

"No. No. Don't you be sad, sugar."

"You're Southern now too?" I whispered.

Freddie shot me a glare.

"That's right. There's someone just around the corner for you. He's tall and dark and everything we have both dreamed about."

"Don't forget to tell her he's a billionaire with an S and M room."

"That's right. That's right," Freddie said, ignoring me. "You come back any time now, honey pie." Freddie clicked another key and spun his chair to face me. "So? What do you think?"

"About you being an online psychic?" I replied. I took a moment to really give it some thought. "Strangely fitting."

"I know, right?"

We stared at each other for a moment.

"I feel like we should hug or something."

I wrinkled my brow. "I know, but I really don't want to."

"Me neither," he said, nodding quickly. "And I say that with love. Speaking of intimacy issues, though, how did it go with your mother?"

I gave him the rundown of everything that had transpired since I had arrived. Well, almost everything.

"Insurance fraud. Discovering impaled bodies. You really need to visit more often." Freddie got up and walked over to the beer fridge fitted into the built-in mahogany shelves behind the desk. He held up a bottle to me, but I waved him off. He twisted the cap and took a swig. "So are you traumatized?"

"I don't know," I replied, shrugging my shoulders. "I don't know what I'm supposed to feel. Dickie wasn't a great guy, and he definitely was a pervert." Freddie nodded his head in agreement. "But I've known him forever. It wasn't nice what I saw. I want to unsee it."

"I hear you. It's sad, but also it's hard to really feel bad for the guy. He was such a jerk in high school. Remember that time they locked me up in that cage thingy on wheels with all the dodge balls? And then rolled me out to the parking lot?"

"I remember."

"But then you came to find me," he said, crossing his hands over his heart, "and we put all the balls in Tommy's truck."

I smiled at the memory. "Yeah, they all rolled out onto him when he opened the door."

"I think Tommy was always just a little bit afraid of you. Must have been the bite back in the first grade." Suddenly he slapped the desk. "You know who you were like? Rudolph the Red Nosed Reindeer! Always making sure Santa found a place for the misfit toys . . . a place for everyone but you."

I furrowed my brow.

"What? Rudolph's cool," he said. "And you know, in some ways, those three, now two, have just gotten worse. Lately, they've been tearing up the lake with Tommy's new boat. Totally obnoxious stuff."

"Really?" I suddenly remembered my senior class standing on the gymnasium stage for graduation. I bet none of us imagined our futures turning out quite like they had. "That's so sad on a lot of levels."

"Yup," Freddie replied. His eyes were distant for a moment before snapping back into focus. "And what about Grady? Was he there?"

"Grady who?"

"That's cute. Grady who." He smiled over the spout of his beer. "You know, Grady? The Grady who is the proto-type for the teenaged boy every girl dreams about? The Grady you could never seem to shake? The Grady who may or may not have shot JFK? Whoops, I'm getting my conspiracy theories confused. I meant the Grady who may or may not have been responsible for that night?"

"Oh, that Grady," I muttered.

"So he was there."

I sighed heavily through my nose. "I didn't talk to him."

"Good," Freddie said, again slapping the desk.

"Why are we even talking about him?" I asked. "That was a lifetime ago. I've dated plenty since then. I have built a whole new life for myself back in Chicago. I have a fabulous job, more friends than I can count—"

Suddenly Freddie made a face.

"What? What is that face?"

"Erica, you don't have to lie to me about the friends situation."

I straightened. "What are you talking about?

"It's okay. I'm not even sure it's your fault. And look at me. I'm no better. Why do you think I'm still living in Otter Lake? It changes you. We're not like the rest of the world," he said, shaking his head. "Here, everybody knows my name. I can't go into town without at least one person shouting, *Hey, it's the Gay Guy! How's it going, Gay Guy?*"

"That's messed up, Freddie."

"Meh." He shrugged his shoulders. "I may be exaggerating a little bit."

"That's still terrible." I recrossed my arms over my chest. "And not to take away from any of it, but that's your experience. Not mine. I have made a life for myself in Chicago. I run. I play Ultimate Frisbee twice a week in the summer. My teammates call me the Enforcer."

"Of course they do."

I squinted my eyes at him in warning but moved on. "In the winters, well, I *was* going to a book club, but they kicked me out for not reading the books." Suddenly I snapped my fingers and pointed at him. "Every second Thursday I go out for drinks with the other clerks from work. And I plan to renew my gym membership and join a spin class in the fall."

"What about dating?"

"I date. All the time!" My cheeks suddenly felt hot. "Not a lot of second dates, but that's just because I haven't met the right guy, and—"

"And all these friends of yours?"

"What about them?"

"Name one."

Faces and names rattled through my brain, but they were all from work and were really more like friendly acquaintances. Huh, this was weird. I hadn't spent much time thinking about the lack of people in my life. I did work a lot. Maybe too much, but I had friends. I just couldn't think of any of them right now. Whatever the case, I liked my life in Chicago. It was calm, predictable, drama-free. I liked my job. I liked my Ultimate Frisbee team. I really liked the new cable package I just subscribed to that had all those shows I never got around to watching. Huh, that was a lot of *likes*. Clearly, I needed to give this some more thought later, but in the meantime, I wasn't about to give Freddie the satisfaction of winning this argument.

"Sophie Myers," I blurted out. "You've seen her. She's on my Facebook."

"Oh, Erica," he said, shaking his head.

"What?"

"It's time you knew."

"Knew what?"

"I'm Sophie Myers."

"What?"

"I'm Sophie Myers."

Gears slowly turned in my brain. "You . . . catfished me?"

"I did."

"Why? Why would you do that?" I suddenly found myself leaning into the beer fridge grasping at bottles. Apparently, I was thirsty after all.

"I felt bad for you."

"Wait," I said, slowly pointing a finger at him. "Are you . . . are you Brandi from Montreal?"

"And Dave from Pittsburgh," he said. Freddie studied the beer bottle in his hand before tipping the top toward me. "And Mike from Chicago."

"I can't believe this." I slammed shut the door of the fridge with the side of my knee. "I . . . I don't even know what to say to you right now."

He grimaced. "I know. It's weird and creepy. But before I found my calling as Madame Freddie, Conduit to the Stars, I got bored a lot. Besides, you know they say that if you have less than a hundred friends, you probably aren't real. I was validating your existence."

"Gee, thanks."

"Don't mention it," he said quickly. "But this brings up the much bigger issue of why you need to stay away from Grady."

I took a sip of my beer, trying to process how everything I thought I knew about myself was being questioned in less than two days of being home. "Wait. We're not done with this whole catfishing thing, but, out of curiosity, why do you think I need to stay away from Grady?"

"Listen. That night at the Raspberry Social, it was a strange and epic night." He leaned back in his chair and took on the faraway look of a storyteller.

I kicked his seat, throwing him off balance enough that he had to grab the desk with his free hand. "Okay, first, stop that," I said. "Second, you weren't even there! You had a cold!"

He nodded. "More's the pity. And let me tell you, the social's been a real snoozefest ever since you left. It's like everybody goes expecting something to happen, but it never does. Well, there was that one time Kelly Winterburn had a little too much to drink." Freddie smiled. "She tried to get up onto the stage to dance with the band, but fell off and landed on the tart table."

"Fascinating."

"But the point is, even though I wasn't there, I know the legend, and it worked on many levels. It had a peculiar brilliance, but we're getting off track. For you, it was not great. Well, the end was great . . . when you totally lost it, and you were all like, *Fine! You want a show! Here's a—*"

"What? I did not say that! Who are you getting this from?"

"Doesn't matter. You and Grady are like two ships meeting in the night," he said sagely. "Ships that collide and then explode and all the passengers die. Betsy learned that the hard way. It shouldn't happen. You're both young and hot . . . but riddled with issues."

"I'm not *riddled* with issues," I said, slumping back onto the desk.

He sighed. "Here, look at it this way. Your mom, well, she brings a whole lot of crazy to the world. And as her daughter you had to absorb a lot of that crazy, like radiation."

"I am nothing like my mother."

"That's it, right there. Exactly," he said, pointing at me. "You never wanted to be like your mother. So you kept all the crazy in. Like a pressure cooker. And that's really hard in Otter Lake."

"I did n—"

"Let me finish," Freddie said, jumping to his feet. "I've so got this now. So you're walking around all pressure cooker like, and it's fine. Every now and then you'd let out a little steam like when Tommy was picking on somebody, but for the most part you keep a lid on all of your bubbly emotions. Then Grady comes along"—Freddie smacked his hands together—"and POW!"

"Oh, please." I rolled my eyes. "Pow?"

Freddie held one finger up. "That's probably why you're not going on any second dates back in the Windy City. You're afraid of what might come out if you let your guard down."

"Oh, come on."

"I'm sorry, Erica, but sometimes watching you around him was like watching an episode of *I Love Lucy*. You could never be sure what might happen. And as for Grady, well, he's just too pretty for his own good."

"What are you even talking about? That is so not tr—"

"Trust Madame Freddie on this one. Grady is the nitro to your glycerin. You can't handle it. I can't handle it."

"Pfft," I replied. "More like Grady couldn't handle the awesome mature woman I've become, and he would, like, embarrass himself in uniform and become, like—"

"Just stop," Freddie said, putting his bejeweled hand up to my face. "It's happening already. Look, I like having you back. I want you to come back more, but if you see Grady, God only knows what will happen. Then it will be another decade before I see you again."

"Huh." I swirled my beer around in the bottle. "Are you . . . wait . . . even Joan from Delaware?"

"Even Joan from Delaware."

"Huh."

I spent the next couple of hours raiding Freddie's fridge for meat products before leaving to head back to camp. The beer's happy effect had long since worn off, and I felt tired and headachy as I walked down the dock toward my boat.

It was all too much.

I knew coming home wasn't a good idea. Despite Freddie's big reveal regarding my social status, I had a good life back in Chicago, and, again, I knew a cute assistant DA who smiled at me a lot.

It was time I smiled back.

Yeah. I was going to smile so big, he wouldn't know what hit him. Yeah. Good plan.

Trust Madame Freddie.

Please. I mean what did Freddie know anyway? He really needed to move to Chicago with me. There was more to the world than Otter Lake. I could show him. Yeah. That was an even better plan. And I never lost my cool anymore. I was the calmest, coolest, most collected person I knew. Granted, it turned out most of the people I knew were fake, but the argument was still there.

I jumped in my mom's boat, grasped the T-shaped lever on the pull cord starter and gave the rickety motor a good yank.

Nothing.

"Come on," I muttered, giving it another pull as sweat trailed from the back of my neck down between my shoulder blades.

He was probably right about staying away from Grady though. Not that I believed we were two exploding ships, but because the Grady years were over. I mean we had only hung out a few times. And sure, we'd had undeniable chemistry, but we were teenagers. All teenagers are . . . chemical.

I yanked at the motor again.

Still nothing.

I swiped my bangs away from my forehead with the back of my hand. It was time to let the Otter Lake Erica from my childhood go completely. I wasn't the kid with the dippy mom anymore. I wasn't the kid who bit people on the shoulder. And I definitely wasn't the girl who desperately followed Grady Forrester around trying to get his attention and then freaking out when I finally did.

I yanked the pull cord again.

Nothing.

"Come on!" I hopped up and down in frustration.

Just then a large hand slid up from the water over the lip of my boat.

"Wah!"

I jumped back, my foot landing awkwardly on a life jacket. Before I knew it, I was on my butt, dirty water from the floor of the boat seeping through my jean shorts.

I struggled to my feet, eyes never leaving the hand. As I stood, I could see that those manly digits led up to a rippling forearm . . . and then to a bulging bicep.

Oh, crap.

I knew where that arm led.

My heart fluttered in my chest, unable to catch a rhythm.

Suddenly his wet, chiseled face appeared . . .

My heart gave up trying to beat.

 . . . his free hand slicked back his hair, sending wet trails of water running over the planes of his nose, his lips . . .

Shaky breath escaped my lips.

"Erica Bloom," Grady said, squinting his blue eyes against the sun. "Can I give you a hand?"

Chapter Four

It took me a second to shake off the slow-motion moment I was having in my head. No, I mean, yes . . . he was beautiful. So very beautiful. But I needed to get a hold of myself. I could handle this. Obviously the universe wasn't on board with my staying-away-from-Grady plan, but it was okay. Everything was different now. I was different now. It was time for Grady to meet the new and improved Erica, Chicago Edition.

I wiped a droplet of sweat from my nose before meeting Grady's gaze. "Thank you for the offer—it's lovely to see you by the way—but I'm fine."

"Really? It looks like you're having engine trouble." He planted his large hands on the edge of the boat and began to push himself up, muscles rolling over his shoulders.

It was all happening too fast.

Before I knew it, those shoulders rose up, revealing honeyed pecs . . . then the first two bumps of his six-pack.

Alarm bells rang in my head.

He was going to mount my vessel!

The last thing this situation needed was a better view of Grady's half-naked body.

"No! Put your chest away!" I shouted, thrusting out my palms in a stop gesture. Then I froze, turned my palms in, and let them drop. "I mean, I'm fine. Really," I said with an attempt at a breezy laugh.

I turned and gave another yank on the pull cord, allowing myself a second to close my eyes and regroup. Apparently the Chicago Edition of Erica Bloom still had a few kinks to work out. Yup, this cool, confident thing felt a little unstable.

I glanced over my shoulder.

Grady had lowered himself back into the water but left his arms crossed over the edge, his head cocked adorably to one side. The sun caught the droplets of water on his skin, nearly blinding me. I squeezed my eyes shut. What was wrong with me?

It was this place.

I was de-evolving. All my baser instincts were coming out. I needed to get out of here before it got any worse.

"I was going to come by and see you later," he called to my back. "Make sure you're okay after what happened."

I turned, nodded quickly at his bobbing form, then swiveled back to the engine.

"Actually, I'd wanted to see you yesterday. I'd heard you were in town, and I thought maybe we could catch up." I could hear the smile in his voice, and I did not like just how much I liked the way those words sounded coming out of his mouth. But wait, he'd been visiting in uniform? Coincidence, or had he done that for my benefit? "Oh, that's sweet, but . . ."

"It's been what?" he said, tossing a wet flop of hair from his eyes. "Five . . . six years?"

"Eight. Almost eight." I inhaled deeply through my nose.

"Are you all right?" he asked, furrowing his brow. "You seem tense."

"Completely! I mean, I'm fine." I could hear the nervous laughter coming out of my mouth, but I just couldn't do anything to stop it.

"I think I know what's going on."

My eyebrows jerked up in question.

"Well, aside from Dickie . . . there's the social." He pursed his lips before saying, "You know, I always wanted to explain what happened. You left town so quickly afterward."

The social again. Why was everybody always bringing up the freaking social? I yanked at the motor in hard, rapid bursts. "I was off to school," I muttered quickly. "You knew that."

"You know, I never got a chance to tell you my side of things. You didn't even say good-bye," he said, cocking his head again.

"Oh . . . well, good-bye. And now hello again," I said, chuckling painfully. "And good-bye once more." I mentally slapped myself on the forehead.

"I know you never were one to talk about your feelings—"

I cut him off with something that sounded a little like a shout. His eyes widened. I stopped to take a breath before saying, "I just think that night is one of those memories in life that is better left untouched. You know, it's like when a dog has an accident indoors, and even though you clean it up, he keeps going back to that spot, over and over, to give it another sniff. I don't want to be that dog. Do you want to be that dog?"

Grady blinked his eyes slowly a few times before saying, "I . . . I'm not sure."

I pressed my lips tightly together. Panic fluttered in my chest. This was exactly what I didn't want. All these emotions. Explanations. I didn't need to know why any of it happened the way it did. It was done. And it really wasn't that big of a deal.

I glanced at the water. Maybe I could outswim him.

"I was thinking that I could hitch a ride with you to the retreat—"

"Nope. I don't th—"

"I need to talk to your mother."

"Nope . . . wait. What?"

"About the well."

My yanking arm collapsed to my side. I turned to face him. "The well? What about the well?"

He propped himself more comfortably on the edge of the boat. "Oh, you know, routine stuff, like when was the last time she checked to make sure it was secure. When the cover was last replaced. That kind of thing."

I stepped back and crossed my arms across the sweat-drenched fabric of my tank top. "My mother's not in trouble, is she?" I said quickly. "Because she's already having some difficulty with her ins—"

"Slow down," he said, body still rising and falling with the water. "Nobody's accusing anyone of anything. I just want to be thorough."

"Pfft."

His eyebrows furrowed in a very coplike expression. "I'm sorry? Did you just say *pfft*?"

I wasn't exactly sure why I had made that sound. I certainly didn't intend to make that sound.

"Pfft." Or that one.

"Again," he said with a point. "I distinctly heard a *pfft*."

I rolled my eyes to the sky. "Must be all the water in your ears."

God, what was I doing? That sounded angry. I wasn't angry at Grady, was I? I did a quick body check. Clenched fists. Gritted teeth. *Uh-oh.* Maybe I wasn't mad. But I was *something.* This all was headed in a very bad direction.

He smiled. "Same ol' Erica."

Heat rolled up from my chest to my face. "Okay, you know what? Something has been bothering me. And it's not that I'm interested because I'm really not," I said, with probably too much hand waving. That seemed to be my new thing. "But how exactly did you get to be sheriff?"

He tilted his head and flashed me another grin. "What exactly are you implying?"

"See!" I pointed at his lips. "You know exactly what I mean. The Grady Forrester I knew was not exactly Mr. Responsible. In fact, when I think of the Grady Forrester I knew, I think of beer, pickup trucks, snowmobiles—"

"All good things."

"I think of speeding, womanizing"—I was on a roll now. Maybe too much of a roll because I didn't see where I was headed—"hockey brawls, stupid-guy high fives, and immature practical jokes that, I guess, are supposed to be funny, but are actually pretty cruel and deserve a kick in the n—"

"And there it is." Grady's hands once again clutched the side of my boat. "We are going to hash this out once and for all." There were those pecs coming aboard again. "I don't think you really know all that happened that night."

I grasped for the pull cord and desperately resumed yanking. "I don't need to. I have a pretty clear recollection of that night, and I don't need to know what little misunderstanding happened before the main event."

"Erica—"

"Stop!" I paused for a moment and took a deep breath. Once I was sure I had myself under control, I said, "Seriously. It doesn't bother me. Nobody but you really saw anything anyway."

"Exactly, and I—"

"In fact." I jabbed a finger toward Grady's face, making his eyes go wide. *Uh-oh.* Not done freaking out. "The only thing that bothers me is that people keep bringing it up!" I felt some spittle hit my chin. Wow, really not done. "And you know what's even worse than people bringing it up?"

Grady quickly shook his head no.

"People feeling bad for me! Because then I start thinking, hey, maybe they have a reason to feel bad for me." I tapped my finger to my chin. "I wasn't feeling sorry for myself. But if everyone else is feeling sorry for me, then maybe there is something to feel sorry about. And really," I said, chuckling, "I'm awesome!" I snapped my mouth shut, swallowed then tagged on a casual, "You know?"

Nothing like shouting, *I'm awesome!,* to your ex-*something* like a crazy person to get the point across that you're awesome.

This just wasn't working. Freddie might have been on to something with the whole *POW!* thing. It was really time to go.

"Erica, I'd still like t—"

I cut him off by giving the pull cord one last, hard yank. Finally, with an eruption of black smoke, the engine roared to life.

I shot a look back to Grady. One leg had already straddled the boat.

"You need to get off, Grady."

He froze. Half in, half out of the boat. "You can't leave yet, Erica."

I revved the engine. "Get off my boat, Grady. You're good. I'm good. It's all good. And I'm leaving."

"You can't—"

I pushed the motor into the water. My mother's loyal little boat jumped forward. Then it slammed back.

A loud crack sounded behind me.

"You're still tied to the dock."

I looked back. A wooden post lay in the water attached to my boat by rope. I looked over to Grady, treading water a few feet away . . . chuckling.

"Gah!"

I pushed the throttle again and took off across the lake, the trailing dock post bouncing on the waves behind me.

The short boat ride did nothing to improve my mood. Thankfully, the retreat looked deserted as I climbed the lodge's stairs. Okay, what had happened with Grady wasn't great. Certainly not how I had imagined it. But I could regroup. It was a one-off type of deal. I wasn't mad at Grady. I didn't care about this social. It was this place.

I needed a new approach. It was now time to avoid everyone and everything. Just hunker down and wait this trip out. It was just too soon. I had thought eight years was too long. But obviously it was too short. I loved my mother, and Freddie too for that matter, with all of his alter egos, but I needed to love them from a distance.

I made it halfway to my bedroom when I heard a loud *thunk*.

What the heck was that?

Thunk!

It came from the kitchen.

I backpedaled slowly and craned my head to peek in.

Laurie Day stood behind the rustic wooden island slamming a heavy cleaver down on a whole pile of plucked chicken carcasses.

I froze. Part of me felt I should really go talk to her. She was grieving after all. I should express my condolences. The other part of me, however, did not like the way she was throwing that meat cleaver around.

I turned away slowly, deciding this really wasn't my place. After all, I barely knew her in high school. And how could I possibly relate to someone who would sleep with Dickie—God rest his soul—let alone comfort her about his death? Besides, she probably wanted to be alone.

I didn't even make it a step down the hallway before I heard, "Erica?"

Condolences it would have to be.

I turned back to the kitchen. "Laurie. Hi. You shouldn't be here. How are you . . . honey?" I asked in an unnaturally soft voice. Freddie was right. Maybe I did have issues. Expressing condolences felt about as natural to me as a third leg.

Laurie's lean muscled arm slammed the cleaver down on the meat block again. I jumped . . . just a little.

She had always been tall and slender, but never soft. Nope, Laurie was all gristle. Every muscle in her body formed a hard edge that looked a little dangerous. Today, in a green fatigue tank top, she looked downright terrifying.

"I'm fine."

"Are you sure?" I asked with my careful, "please don't hurt me" voice. "Because you look a little upset."

"Upset?" she asked, chuckling. "Upset? Why would I be upset? Just because I invested thirteen years in that asshat and have nothing to show for it?" she asked, pointing the cleaver at me. "Do I have a ring? Do I get the dress?

No, I get a dead Dickie on a hot-dog stick." She banged the chicken three more times. Bits of raw flesh flew about the kitchen. Maybe my mom was on to something with her whole veganism thing.

I had no idea what to say next, but I felt like I had to say something. "Laurie—"

"This is all Tommy's fault." Her eyes fixed onto mine.

"Tommy?"

She dropped the cleaver onto the counter and cracked the knuckles on each of her fists. "He always ruins everything for everyone. He always did."

My eyes quickly ran over Laurie's face. She was distracted, talking more to herself than me.

"You mean because of the pranks and stuff?"

Her eyes focused back on mine. She pinned me for a moment in her glare before looking back down at the chicken. "I don't know what I mean. I'm just upset."

"Laurie, I'm sure what happened to Dickie was an accident," I said cautiously. "I'm not sure why he was wandering around the island with a skewer, but it was just a horrible accident."

She licked her lips. "Right."

"Laurie, if you know something about what happened—"

"No. I know it was an accident. I'm just in shock," she said, laying the cleaver down and taking a breath. She then planted both hands on the counter and leaned forward. "So was this the homecoming you were expecting?"

"It's fine," I replied, shaking my head. "I'm just sorry for what you're going through."

She picked up the cleaver again. This time her hand was shaking. "And it isn't over yet."

I spent the rest of the afternoon lying facedown on my bed listening to Laurie bang around the kitchen.

A couple more days. I just needed to get through a couple more days.

I must have fallen asleep, because when I rolled over, the sun lay low on the horizon. I ran a hand over my face. I could hear the animated chatter of women in the front room. I looked to the frog clock hanging on my wall. His fishing poles told me I had missed supper, which explained the grumbling in my stomach, so it was either face the women or starve in my room.

Hunger won the day.

I padded my way softly down the hall. Loud laughter seem to fill the entire lodge. Maybe they wouldn't notice me if I walked really—

"Erica! Honey!" my mom's voice called out.

I turned to look at the room full of women in pajamas holding mugs of tea.

"We missed you today! We weren't able to do our regular therapy exercises because you weren't there," she said with the slightest bit of strain in her voice. She also darted her eyes, not very subtly, over to the insurance agent, Lydia Morgan, who didn't seem to notice anything but the muffin in her hand.

"I am so sorry," I said. "I . . ." *Think, Erica. Think.* I shot my mother yet another look to remind her of how much I hated being put in this position. She just smiled. I inhaled deeply and pushed my shoulders back. "I had a pretty bad allergy attack, and . . . I had to get some medicine! Antihistamines. Knocked me right out." I tried faking a sneeze but ended up spitting on myself.

All the women were still looking at me as though they were expecting more.

"But," I said with what I hoped was a reassuring nod. "I did spend some time last night—hours in fact—going over some exercises we might try to, uh, relieve some of the pressure from all of our unresolved feelings." As soon as the words were out, I felt my lungs deflate. Had I just said *exercises*? I didn't have any exercises! I—

"Yes, I got your notes, darling! We're going to try out all those exercises tonight! We were just waiting for you!" My mother swung her arms widely, embracing the room.

"Great!" I said, finally able to breathe again. "Great."

I guess my *great* wasn't all too convincing, because someone said, "I know what's going on here."

The voice came from Maria Franelli standing by the fireplace in her leopard-print pajamas. The way she was swinging her mug about made me think she'd found Kit Kat and Tweety's gin.

"You do?" I asked quickly. I looked over to my mother, who stood frozen by an armchair, before switching my gaze to Lydia Morgan, who had stopped eating her muffin and was now paying close attention to the woman with the shellacked hair.

"You," she said, pointing a finger first at me then at my mother, "have mother-daughter issues."

My mom said, "Nonsense," at the exact same moment I said, "Absolutely."

The women froze before dissolving into laughter.

"Ah, well," my mother said, clapping her hands together. "You have caught us." She hung her head dramatically before swinging it back up. "Is there any relationship more complicated than that of mother and daughter?"

The women all nodded their heads in agreement while my eyes rolled violently.

"Even my daughter, a brilliant psychologist in her own right, can't help but roll her eyes when her mother speaks."

All the women turned to look at me again. I smiled, but the corners of my mouth felt like they weighed about a hundred pounds.

"But ladies, this week is about you!" my mother announced, grabbing back their attention. "Don't let our foibles get in the way. Erica and I are professionals. Let's turn our attention to you and your healing," she said, smiling and nodding at each one. "Erica, honey, sit down."

"I'll be right there," I said through my faltering smile. "I'm going to get something to eat."

I walked into the kitchen listening to a woman behind me mutter, "My daughter is exactly the same way."

I grumbled my way over to a drawer and yanked it open before I realized I wasn't alone.

"Oh, I'm sorry," a cheerful voice said.

I turned to see a woman about my age pouring water from the kettle into a mug. "I was just getting some . . . some . . ." She turned a package over in her hand. "Vegan berry soul rejuvenation tea." She put the package down. "Then I have to find Kit Kat's tonic."

"Tonic?" I replied, taking in the woman in front of me. She was petite and pretty, with just-styled blond hair and dimples. I doubted she had a frog-themed room growing up.

"You must be Erica. I'm Candace," she said, stepping forward, big smile on her face. "I'm trying really hard not to hug you right now, but I feel like I already know you."

I blinked my eyes a few times.

She gave me a hopeful smile. "Unless you're a hugger too?"

I laughed and took a step back.

Candace? How did I know that name? My brain flashed to my earlier conversation with Freddie. "Oh, Candace. The PR person for the developer."

"That's me, the one and only, working for the evil developer threatening to destroy Otter Lake." She bared her teeth and growled cutely. "I left my tail and horns back in town though."

I chuckled. "Yeah, I don't think they make them in your size." I shut the drawer I had opened and eyed the fridge. "You're not here for the 'We hath mo' healing' session, are you?"

"Oh, no. More like community outreach." She popped a piece of something into her mouth then turned back to the cupboard. "And the muffins. Your mom makes really great muffins." She rummaged around in the cupboards with a level of familiarity that made me frown. "Oh, this must be what Kit Kat was talking about," she said, pulling out an unlabeled bottle with clear liquid in it. "Some natural-medicine thing. She said it helps with her knees."

"I bet it does." Leave it to Kit Kat and Tweety to keep a stash in my mom's kitchen. I pulled open the fridge and spotted some breaded chicken on a plate under plastic wrap. "So I guess Otter Lake hasn't exactly rolled out the welcome mat for you," I said loudly, head still in the fridge.

I heard a sigh. "Actually, the people here are great. It's the job that's killing me." I turned around, chicken in hand, to see Candace lean against the counter. "Don't get me wrong. The money's terrific, and there are worse places to spend the summer, but this job is impossible . . . on both ends."

"Really?" I popped a piece of chicken in my mouth and forced myself to lean against the counter, mirroring Candace. Ever since my conversation with Freddie, I had a burning desire to prove that I could make friends. I liked people . . . generally speaking. Even if they were blond huggers. "Why both ends?"

"Well, the people of Otter Lake don't want change. And

my boss, well, he seems to think I can gentrify this place all by myself. The buyers we're trying to attract are families from the city, and, when they look around, all they see are hillbillies with banjos."

My mouth froze. Otter Lake was kind of like an annoying little brother or sister. Which meant it was fine for me to pick on it, but anybody else? That was an entirely different story.

"I don't see it that way," she said, holding up her palms, "but the people the development is targeting do. And now with poor Dickie falling down a well." Her eyes sadly blinked their way to mine. "Did you know him?"

I shrugged, but my frown deepened. Candace, here, didn't seem to realize that she was the outsider, not me.

"What will the Musketeers do without one of their members?"

I choked a little on my chicken. Suddenly I was feeling kind of silly for calling them Fluffateers myself. We were all adults. "You know it isn't really *Musketeers*. It's—"

She held up a hand. "Oh! Stop right there. I'm not much of a swearer," she said, wrinkling her nose with a smile.

Huh, maybe I needed to start my whole liking-people kick with someone a little easier.

"Anyway, it's a tragedy, and my boss thinks nobody is going to buy out here until the locals have all been cleaned up, or better yet, moved out."

"And that's not going to happen," I said, taking another bite of chicken. Laurie Day sure knew how to tenderize a piece of meat.

"Exactly. It's impossible. That and the snapping turtles."

"Snapping turtles?" I mumbled through my chicken-filled mouth.

"Do you have any idea how many snapping turtles there are in Otter Lake?" She suddenly moved toward me and grabbed a piece of chicken off my plate. I would have stabbed her hand with my fork, if I had been using one.

"Sorry. I'm a sharer. You don't mind, do you?"

I couldn't think of a single appropriate thing to say.

"Are you okay?" she asked, pointing to my face with the fingers holding my chicken. "Your cheek is twitching."

I nodded.

"Anyway, there are so many turtles. And they scare the helicopter moms. I don't blame them. Baby toes are so precious," she said through the hand that was covering her mouth. "I sound completely crazy, don't I?"

I unclenched my jaw. "Not at all."

"Mmm, that was really good."

I moved my plate safely to the counter behind me.

"So how long are you here for, Erica?"

"Just a few more days."

She pulled a phone out of her pocket. "We have to hang out," she said. "What's your number?"

A strangled sound escaped my throat.

"What about tonight? We could head over to the Dawg! Oh, wait . . . I can't tonight," she said, still poking at her phone. A new kind of smile spread over her face. "I'm meeting somebody for drinks."

"Really?" I asked. My mind shuffled through all of the available men in Otter Lake. It was bound to be someone I knew. "Who?"

"Grady Forrester," she said, looking up at me. "Do you know him?"

Candace excused herself shortly thereafter, and I spent the next hour and a half in a fog. My mother, always the survivor, put a pen and notepad in my lap, and I tried really, really hard to play the role of a therapist deep in thought, but the women's stories blew right over my head.

Candace was having drinks with Grady.

Drinks.

With Grady.

It was stupid. I shouldn't care. I mean, it had been a long time. Grady probably had had lots of drinks with lots of Candaces. Probably some Melissas too. Maybe even some Tiffanys.

I moved my pen randomly over the pad on my lap.

It was none of my business if he went on dates with dimpled PR girls. And what was with those dimples? They were big enough to serve soup in. I looked down at my notepad. Huh, and was that a picture of a dimpled woman swimming from a snapping turtle? I grabbed the pen and quickly scribbled over my doodle before getting to my feet. I needed a break.

"Erica, darling. Where are you going?" my mother asked sweetly while stepping around an invisible box of pain belonging to Susan Anderson, the woman who cried every day. She was miming her prison of sorrow.

"I need a breath of fresh air . . . and, and to think about individualized treatment plans."

"Of course. You'll be right back? We're all anxious to hear your thoughts." she said, clasping her hands ever so sweetly to her chest.

I clasped my hands so tightly my knuckles cracked. "Righto."

The screen door banged behind me as I stepped onto the dark porch. I walked over to the railing and took a deep breath.

"I can do this," I whispered softly.

Saying the words out loud actually felt kind of good. Maybe everything my mom taught wasn't hooey.

"I can do this," I said a little more loudly.

Huh, it felt even better louder.

"I can do this!" I yelled into the night sky.

"She's losing it," a voice behind me said.

"Wah!" I spun around, bracing myself on the ban-nister.

Kit Kat and Tweety, white hair glowing in the dark, clunked their mugs together before taking long sips.

"Nice," I muttered. "You two need bells on those mugs, so people know when you're around."

"Then we'd miss all the good stuff," Tweety said. " 'I can do this,' " she mimicked, holding her cup in the air while her sister laughed. "Priceless."

I crossed my arms over my chest. "I see Candace fetched your medicine."

"Great girl that Candace. Knows how to respect her elders."

"Yeah, she tells me your knees are acting up."

"They are when someone else is willing to make a kitchen run," she said, again clinking mugs with her sister. She then patted the bench beside her. "Come sit. You don't really want to go back in there, do you?" She jerked her thumb to the window glowing with yellow light behind her. It looked like all the women were miming now, smash-ing their fists at Susan Anderson's invisible walls. One might have been swinging a pickax.

"Nope," I said, taking a seat.

We sat for a few moments in silence.

Tweety cleared her throat. "So, Erica, how—"

"So not only does my mother have me committing in-surance fraud, but I drove off with my boat still tied to a dock today, tearing off a big chunk of said dock in front of Grady Forrester, no less, who is going out for drinks," I said, making big air quotes around *drinks,* "with your great girl, Candace, who has totally obnoxious dimples . . . all . . . ALL after finding the dead body of a guy I knew back in high school, but didn't particularly like, which is making me feel kind of guilty and traumatized all at the same time. That's how I am!" I said, flopping back on the bench.

Neither twin said anything for a moment.

"I was going to ask how long you were staying."

I threw my hands into the air then let them drop back onto my lap. "A few more days. Till the end of the retreat."

The twins nodded.

We sat in silence again.

This time it was Tweety who broke the silence. "So, why—"

"Why does my mother do the things that she does?" I asked, nodding quickly. "I don't know. You tell me." I jumped to my feet. "I mean I know she loves me, but she doesn't exactly make things easy for me. And then she complains when I don't come to visit. If you were me, would you visit my mother?" I didn't give them time to answer. "No, you wouldn't. No sane person would!"

"I was going to say why—"

"Why does my mother teach honesty and authenticity, yet refuses to practice it in her own life?" I asked, nodding angrily. "Did you know that my mother has never even told me who my father is? Refuses to even discuss it. Says it doesn't matter. Doesn't matter! She probably doesn't know. That's my guess. I was probably conceived with the moon and stars!"

"Erica, honey, keep it together."

"I mean, why does anyone behave the way they do? Why does Grady Forrester charm ladies only to break their hearts? Why does he try to mount somebody's boat one minute only to take someone else out for drinks the next?"

"I was going to say—"

"Oh, stop right there," I said, pointing at Tweety or maybe it was Kit Kat. It was hard to tell in the dark. "I know your routine. I'm spilling my guts and you're going to say something like I was just going to ask why don't I take the four o'clock bus into the city instead of the eight-thirty, or something else to make me look like I'm freaking hysterical!"

Tweety cleared her throat. "Actually, I was going to say, why are you letting everyone push you around?"

"I was going to say the bus thing," Kit Kat muttered over her mug.

I stood frozen for a moment, derailed from my rant. "I don't let everyone push me around. In fact, I'm known for standing up for other p—" Something big and furry hit me in the back of the leg. I stumbled forward. I turned back to see Caesar standing where I had stood just a few seconds ago, licking his paw.

A little gin sprayed from Kit Kat's lips.

"Okay, morbidly obese cats notwithstanding, I do not let people push me around. This is not me," I said, waving my arms around in the air. "I have a life back in Chicago. I—"

"Ran away."

"I did not run away!"

"You ran away because you couldn't . . . what does her mother call it when she's talking to those women who still do their ex-husbands' laundry?" Tweety said, looking to Kit Kat.

"Boundaries."

"Boundaries!" she said, turning back to me. "You couldn't put boundaries up around your mother."

"Putting boundaries around my mother is like putting boundaries around air," I said. "But—"

"Yeah, you don't manage your emotions very well. Like the night at the Raspberry Social," Kit Kat said. "Although it was pretty great when you started screaming, *You want a show! I'll give you a show! Let me introduce you to my little friend!*"

"I did not say, *Let me introduce you to my little friend.* Where do you people keep getting this stuff?"

The twins shrugged in identical motions.

I once again folded my arms over my chest. "You guys don't know what you're talking about." I turned away from them and slapped my hands down on the rough wood of the railing. "Unbelievable," I muttered. "First, there's Freddie saying I have people issues. Now you—"

"Oh, yeah, that too," said Tweety, raising her voice to my turned back. "People issues. You should explore that. That's good."

I shot a glare over my shoulder.

"How many of my mother's sessions have you been to?"

"It's been nearly thirty years. Some of it ain't bad. Hilarious, but not bad."

"Well, thank you, Drs. Freud and Jung, for your brilliant slapdash analysis. I'm sure it will change my life."

"Now you're . . . what's it called?" Tweety snapped her geriatric fingers. "Regressing."

I made a face at her before saying, "And I will have you know, I don't have any *issues* back in Chicago. So maybe it's not me. Maybe it's all you crazy people."

Tweety shook her head. "Nah."

"Hey, quiet down," Kit Kat whispered. "What's going on over there?"

I followed her crooked finger. Over at the crest of the hill at the top of the stairs stood two people, a man and a woman. A shot of fear zinged through me before I realized the woman was Laurie Day and the man, well, by the toss of the hair, the man had to be Harry.

"What are they doing here?" I asked no one in particular.

I remembered my mom had hired Laurie to do some housekeeping for the cabins along with the cooking, so it was possible she was finishing up, but what was Harry doing here?

"I don't know, but Laurie looks *angry,*" Tweety announced with the excitement of a boxing commentator.

I rolled my eyes, but I couldn't help but agree. Laurie did look angry. She wasn't yelling—we would have been able to hear her—but her arms were flailing.

"Laurie's always angry. Now *she* should maybe learn to repress a little bit," Kit Kat replied before leaning forward to slap my hip. "Move, Erica. I can't see."

I shuffled over to the side.

"We probably shouldn't be spying on them," I whispered, unable to peel my eyes away.

"You're welcome to go back inside," Kit Kat added. "But my guess is she's just about to hit him, so you might want to wait."

I scoffed. "Come on. We're not kids anymore. Laurie's not going to—"

"Whoa!" all three of us shouted at once.

Not only did Laurie hit Harry, she clocked him.

"Man down!" Both Kit Kat and Tweety were struggling to their feet.

I waved them back. The twins were always up for a fight, and I didn't want this situation to turn into a Royal Rumble. "I'll go."

I jumped down the porch steps and ran over the best I

could in my flip-flops. As I approached, Laurie disappeared down the stairs leading to the lake. Harry stayed on the ground, hand at his cheek.

"Hey!" I called out, trotting up to where Harry was sitting. "You all right?"

"Erica! What are you doing here?"

I didn't answer right away. I thought it more polite to give him a moment to catch up.

"Oh ho ho, right. You live here."

"My mom lives here," I corrected.

"Right. Right. It all makes sense now," he said, smiling and nodding. If I didn't know Harry, I might have been concerned that Laurie's whack had given him brain damage.

I offered him a hand up, but he waved me off. "I'm cool."

"So what was that all about?" I asked, looking below to Laurie's boat pulling away. I noticed another boat still tied to the dock. That had to be Harry's.

"Nothing. Nothing," he said, still smiling. "I was cruising by, and I saw Laurie's boat and thought, *Hey, I should totally go up there and give Laurie my grieving gift,* but she didn't want it."

"Your grieving gift?"

Harry's hand shot out, tossing a package at me. I fumbled with it a little before pinning it to my chest.

"Harry, is this a bag of weed?"

"Yup, the perfect grieving gift," he said, nodding sagely. "It's also good for dumping people. Take it from me. Your next dumpee will appreciate it."

"I'll keep that in mind," I said, tossing it back to Harry. "So Laurie decked you because you offered her weed?"

"Nah . . . yeah, kind of. You know, she's probably just upset about Dickie." His face turned sad.

I nodded. "How are you doing with everything?"

"Okay." He folded his arms around his knees before adding, "Hey, do you want to make out or something?"

"Not really."

He nodded. "Yeah, me neither. I kind of just want to smoke the weed." He caressed the bag in his lap.

I gave him a smile, but said, "You know you can't do that here, right? But should you be boating?"

"No, totally. I haven't started yet. I'll go home, tie off the boat, and then just float and look at the stars . . . think about what Dickie's doing. If he's in heaven, he's probably rolling around in a bed of boobs right now."

That was too much image for me to respond to.

"Yeah, he'd like that." Harry struggled to his feet. "All right, see ya, Erica."

"Yeah, see ya."

I watched Harry stumble down the steps and push off in his boat before turning back to the lodge. Just then I heard Tweety yell something, but I couldn't quite make out the words.

"What's that?" I shouted back, straining to hear her response.

She yelled louder.

I closed my eyes and shook my head.

"No, Tweety, I didn't keep the weed," I said, stomping back up to the retreat. "And, isn't it time for you to go home?"

Three more days.

I blinked away the morning rays blasting through my bedroom window.

Two really.

Actually, maybe one and a half.

I just needed to get through today, and then I could take

the early bus out tomorrow morning. The women would leave the following day. My mom could work that out with Lydia and cancel next week's retreat.

I popped out of bed and stretched my arms high into the air, ignoring Caesar anchored to the floor by his rolls of fat.

This trip had given me lots to think about, but I could put all of that on hold until I was back in my safe little apartment in Chicago, eating something with lots of meat.

One day really.

I could do this.

I would lie low and say nothing.

And most important of all?

I would stay on the island.

Grady was the biggest problem. Seeing him did stir up all sorts of emotions. And all those emotions led straight to crazy Erica. I couldn't handle both Grady and my mother. And I couldn't embarrass myself in front of Grady if I didn't see him. Thankfully, that really shouldn't be too much of a problem. The Crime Unit had scoured the well site, and I had been questioned. So Grady had no reason to bring his police butt out here—especially considering it was probably still naked in bed with Candace.

I slammed the heels of my hands against my temples.

Gah! Where had that come from?

No, no, no. No naked Grady images in bed with Candace.

Why did I care?

It was ancient history.

I rolled my shoulders again and stretched my head from side to side.

It didn't matter what I had to do to make it happen, this was going to be a good day.

* * *

"Sweet Mother of God, I don't want to die!"

A startled flock of birds rose up from the trees.

"You're fine, Maria!" my mother called up to the woman clinging to the pole supporting the wooden platform. The rest of the women stood a short distance behind my mother, waiting their turns. "This is a trust exercise. Step out onto the rope and make your way to the other side toward Lydia. You need to trust in me! I won't let you fall! You need to trust in yourself!"

I sighed and wiped a bit of sweat from my brow. This could take a while.

I stood at the other end of the course, holding the ropes for Lydia Morgan. The helmeted insurance agent beamed down at me and gave a friendly wave which I did my best to return. Yup, this could definitely take a while.

The course consisted of two pairs of parallel ropes— one pair for the feet, the other for hands—running between two suspended wooden platforms. The way this exercise ran, the women would start from either end, they would meet in the middle, take a brief moment of strength by staring deeply into each other's eyes, and then continue their respective journeys to the other end. The entire time, my mother and I would guide them from below, holding on to the safety ropes that attached to their harnesses, just in case they fell or simply bailed. Thankfully, the device was designed in such a way that it didn't take much strength on our part to guide them to the ground.

"I can't do it! I can't do it!"

"Trust in us, Maria! We won't let you fall! This is your turning point of power! I can feel it!"

I shifted my weight back and forth. My hips were beginning to ache standing on the uneven ground. As a teenager

I had begged my mother, over and over, to skip the ropes course, but she never would. I just couldn't help but think there had to be a faster, less sweaty, way to build trust.

"One step, Maria! Just take one step!"

"Okay! For you, I'll do it!"

"Don't do it for me! Do it for you!" my mother shouted back.

Maria Franelli pointed one shaky toe toward the rope. Finally.

I adjusted my grip, looked up to Lydia and nodded. She took a step.

"I caaan't!" Maria screamed.

"Oh, for the love of God, come on!"

I started. Who had said that?

All eyes landed on me.

Oh . . . uh-oh.

Then all the women began to shout.

"She's right!"

"Come on, Maria! You can do it!"

"Show that cheating bastard how strong you are!"

Maria's hair had found every possible way out of her helmet, and black mascara ran in thick trails down her face. I had never not seen a woman eventually make it across with my mother's encouragement, but she might be a first.

Then, almost in an instant, a different look came across her face. For a brief second, she looked stunned and then focused . . . superfocused.

She took a step . . . and then another.

I jumped to attention and gave Lydia another nod.

Lydia kept a good pace, but she was nowhere near as quick as Maria, who was now making a beeline across the rope.

Then just as suddenly she stopped.

"You're doing beautifully, Maria! Don't give up now!"

I looked again to Maria's face. Her look stayed intent.

Realization dawned on me. She wasn't focused on the course. She was focused on the woods behind me, like she was angling to get a better view.

"Oh my God," she said in a daze. "Who is that? Tell me he's the prize for making it across."

I looked over my shoulder. Of course. Well, at least I wasn't the only one he had that effect on.

All the women froze as Grady broke through the trees. His sheriff's hat hid his face, just as it had that morning when I watched him crest the hill. He brushed a branch from his path.

Then bam!

He looked up just as he stepped into the full strength of the sun.

A chorus of women gasped in unison. His slow smile slid across his face at the sound, revealing his perfect white teeth.

I snorted. He so did that on purpose.

The women oohed then began murmuring in fast, hushed voices.

"Have you ever seen anything so beautiful?"

"His thighs. Oh my God, would you look at his thighs?"

"Just once. Just once, I want to be arrested. Why do I never get arrested?"

"He's walking over to Summer's daughter."

"You don't think they're together, do you?"

"She's not in his league."

"Nobody is in his league."

"I'm standing right here!" I shouted.

The women startled.

"Well, good morning, ladies!" Grady called out, voice riddled with enjoyment.

They tittered while I rolled my eyes so violently something hurt deep in my head.

"Don't let me disturb you," he said, holding his hand up in a way that flexed his bicep. The women clutched each other for strength. "Please continue what you're doing. I just need a few words with Erica."

The women didn't move.

"Ladies," he said. "Please. If I'm interrupting, I'll have to go."

Well, that got them moving. Luckily, it also allowed me to look up and focus on Lydia instead of him. Not that it really mattered. I had already decided today was going to be a good day, no matter what.

I was ready for my do-over with Grady. Calm, cool Erica was back.

"Good morn—"

I cut him off. "Well, don't you look all bright eyed and bushy tailed after your date." Nope, Crazy Erica was apparently still in the building.

"I'm sorry?"

I cleared my throat. "I had the pleasure of meeting Candace last night. Sweet girl. Very . . . um, blond. A hugger too. You have to love a hugger."

"Oh, right," he said. I could hear the smile sliding back over his face.

I closed my eyes. "Why are you here? I . . . I really thought we left things in a good place yesterday."

He gave me a look that clearly spoke the fact that he too was now questioning my sanity, but said, "I need to ask you something—it's not about the social—and I don't want you to take it the wrong way."

I inhaled deeply. "Of course," I said, forcing a smile. I kept my eyes on the women above me, but I wasn't really seeing them anymore. "What can I help you with?"

"How do I put this," he said before pausing. "I'm just going to ask it."

"Please do."

"Erica Bloom, are you a serial killer?"

Chapter Five

"Uh, I think you're supposed to keep a hold of that rope."

I stared into Grady's face, not moving.

He motioned his eyes from me over to the rope dangling midair.

I quickly grabbed it. "You're joking, right?" I asked, not quite able to tear my gaze from his face. There was something serious there that I did not like at all.

He sighed. "Bad joke for an even worse situation. Harry Drummond was in an accident last night."

A cold rush swept over my body despite the morning heat. "He's not . . ."

"He's in a coma over at St. Elizabeth."

I exhaled until my chest felt still and empty. "Oh, no, poor Harry." I was a little surprised by how sad I felt. I mean, Harry wasn't a big part of my life, but he was endearing in his own way. "What happened? Can I see him?"

Grady swallowed before answering. "The hospital isn't allowing anyone but family to see him at the moment. And as for what happened, I can't give you any details right now."

"Why not?" I asked and glanced back and forth from him to Lydia's form up above. She and Maria were holding hands, now at the halfway point. Unfortunately, this also meant my mother was directly across from us, listening to every word.

"Is there someone who can take over for you?" Grady looked around to the other women. They were still all looking at him with dumb smiles on their faces. He gave them a group nod.

"Believe me. There's no one," I said, shaking my head. "And what are you talking about? What does Harry's accident have to do with me?"

"Yes, what does Harry's accident have to do with my daughter?" my mother asked sharply. "You know, my brother is a very influential lawyer. Should I call him?"

Both Grady and I looked over at my mother. Her already large eyes had widened to near-hysterical proportions.

"Mom, I thought you guys weren't speaking, and . . . and, this is crazy. You don't need to call Uncle Jack."

Grady cleared his throat. "You might want to call Uncle Jack."

My eyes flashed back to his. He was serious.

My mother was about to speak, but luckily, the women above were parting ways, and we began to sidestep in opposite directions.

Grady waited until we were a few steps over before he resumed speaking.

"Did I say Harry was in an accident?"

I nodded.

"Well, it may not have been an accident."

A new rush of chills raced over my damp skin. "Okay." I did not like where this conversation was headed. My eyes darted over Grady's face.

"And it seems as far as Dickie is concerned," he said

before taking a breath, "it looks like he may have been stabbed before he fell into the well, but we don't have the murder weapon." He studied my face for a moment. "You're sure you saw a weenie skewer?"

"Yeah, I'm sure," I said, my mind sussing out all this new information. "You mean it wasn't at the scene?"

He shook his head no.

"So somebody got down into the well and pulled it . . . pulled it out of his body . . . in the time it took for me to run to the retreat and get you?"

"Yeah, sounds kind of implausible," Grady said. "It would have made more sense for the murderer to stab him, keep the weapon, and push him into the well."

"But I saw the skewer!"

"So you say." His tone was neutral, but I did not like what those words implied.

"I can't believe this is happening."

"Yoo-hoo!" a voice from above called down. "Did I hear you say something was wrong with the retreat's well? If so, as your insurance provider—"

My gaze flipped up. "Oh, no, Ms. Morgan, Officer—"

"Sheriff," Grady corrected.

"Pfft," I replied, not sparing him a glance.

"Why do you keep *pffting* my credentials?" he asked quickly, eyes darting around to the other women. "I am a real cop, you know."

"I know. You have the uniform and everything," I said, shaking my head before turning my face back skyward. "Sorry, Ms. Morgan . . . Lydia," I corrected. "Grady here is just looking for . . . directions."

"Oh, okay," Lydia called down. "Thanks for the support, Dr. Bloom."

"Dr. Bloom?"

I felt my cheeks flush. I gave him a sideways look,

and said through my teeth, "Grady, you have caused enough horribleness in my life for one man. Just leave it alone."

Our eyes met and warred for a bit before he shook his head in defeat.

"I don't want to know anything that's going on with this," he said, waving his hands around the retreat. "You're already in enough trouble."

"But the missing skewer alone can't implicate me in all this mess. That's really circumstantial. Or inconclusive. Or something like that. You have got to have more than that to go on before you even consider me to be a suspect."

"We do."

Before I could stop it my jaw dropped again. "You do?"

"Fingerprints."

"Fingerprints?"

"We found your fingerprints on a bag of weed Harry had in his possession." My brain was clicking all the pieces together before Grady even finished speaking.

"I can explain that," I said quickly. "You know my prints are only in the system as a job requirement for the courthouse, and as for last night, I only touched—"

"Stop," he said, putting his hand up. "You're not under arrest. And I don't want your answers until you've consulted an attorney. I figure it's the least I can do. But if you saw Harry last night, that may very well make you the last person to see him before his hair got caught in that propeller and—"

"Propeller! What propeller? His boat propeller? Oh my God, poor Harry. I can't—"

"Forget I said that. I wasn't . . . never mind." Grady ran a hand over his face.

"Okay, but why would I want to kill Harry? Dickie,

maybe. Everybody has wanted to kill Dickie at some point, but not Harry. What would my motive be?"

Grady looked me in the eye.

"So help me God, Grady, if you say the social, I'll—"

He held up his hand again. "I'm not saying anything. Some people think that maybe the social was your 'pig's blood on prom night' moment, but I don't think that."

I put a hand to my forehead. "I can't believe this is happening."

"Look, believe it or not, Erica, I'm here to help you." He moved to touch my arm then pulled away. "I've gotta go," he said, taking a few steps back. "But listen, until we get this whole thing sorted out, I don't want you talking to anyone."

"Right," I said more to myself than him. "Don't talk to anyone."

"Oh, and Erica?"

I looked over my shoulder to his departing form. He was pointing back to me. "Don't leave town."

Time stopped.

The next thing I remember somebody was shouting something about a rope.

"Well, the hospital called," my mother said, walking into the common room. It was early evening. The women were once again in their jammies drinking tea. I sat in the middle of them like a guilty dog staring at its paws. "Lydia's going to be fine. Maybe a little whiplash from the safety lock catching her the way it did, but fine. I've sent Red over to get her. She'll be back within the hour."

The women murmured relief in response.

Yup, I'd dropped Lydia Morgan.

I'd dropped the insurance agent who held my mother's business in her hands.

Well, technically, I didn't drop her. I'd just failed to catch her.

Apparently, she was stepping onto the platform just as Grady told me not to leave town. Startled, she missed her footing.

I picked at a loose thread of denim hanging from my shorts.

Maybe I was some sort of deranged killer and didn't know it.

Did that happen?

A psychologist would know.

Maybe coming home had caused some sort of psychotic break. It all fit, really. I could already see my neighbors on the nightly news saying, *She was quiet. Kept to herself. Bit of a loner.* Then all of my fake friends on social media would be discovered. Yup, and it would only go downhill from there. *She was raised by a single mother,* they'd say, *practicing alternative religions.* And then they'd come up with names. I'd be known as the Earth Mother Executioner, the Raspberry Social Satanist, the Hippie Horror, the—

"Okay," my mother said, clasping her hands together. "I know everyone is upset by the day's events, but that's life for you! Not every day is going to be perfect. This is a learning opportunity. I think what we need to do is have everyone gather around, and then we can talk about our feelings openly and honestly."

I couldn't help it. Before I even realized what was happening, I found my head shaking back and forth in my hands, and I was making the most peculiar sound—not quite sure what it was all muffled in my hands.

"Is she all right?" I heard one of the women whisper.

"No. No. No. No. NO!"

Oh, that's what I was trying to say.

"Erica, darling?" my mother murmured with lots of warning.

Suddenly I was on my feet.

"No! I don't want to talk about my feelings! And I don't want to talk about your feelings!" I said, pointing at a random woman. She froze, teacup hovering mid-sip. "Or yours!" I said, turning on another. "I don't want to talk about anything! Ever again!" Some rational part of my brain was sitting far up in the nosebleeds watching my crazy show unfold, but it was too far away to do any good. "Let's try that therapy! Let's all take a vow of silence! Every single one of us! You! You! And especially you!" My finger jumped from woman to woman. They were ducking, maybe a little worried my finger was loaded.

I felt my mother's hands on my shoulders, guiding me away from the herd of frightened women.

"I think you need a break, sweetheart," she said, leading me to the door.

"I don't need a break! I haven't even gotten started! You know how I know?" I asked, the roundness of my eyes matching my mother's. She gave me the *Why don't you tell me, sweetheart?* smile nurses give mentally ill patients. "Because we're still talking!"

"Okay, now." My mother pushed me out the front door. "You get yourself some fresh air, and I'll check on you in a little bit."

I whipped around to face her as the screen door banged shut between us. I saw her mouth the words, *What is wrong with you?* I would have answered, but she shut the wood door too.

"Gah!" I yelled before spinning around. I walked over to the railing, planted my hands, and took a few deep breaths of night air before I realized something was hissing at me.

Caesar.

How he managed to launch his massive body onto the bannister was beyond me, but there he was, a fur-covered beach ball stalking toward me.

"Oh, you want me to move?" I asked him.

He padded another paw forward, still hissing.

"Am I touching your cat space?"

He hissed again. This time some spittle landed on my hand.

"Oh, that's it!" I grabbed the bannister and shook it with everything I had in me. The wood was well anchored, but I just needed a jiggle.

Then it happened.

Caesar's eyes widened, and he tipped over the side, paws in the air, right down into the hydrangeas below.

I gasped and quickly looked over the edge. Caesar lay on his back, wiggling, in an attempt to flip over. Our eyes met. Sure, his were filled with hatred, but there was something else there. Something that had never been there before.

Respect.

Everything suddenly became very clear.

I whipped my phone out of my pocket, mumbling.

The phone rang twice then before I could say anything, Freddie's voice sounded on the other end. "Where have you been? I've been calling and calling! I heard you went on a rampage at the retreat and killed eight people with an axe!"

"Never mind all that."

"Never min—"

"Look, I need your help."

"Why . . . with what?"

"With solving the murder of Dickie Morrison."

Chapter Six

By seven the next morning, I was halfway across the lake to Freddie's house. It didn't take much convincing to get him on board. I guess he had a thirst for adventure that fortune-telling alone couldn't satisfy. I had called my boss back in Chicago the night before asking for more time. She didn't seem annoyed by all the rescheduling this would mean. In fact, she seemed really happy that I was, quote, *working on my personal life.*

I had avoided the women completely by climbing out of my bedroom window. I didn't have time for any more distractions. I needed to get out of Otter Lake before I truly did lose my mind, and to do that, I needed to find out what happened to both Dickie and Harry. While the details were sketchy, I was sure that this whole mess could be wrapped up fairly easily. I had, after all, recorded dozens of murder trials, so it shouldn't be too hard. Then, once I had unmasked the murderer, I could plunk a stack of conclusive evidence on Grady Forrester's desk and tear out of this town, leaving it in a big cloud of dust.

Oh, and it all had to happen before the Raspberry Social.

Five days. No problem.

I waited a minute after ringing the bell on Freddie's door before I did it again.

Finally, it swung open.

"No."

"What?" Freddie asked, all wide-eyed.

"You're not wearing that."

He stepped back and looked down at himself. "I thought, given the circumstances, this outfit was perfect."

I gave him another once-over. The lower half was fine, albeit a little casual. He wore sandals, oversized Hawaiian shorts, and a worn Hooters shirt. It was the hat I was having a little trouble with.

"You can't wear a Sherlock Holmes hat."

"Why not?"

"How do I even begin to answer that question?"

Freddie planted his fists on his hips. "Do you want my help or not?"

I closed my eyes and sighed. "I don't know anymore."

He started to shut his door. I pushed it back open with my hand.

"Fine. You can keep the hat."

"Excellent," he said with a skip over the threshold. "So where are we going first?"

I had given this a lot of thought. "Laurie Day's."

"Why Laurie's?"

I walked ahead, leading the way toward Freddie's far superior boat. "Because she knows more than she's saying."

Suddenly I was the only one still walking.

I turned around to see that Freddie had stopped, annoyed look on his face.

"What?"

"You're giving me grief about the hat, but you get to say stuff like that?"

"Like what?"

Freddie tucked his chin into his chest and deepened his voice. " 'She knows more than she's saying.' "

"I see your point. I'll stop."

"No, don't stop. That was awesome. Just don't be greedy with the coolness."

Twenty minutes later, we were stepping around rusted-out rabbit cages to knock on the door of Laurie's trailer.

The sound of yipping dogs started up from the cabin behind us. It belonged to Grandpa Day, who had seemed about a hundred twenty years ago. I wondered briefly if we should go knock on his door next. The thought wasn't exactly appealing. Grandpa Day was a bit eccentric.

"Either she's not home, or she's a heavy sleeper."

"I'm going to look in the window," Freddie said, flipping an old cinder block on its side by the edge of the trailer. He stepped up, and pressed his face against the grimy glass, Sherlock hat slipping back on his head. "Erica, you gotta see this."

Freddie stepped down, giving me room. It was hard to see through the dirty glass. I cupped my hands by either side of my face to block out the sun.

"Is that a suitcase?" I asked.

"Sure looked like it to me," Freddie replied. "Half packed too."

"Hey! What are you two doing over there!" a voice shouted out.

"Uh-oh. Is that Laurie's grandfather?" I asked, grabbing Freddie's arm to jump down.

"Yeah," Freddie replied, slowly leading me toward the back of the trailer. "And he's armed."

I jerked around to squint up at the cabin. Yup, Laurie's grandfather holding a shotgun that was nearly as tall as he was.

"Who's out there!" he called again.

"We're friends of Laurie, Mr. Day!" I shouted back. Then I whispered to Freddie, "What are the odds he'll actually shoot at us?"

"My guess?" Freddie squinted his eyes. "Near a hundred percent."

I looked back at the cabin to see Grandpa Day raising his gun.

Freddie and I hurried our side-shuffle toward the back of the trailer.

"Laurie said to shoot anyone who came sniffing around her stuff!" Grandpa Day yelled, leveling his rifle in a shaky motion.

"Time to go!"

Freddie and I sprinted toward the dock.

BAM!

My hands flew to my head as my knees buckled.

I hit the ground.

Holy cow!

My fingers flew over my body. No holes . . . on me. But what about Freddie?

I spun to see Freddie cradling his hat in his arms.

"My hat!" Freddie yelled. "He shot my hat!"

"Freddie, come on!" I screamed, jumping to my feet. "Leave the hat!"

"Oh, it's fine," he said, sticking a finger through the hole in his deerstalker before jerking his head in a motion for me to look behind him. "Grandpa down."

I looked up at the cabin. The shot had knocked Grandpa Day onto his back. He was wriggling around a little, much like Caesar from the night before.

Freddie got to his feet. "Come on." He turned and began walking toward the cabin.

I stayed frozen to the spot. "What are you doing?"

"Well, we can't just leave him there," Freddie said, walking back into the range of fire. "I still have to live with these people, you know."

"He tried to shoot you in the head!"

"Right. Like he could aim that thing," Freddie replied with a huff. "Man, you have been gone a long time. It's Otter Lake. What's a single gunshot between neighbors?"

I ran and caught up to Freddie, making sure to use his body as cover.

Grandpa Day was still on his back when we got to the porch.

"Stay back!" he warned. "The first shot was a warning."

"Here. Let me give you a hand," Freddie said, kneeling down, carefully sliding the shotgun away with his foot.

"Hey, you're that fat Asian kid with the rich parents."

"Yes, yes, I am," Freddie replied, raising Grandpa Day by the shoulders to a seated position.

"And you're the Boobsie girl," he said, pointing at me, "with the wing-nut mom."

"That's right."

I sat on the top step of the porch. Despite the adrenaline pounding through my veins, I realized that Freddie was right to come back. This was starting to look like an opportunity.

"Sorry about shooting at you like that. If I had known it was you—"

I waved him off. "Mr. Day, did Laurie really tell you to shoot anyone who came by her trailer?"

"That she did, young lady," he said, letting Freddie help him get to his feet. "She was real serious about it too."

Freddie and I exchanged looks. "Did she tell you why?"

He scrunched his face in concentration, his features nearly disappearing into the folds of his wrinkles. "No, I don't think she did."

"You didn't ask her?" I pressed.

He shrugged his thin shoulders.

Freddie and I exchanged another look before he added, "Do you know where she got off to this morning?"

"Nah, but she took the boat out real early. I didn't even have my teeth in," he said, scratching the white stubble poking out from his chin. "I would have thought she'd be at your place."

"Maybe," I said, but I knew that wasn't the case. My mom handled breakfasts. She couldn't afford to have Laurie do all three meals.

"Well, thanks, sir," I said, grabbing Freddie by the arm. "We'll let you get on with your day."

"Thanks, kids. Sorry again about your hat." He tipped his own John Deere cap.

"No problem," Freddie mumbled halfheartedly, again poking at the hole with his finger.

"Do you think we should take his gun?" I whispered as we walked down the porch steps.

Freddie gave me a look that clearly said I was nuts. "Yeah, let's take the old white man's gun. In case you haven't noticed, I'm a visible minority . . . an endangered species in Otter Lake. Actually, I guess I can't be endangered. My kind was never established in the first place. Although I probably share more DNA with Native—"

I groaned loudly.

"You never take a white man's gun." Freddie stepped into his boat.

I shrugged my shoulders. "I just thought he might—"

"Are you trying to get me killed?"

"All right! I get it," I said, untying the mooring rope and tossing it into the boat.

Freddie revved the engine. "What, do you think you're in freaking Canada?"

"All right already," I shouted. "Enough!"

Freddie pulled away from the dock. "Hippie."

I gorged myself on processed meat at Freddie's before heading back to the retreat. During lunch, we tossed around a number of wild theories about Dickie's death—none as crazy as my being a serial killer. Obviously, Laurie was somehow involved with all this mess. Maybe they had all gotten into something illegal and were now paying the price. At some point, I needed to see Tommy. There's no way his two best friends would have been involved in something without him.

By the time my mom's boat coughed and sputtered its way back to the retreat it was mid-afternoon. I would have stayed at Freddie's all day, but I had to face the music at some point. I wanted to apologize to Lydia before I was consumed by the bitterness of the lawsuit I was pretty sure she would slap me with.

I took a steadying breath as I walked up the porch steps.

I could hear the women's voices from inside.

I suddenly remembered my outburst from the night before. Maybe they'd give me a wide berth now. You know, the kind you give the apocalypse criers on the street.

"Erica!" my mom called out as I stepped in the door.

"There she is," one of the women said, clutching her hands to her chest. "She's back."

I couldn't remember her name, but her husband had spent their life savings on the Web site Naughty Robots!

A second later, all the women were on their feet, coming at me with open arms.

"What the—" My words were cut off by a group hug.

I froze. I once read that playing dead could ward off bear attacks. That advice seemed sound in this situation too.

Before I knew it, I was being ushered into the common room toward a couch with Lydia Morgan sitting on it. She wore a neck brace, my guilt painted all over it.

I tried to plant my feet, but the wave of women swept me forward.

Then Lydia did the strangest thing.

She patted the spot beside her on the couch.

My eyes flew in a panic to my mother. She flashed a reassuring smile, but it did not have its intended effect.

I sat down slowly beside Lydia, keeping my front rigidly forward. I could feel her body turning toward mine, inviting me to face her, but I pinned my hands between my knees.

A few moments of silence passed.

My eyes flitted about the room. All the women were looking at us smiling . . . waiting.

I licked my lips. I needed to say something first. "Lydia, I'm so sor—"

Suddenly Lydia's arm was around me, and her forehead was on my shoulder.

"I forgive you," she said. "I forgive you."

All the women began to laugh and clap.

All right, what the hell was going on?

This time I looked at my mother with as much suspicion as I could physically muster.

"Erica, darling, after you left last night, the women and I had a deep session on forgiveness."

"Ooookay."

"We talked about the freeing power it has. How it's a gift one gives to oneself."

"Right," I said, slowly looking sideways at Lydia, who had thankfully removed her forehead from my shoulder.

"I'll admit," she said, looking far more deeply into my eyes than I was comfortable with. "It wasn't easy. I mean dropping me in a trust exercise? But when your mother had the courage to tell us the truth . . ."

"The truth?"

This was the first bit of good news I had heard in a while.

Something like happiness ran over my body. I couldn't believe my mom had actually come clean. It was strange, being an insurance agent, that Lydia was so cool with the whole thing, but my mother could be persuasive when she wanted to be.

My shoulders eased down for the first time in days. I looked around the room at the smiling women, and actually started to smile back.

"Wow. This is great news," I said. "It's really amazing how supportive you women are. I thought you might be mad that—"

"Mad? Mad?" my mother cut in. "Erica, you underestimate the friendship and love your fellow sisters are capable of. When I told them what Grady Forrester and his cousin did to me . . . did to you . . . all those years ago at that wretched social, they immediately understood why you were acting so, so . . ."

My mother looked about the room for help.

One of the women made a cuckoo gesture, finger twirling about her ear.

"The social?" The gears in my brain ground to a halt.

"And then him showing up like that? Accusing you of all sorts of terrible things?"

I blinked a few times. "You told about the social?"

All the women nodded and one said, "Can you imagine? Him luring you into skinny-dipping?"

I closed my eyes and shook my head. "He didn't lure me. I actually wanted to go swimming because . . . well, because, my mother," I said, flashing my eyes open, casting a pretty accusatory look in her direction, "was insisting on going ahead with an ill-advised interpretative dance in front of the entire town."

My mother smiled and nodded, completely ignoring my tone. "It was going to be a beautiful performance inspired by the legend of Diana the huntress, but in my interpretation she realizes the evils of eating meat and—"

"Anyway, the skinny-dipping just kind of happened." I shook my head. "It wasn't a big deal, and—"

"And he ran off with your clothes."

"You can't trust men who are that good-looking," Maria Franelli interrupted, nodding vigorously. "Everything comes just a little too easily to them." Her eyes flashed through her sparkly purple eye shadow. "And I thought my husband was a bastard."

"But your mother never told us how you got up on that stage. What happened?"

"Wait, don't answer," another woman piped in. "I have to go to the washroom. I don't want to miss this."

Another woman jumped up from the couch. "Oh! And I've got marshmallows. We could cook them in the firep—"

"No! No! No!"

"Uh-oh, there she goes with the *no*s again," somebody muttered.

"Erica's right. There's no reason to rehash. I told them it's probably why you went into psychology in the first place," my mother said, placing her hands on the shoulders of one of the women beside her. "You needed to process the trauma. Although I'm sure you'll disagree."

"I do. I do disagree."

"But sometimes you have to trust your mother," she said

brightly. "All right, ladies, get your walking shoes. It's time for our sing-a-long through the forest." As the women headed for the door, I made a grab for my mother.

"Are you coming, sweetheart?"

"I think I'll pass," I said, pulling her aside. "And don't think we're not going to talk about all this later, but in the meantime, I need to ask you something."

"What, darling?"

"Did Laurie come in today?"

"No, she didn't as a matter of fact," my mother said, eyes shrewd. "But it was fine. All the women pitched in. We made squash stew for lunch. But now you tell me something. How much trouble are you in? I've called your uncle, but he hasn't gotten back to me. Is there something I don't know? Did you do something to break the law?"

"Really? Really?" I said, straining to keep my voice at a whisper. "Now you're worried about the law?"

"I do wish you would work on your codependent relationship with sarcasm."

I closed my eyes as though that would make the horror of my situation disappear. "Mom, that doesn't even make sense."

"Well, I'm not the one with the Ph.D.," she said, spinning around, bangles jangling in the air. "Shall we go, ladies? Don't wait up, sweetheart. We're having supper in town."

After the women left, I called the hospital to check up on Harry. He was out of intensive care, but still in a coma. His parents, now residents of Florida, had flown in and weren't allowing any visitors. Made sense given the circumstances. I intended to spend the rest of the afternoon mulling over everything that had happened so far, but it turned out my bed wasn't a good mulling spot, and I fell asleep. It was quarter to nine when my phone rang.

"Hello?"

A Southern-accented voice filled my ear. "Sugar plum, didn't I tell you this would happen? You can bathe a dog in vinegar, but all you'll have is stinky fleas."

I took my phone away from my ear to look at the number. "Freddie?"

"Yeah, hang on. I'm working."

I flopped back in bed.

"No, you're welcome, Mint Julep. Just remember to come back to Madame F for all your fortune-telling needs." There was slight pause before, "Erica?"

"Madame F?"

"Oh, stop it," Freddie replied. "I don't have much time. I have like eight people waiting for me to tell them what they want to hear. So listen up. I've got us a lead."

"You do?"

"Remember how on that first day when you came home, you were talking about Tommy's boat?"

I absentmindedly ran my toe along the edge of the window frame by my bed. "Yeah, it is a pretty nice boat."

"Exactly. It got me to thinking. How could Tommy afford a boat like that? He hasn't had a steady job, well, ever."

I pushed myself up and crossed my legs. "Okay."

"First I thought maybe he got a bucketload of credit, so I contacted Kevin Mutt because he took over his dad's boat shop, and—"

"Wait a minute, doesn't Kevin Mutt hate you?" I asked, furrowing my brow.

"Yeah, but he doesn't hate Brandi from Montreal."

My eyes rolled up to the beams of my ceiling. "You're catfishing Kevin Mutt?"

"What? You thought all that effort was just for you?"

"Freddie, you can't still be holding a torch for him. He used to throw you in lockers, so people wouldn't think he liked you."

"Hey! Don't judge. The heart wants what the heart wants," Freddie said quickly before adding, "We're getting off topic."

"Sorry. Continue."

"Anyway," Freddie replied dramatically. "I found out that, yeah, some of it is on credit, but, get this, he put twenty grand down on it . . . in cash."

"Huh."

"Huh? That's it?"

"I'm still thinking," I said.

"Well, hurry up!" Freddie yelled. "Where did Tommy get twenty grand?"

I chewed the edge of my thumbnail. "I don't know."

"Me neither. But I do know he didn't save it up, because he's a moron. So that means twenty grand fell into his lap mere weeks before someone kills Dickie and someone else tries to kill Harry."

"Huh."

"Okay, this is painful for me. If we're going to be a detectiving team, you need to show a little more enthusiasm."

"I just woke up. Cut me some slack. So how do we find out where he got the money? You wouldn't happen to be catfishing someone at the bank, would you?"

"Brandi's not a slut."

I flopped back down in bed. "Fine. I'm going to have to break into Tommy's place and look for clues."

"I'm sorry . . . you're going to have to do what now?"

"Freddie, the women have started group-hugging me."

The sound of Freddie sucking air through his teeth came through the phone. "Oh, that's a shame."

"Yeah, besides, what day is it? Tommy's probably at the Salty Dawg, right?"

"I don't think the actual day really matters," he said. "Why don't you wait until tomorrow, and then I can come too. I've got balaclavas," he added with game show enthusiasm.

"I can't wait. I've got to get out of here. If I find a bit of evidence, pointing in a direction other than me, Grady might actually let me leave town."

"Of course, he might not be happy about you breaking into his cousin's place."

I rubbed my forehead with my thumb and forefinger. He had a point. "I'll think of something."

"Fine, but I am not happy about this. We were just starting to have fun."

It was crazy, but despite everything, it had been a lot of fun hanging out with Freddie. There was no way, however, that I was sticking around for the social. I had thought everyone would have forgotten it by now. But obviously I was wrong.

I ended the call with Freddie, and slipped on a pair of jeans and a black T-shirt. I checked myself in the mirror. The outfit did kind of look like it needed a balaclava, but it would have to do.

I glanced around my room to see if there was anything else I needed to bring. A screwdriver stood out on my dresser. My mom was always starting jobs and leaving tools lying around. I slipped it into my back pocket. I wasn't sure exactly how it would help me, but it couldn't hurt to take it.

Right.

I rolled my shoulders a few times, tightened my ponytail, and swung the door open.

"Wah!"

Kit Kat and Tweety stood on the side. Tweety twirled a
set of keys around her finger and said, "I'm driving."

Chapter Seven

"You two are not coming." I trotted quickly through the front door of the lodge and jumped down the steps in a single leap. "And didn't anyone ever tell you it's rude to eavesdrop?"

Tweety shouted something from behind me, but I couldn't hear what it was.

Crazy old ladies. Like I was going to let them ride along on my first—and God willing only—break and enter. I didn't need their boat. I had—

I was midway down the stairs to the lake when I saw the empty spot where my mother's boat should have been. Argh. Dinner in town. They must have taken both her boat and Red's.

Doesn't matter, I thought, resuming my steps. I could always take the canoe.

Except that was gone too.

Someone must have carted it back to the other side of the lake.

I looked over my shoulder. Kit Kat and Tweety were at the top of the stairs, dentures glowing in the darkness.

I'd swim . . . except it was pretty far. I'd probably drown.

My head slumped forward just as the twins stepped down beside me.

"Give an old lady a hand, would ya?" Tweety said, linking her arm around mine. "These stairs are a bitch."

Twenty minutes later, Tweety killed the engine on the boat as we glided toward a little bit of beach about a quarter mile from Tommy's place. Just as I figured, his boat was gone. At least we didn't have to worry about getting caught. Even better, it was a still night. We'd hear any boats coming a mile away.

"So," Kit Kat whispered. "What do you expect to find inside?"

"Porn."

"Well, aside from that," Tweety said, smacking me on the arm.

"Ow." I rubbed the spot where she had hit me. "I don't know, okay? This is kind of a casual thing. I just want to take a look around and see if anything jumps out."

"So we're going in blind," Kit Kat mused, while staring very seriously at the dark cottage.

I sighed.

"Why are we breaking in though? It seems extreme," Tweety said. "Shouldn't you go question him first?"

"I will talk to him, but I figured this might help me ask the right questions. Tommy's not exactly a forthcoming kind of guy." I licked my lips, avoiding the twins' gaze. "And I don't really look at this as breaking in. We're just having a look-see."

"A look-see. That's adorable. And it's also denial. Your mother would call that denial."

"Well, she's not here, is she?" I stopped and inhaled deeply before speaking again. "I don't suppose there's any chance of you two waiting back here at the boat, is there?"

The twins shook their heads no.

"All right, let's go."

The walk was not an easy one. Tommy's cottage sat on a more obscure part of the lake and thick brush came right up to the shore. I was hoping one or both of the twins would give up, but after twenty minutes of nonstop cursing, all three of us stood on the pathway leading up to the cottage.

I had heard Tommy had bought the place from his parents after their divorce, and it looked like he hadn't done much in the way of keeping it up. From what I could make out, an overgrown garden ran around the outside walls of the cottage and rusted-out tools, car parts, and even an old mattress littered the yard.

"So how do you want to play this?" Kit Kat asked, looking to me.

I frowned. "Um, I don't know." I hadn't really given any of this much thought, and suddenly I was remembering every bumbling *break and enter* I had ever recorded in court. Huh, this probably wasn't such a good idea. We were already probably oozing DNA all over the place.

"Maybe we could try a window? I don't want to break anything. And oh," I said, reaching around for my screwdriver. "I brought this!"

"Honey, there's easier ways to screw your way into a man's place," Kit Kat replied, before slapping her thigh at the brilliance of her joke.

I gave her a dry look. "Hilarious. Well, what do you think we should do?"

"I'm glad you asked. You see, back in the day I was pretty good at jimmying l—"

"It's open!" a voice called out.

Kit Kat and I looked over to see Tweety standing on the back porch holding the screen door open. We looked at each other and shrugged.

"Let's go," I said.

We skulked toward the door. The almost full moon rising in the sky gave us enough light to see pretty well outside, but inside the cottage would be another story.

"Don't suppose you brought a flashlight to go with that screwdriver?" Kit Kat whispered.

"Sorry."

"Some leader you are," Tweety added. "Next time, I'm in charge."

I grumbled something nasty under my breath, but there was no point in arguing the probability of a next time.

For a moment, the three of us stood outside the door peering in. Nobody wanted to say it, but it looked kind of scary in there.

New horrible thoughts skittered around my brain. What if Tommy was the killer? Maybe inside was where he did all of his killing . . . and we were walking right into his trap.

A finger suddenly poked me in the ribs.

I shot a mean look at Tweety. "I guess that means you want me to go first."

I hiked up my jeans and tugged at the collar around my neck before stepping slowly over the lip of the threshold.

I blinked my already night-adjusted eyes several times, but I still couldn't make out anything other than eerie shadows.

My heart hammered in my chest.

Oh, God, what if Tommy had night-vision goggles? What if he was looking at me right now in his dirty white boxers, smiling that poor man's version of Grady's smile!

Suddenly my toe knocked into something and a horrible crash exploded around me.

"Holy crap!"

I tried to turn around and make for the door but every

movement sent my feet crashing into something else. It was a trap! A booby trap! I stumbled forward but tripped and landed on my knees hard.

My arms flew to cover my head. "Don't do it, Tommy! I don't want to die . . ."

Suddenly light filled the room. One of the twins had flicked on a lamp hanging from a chain above the kitchen table.

I looked down at the floor.

Beer cans. Lots and lots of beer cans.

I glanced over to Kit Kat and Tweety chuckling by the door.

"Oh, yuck it up," I said, getting to my feet. "It wasn't like either one of you was offering to go first."

Tweety wiped a tear from the corner of her eye. "That was fantastic."

I tore my nasty look away from the women and took in my surroundings. Along with the beer cans scattered about the floor, dirty laundry and pizza boxes were piled up just about everywhere. At one time, the place must have had a cozy retro feel what with the wood paneling on the walls and the carved ducks resting on the mantel, but the now musty smell of the place was enough to kill any homey vibes.

"Do you think we should leave the lights on?" I looked around at all the windows. "Someone just has to look in the direction of this place and they'll see us."

"We have to leave them on. You might start screaming again," Kit Kat said.

Tweety nodded. "Yeah, that's just as bad. 'Help! I don't want to d—'"

"Have I mentioned I hate you two?" I said, cutting her off. "Let's just get started."

"Got it," she said, pulling a pair of gloves out of her pocket.

Her sister's brow furrowed. "When did you get those?"

Tweety yanked a thumb at me. "I grabbed them from her mother's hallstand when she was on the phone."

"You said you were going to the washroom."

"I did go to the washroom." Tweety pulled the gloves onto her hands, purposely avoiding her sister's glare. "Then I got the gloves."

"Well, did you get any for me?" Kit Kat asked, planting her fists on her boulder-sized hips.

"There was only one pair," she replied, finally looking into her sister's indignant face. "Hey! Sometimes you got to look out for yourself."

"We're identical twins, moron! We have the same fingerprints!"

"No, that's not true. They're similar but not id—"

"This was a terrible idea," I interrupted, rubbing a hand over my face. "Let's just do this thing and get out."

The women grumbled off in different directions.

I looked around the tiny living room, trying not to step on any of the magazines stuck to the floor. Other than a pretty nice gaming system, I didn't see anything out of the ordinary.

I turned back around to see Tweety lifting a pair of well-worn briefs off the kitchen floor, hooking them on the point of a pencil. I shot her a disgusted look. She shrugged and tipped the pencil, letting the underwear slide back into a heap on the floor.

Kit Kat had better luck.

"Hey! Come see this, you two."

Tweety and I followed Kit Kat to the bedroom.

"Well, wouldn't you know," I said mainly to myself.

Lying on Tommy's unmade bed was yet another suitcase, packed and ready to go. It wasn't exactly damning evidence of wrongdoing, but it was something.

"It looks like somebody is getting ready to leave town."

And he's not the only one, I thought.

"Okay, let's keep looking for anything that might tell us where he's going or why." I clapped my hands together. "Let's spread out."

I didn't make it three steps back into the living room before car headlights beamed through the cottage's front window, catching me in their glare.

I didn't think. I hit the ground.

"Kit Kat! Tweety! We gotta go!"

The twins, nimble as elephants, stampeded toward the back door. I scuttled after them on my hands and knees.

One of the twins must have hit the lights because the room plunged back into darkness.

Beer cans skidded across the floor as I flailed in what I hoped was the right direction.

"Go! Go! Go!" one of the two yelled.

We jostled our way through the small door frame and thudded down the rear steps of the porch.

"Come on! Faster!" I cried, pushing on the women's soft backs.

"We're trying! Stop pushing! Somebody's going to break a hip!"

I didn't dare look back until we made it to the water. I turned just in time to see the screen door of the cottage bang open.

"Hurry!" I screamed, pushing the twins harder.

I shot another look behind.

A figure stood on the back porch, making no move to follow us.

"Holy crapfish," Tweety said, whispering again as though that would help. "Is that Tommy?"

"I don't know," I whispered back.

"It can't be," Kit Kat added. "The Forrester boys aren't

the kind of people to sit back and watch. He'd be after us in a second."

"Then who is it?" I asked, not at all enjoying the creeping my flesh was up to.

Neither twin answered.

With one final look, we all turned and walked slowly back toward our boat.

An hour or so later, I was lying on my bed, sheets clutched under my armpits.

Kit Kat and Tweety had dropped me off and gone straight home. I had run up the stairs to the retreat, and for the first time, I had kind of been hoping to find the women hanging out in the living room, but they had already gone to bed. I had even thought, briefly, about dragging Caesar into my room just so I wouldn't be alone, but he seemed to be avoiding me, probably still mad about the tumble into the hydrangeas.

My eyes stared straight up at the ceiling, but all I could really see was the shadowy figure standing on Tommy's back porch. Logic would dictate that it had been Tommy standing there, but I couldn't be sure. It had been too dark. It could have been anyone.

I'm not sure when I fell asleep, but the glowing red numbers on my bedside clock told me it was a little after three when I woke up.

Three o'clock? Why was I awake?

Then I heard it. Quiet, but definite.

Something was moving around outside.

My hands balled into fists as my thoughts ran wild.

Silence.

Maybe I hadn't heard anything.

I stopped breathing for several moments to listen.

There it was again!

Footsteps . . . on the porch.

I glanced toward the window near the foot of my bed. If I leaned forward, I'd be able to peek out.

I watched the flimsy curtains ripple in the breeze.

Maybe it was one of the women. Maybe they needed something. An extra blanket. A carob muffin.

I sat up a little in bed.

Another footstep!

My back hit the mattress.

Or it could be the murderer. It could definitely be the murderer.

But what if it *was* the murderer? Was I going to let him or her kill me in my bed?

And what about my mother? She slept like a log. Was I going to let her be murdered in her bed too?

My ears strained to pick up any sound from outside.

The footsteps had stopped.

Silence.

Crap. Now was the time. I had to do something.

I inched my way back up, staying away from the window, and slowly swiveled to put my feet on the floor.

My eyes shot over to the dresser, searching for my phone. Not there. I had left it charging in the kitchen.

Okay. Now what?

A weapon!

I looked around the room. My eyes landed on the decorative canoe paddle mounted on the wall. Perfect.

I got to my feet just as the footsteps on the porch started up again. Whoever was outside was moving quickly now, purposefully.

Oh God. Oh God. Oh God.

I tiptoed as quickly as I could over to the paddle. I wrapped my hands around the smooth wood and yanked.

Nothing. Not a budge.

The footsteps were coming closer—rounding the corner from the front of the lodge to my side.

My eyes stayed glued to the window as I yanked harder. "Come on!"

The footsteps were almost at my window.

I yanked again. Finally the paddle gave.

Armed, I spun around, right as a dark silhouette glided in front of my window.

"Get away from my room, you murdering psycho freak!" I jabbed the air in front of me with the oar. "You think you want some of this? You don't want this! You can't handle this!"

The figure's shadowy arm shot up in the air.

What the hell was that?

The hand held something long and straight. A tire iron? A machete?

"You stay back!" I warned, now wildly swinging. I barely registered the sound of my mother running down the hall.

I knew I should run, but I was too afraid to take my eyes off the window.

The figure's arm suddenly swung down hard.

Thunk!

I screamed and turned to run for the door just as my mother came flying in.

"Erica! What's going on?"

I pointed at the window with my oar, and watched as my mother turned her head. I cringed, waiting for the horror to come over her face . . . any second now . . . lots of horror.

But it never came.

In fact, she just looked confused.

I glanced over to the window.

Nothing . . . but the curtains gently floating in the breeze.

"Someone was there!" I shouted. "The murderer!"

"What murderer?"

"The murderer was here," I said, grabbing her arms. "Dickie, Harry . . ."

"What are you talking about?" my mother asked, shaking her arms free and stepping toward the window.

"Don't!" I yelled.

"Erica, honey, there's nothing here," my mom said, holding the curtains back. "There's . . . uh-oh."

"What? What?" I rushed over to join her.

"Is that a—"

Right underneath the window, a long piece of metal jutted up from the planks of the porch floor.

"—weenie skewer?"

Chapter Eight

"Rhonda," I said, trying to keep the frustration from show-ing on my face, "if I had killed Dickie, why—"

"I never said you killed Dickie." She looked up from her notepad. "Are you saying you killed Dickie?"

I closed my eyes and counted to ten.

Rhonda had pulled up in her cop boat right as the sun had begun to peek over the horizon. Now, as we stood on the porch, the sun was sitting just above the trees.

Any residual fear I had left long ago. I was tired, hun-gry, and in desperate need of a shower.

"No, Rhonda, I am not saying that I killed Dickie. Please feel free to write that part down." Her pen didn't move. "I was going to say, if I had killed Dickie, why would I call the police to give them the murder weapon?"

"What makes you think it's the murder weapon?"

I pressed my lips together and focused all my effort on scraping a bit of dirt off the porch with my shoe. Maybe if I focused on the dirt, I wouldn't kick an officer of the law. "I'm assuming it's the murder weapon because I was the only witness to the weenie skewer sticking out of Dickie's body, and now there's a weenie skewer rammed into the porch right in front of my bedroom window. Seems a bit of a coincidence." Especially after I had been sneaking around both Laurie's and Tommy's the day before. Rhonda didn't need to know that last part though.

"So you think the murderer planted it there."

"Don't you?"

"You'll know what I think when I think you need to know what I think," she said, raising one of her ginger eyebrows. "So assuming you're not the murderer—"

"Thank you."

"Why would the real murderer leave the skewer with you?"

I blew out some breath noisily. "I don't know."

I couldn't help but think the most logical explanation was that it was a message—trying to scare me off from snooping around. That and it kept the cops focused on me.

But it also had a third effect.

Something the murderer hadn't counted on.

Call me sleep deprived and delusional, but last night had changed things. Whoever that was on my porch had scared me while I was sleeping in my own bed—I mean my old bed. I did not like to be terrorized. Originally, I had started looking into what had happened because I wanted to go home, and, well, as a related point, I didn't want to be charged with murder. Plus, there was the fact that I really liked Harry, and, as for Dickie, well, maybe I didn't like Dickie, but he certainly didn't deserve to die. And all those reasons still stood.

But now this was personal.

"Rhonda, am I under arrest?"

"Not yet," she said.

"Then I'm going to ask you to leave." I had to ramp up my investigation pronto.

"Whoa, settle down there, missy."

I crossed my arms over my chest. "I'm serious."

Rhonda didn't move.

"I mean it."

Rhonda said nothing.

Then something horrifying happened.

"Oh my God, Rhonda." I watched her face crumple, and then something that glistened an awful lot like a tear appeared at the corner of her eye. "Are you okay? You're not . . . are you . . ."

"I'm fine," Rhonda said, retrieving a tissue from her pocket. "It's just that I thought we were friends."

"What?" I asked. "I mean, we are!"

She gave her nose a hard blow. "You never showed up at the Dawg."

"I've been busy!"

"Doing what?" she asked, clicking her pen. "Murder?"

"Rhonda, are you good-cop/bad-copping me right now?"

The corner of her mouth twitched. "Maybe."

"You know you're supposed to have at least two cops for that to work, right?"

"Budget cuts."

I took another steadying breath. "Look, I really have to go. It's the last day of the retreat, and I have to help my mom send all the women on their way."

"Okay," Rhonda said, flipping her notepad shut. "But if anything else murder-related mysteriously turns up on your porch, you call me."

"Will do," I said with a little salute.

"Or if you remember anything else," she said, walking toward the steps that led down to the dock.

"Got it."

"Oh, and Erica?" she said, turning one last time.

"Yeah?"

"In case no one else has told you, don't leave town."

Thankfully my mother decided she didn't need any help discharging the women and sent me to bed. That was one good thing. No more insurance fraud. Now I could focus. I was more resolved than ever to find out who had killed Dickie and tried to kill Harry . . . but after a nap.

I woke up in the late afternoon with another pounding headache and a dry mouth. I stumbled out of bed and headed for the kitchen. I made it halfway down the hall before I froze in my tracks.

My head turned slowly toward the common room.

Women . . . Maria, Susan, Lydia, no-name lady divorcing man with robot porn addiction . . . all the others too.

They were all still here.

I tried to smile, but it probably looked as nauseous as I felt.

"Hi, ladies," I said slowly. "What are you all still doing here?"

"Isn't it wonderful, Erica," my mother said, swooping forward in yet another caftan. "They've all decided to stay a few extra days!"

"There's so much going on around your little lake," one woman said.

Maria laughed. "They want to see if you're going to be arrested."

My mother spun on her. "No one is going to arrest my daughter."

Maria nodded and motioned for my mother to sit down. Surprisingly she did. "I want to see what happens between you and the hot sheriff. Even if he is a bastard."

"Nothing is going to happen between me and the *hot* sheriff." I pressed my thumbs into my temples.

"I wouldn't be so sure. That man looks at you the way a starving dog looks at a plate of sausage." I rolled my eyes.

"Anyway," Lydia said, still wearing the neck brace. "Both you and your mother have come to mean so much to us, and . . ."

I did not like where this was going.

". . . we were thinking maybe we could help? You know, do a little amateur sleuthing. Ask some questions around town. Look for clues." She suddenly made a little wiggle with her hips. "Shake down some suspects."

I looked around the room at all the women with their hopeful faces.

"Wow," I said. "Wow."

"We're going to start with Laurie," someone in the back piped up. "She knows more than she's saying."

I chuckled painfully and muttered, "Kind of thought the same thing myself," before quickly adding, "Wait, has she been back?"

"No," my mother said. "She hasn't called either. It's not like her."

All the women nodded knowingly at this. "And of course we'll need to question you," another woman chimed in.

"Of course." I heard my voice speaking, but my brain had left the building. Then an escape hatch popped into view. "Oh, but the police warned me not to talk to anyone about the case." I made a frowny face.

"What? Did the sheriff tell you that?" a woman asked.

"And you're going to trust him?" Maria added.

"Oh, that's really disappointing," Lydia said, running her hand over her neck brace. "I was so excited by the idea I had almost forgotten all about the accident. Well, if you can call it that. My coworkers would probably call it negligence."

I looked over to my mother.

She smiled and fiddled with her hands.

I silenced a growl forming low in my throat. "Well, I guess it wouldn't hurt to tell you guys the basics."

"And we'll need to know everything that happened between you and the sheriff," Maria added. "Every intimate detail."

"Right."

"Oh, this could take all night," someone in flannel jammies said. "We should make some popcorn."

"I've got vegan butter!" My mother grabbed my arm and rushed me toward the kitchen.

I broke away from her in the hallway and made for the front door.

"Where are you going?" my mother called after me.

"I'll be right back," I muttered.

"But where are you going?"

"To jump in the lake."

I did jump in the lake. Clothes and all.

The sun had gone down, and the shock of the cold water managed to slow the crazy thoughts swirling in my brain.

On the one hand, it was kind of sweet that the women wanted to help. On the other, I didn't really believe they cared all that much about me. My guess was that they were enjoying the murder-mystery twist the retreat had taken.

It made me question what Freddie and I were doing. Were we really any better than the women at investigating homicides? It was hard to actually believe that I was in real trouble, but it was also getting harder to ignore the reality of this bizarro nightmare.

To think, Grady Forrester might actually arrest me.

I pulled myself out of the water and peeled off my wet shirt, leaving my bra. The still hot air felt good on my skin, so I parked myself on the edge of the dock, and dangled my toes in the refreshing water.

I leaned back to look at the millions of stars.

So many stars. Just like the night of the social all those years ago.

That night hadn't started out like a strange mixture of *Jackass* meets *Gilligan's Island*. In fact, it had all started out so right.

A few weeks before the social, Grady and I had started to gravitate toward one another. He was a couple of years older, but, of course, I knew who he was . . . I just couldn't conceive of a universe where he would notice me. Bonfires. Volleyball games. Lake parties. Didn't matter what it was. If all the girls were getting thrown in the lake, Grady suddenly was the one throwing me. If a bunch of us were playing Ultimate Frisbee, more often than not, I'd find myself getting tackled by him. Then, out of nowhere, Freddie started getting invited to all the cool parties, and, of course, he brought me along. Freddie seemed to think it was because his greatness was finally being realized, but I had to wonder. It went on this way for a while. Grady flirting with all the sophistication of a not quite adult male—basically making lewd comments or throwing ice cubes down my shorts—and me pretending not to care even though it felt like my heart was being crushed every time I saw him.

Most of the town noticed and suspected we were an item, but we just hadn't found the right opportunity to really make things click into place. We had definitely seemed to be on the path to . . . something.

Then came the social . . .

The Otter Lake Raspberry Social really amounted to just a bunch of tents filled with tables, a local rock country band, and lots of food, but the meagerness of the event didn't stop anybody from going. The whole town just went—you just did—and that night it didn't take me long to spot Grady.

God, he had looked so good under the tent's twinkling lights in those jeans and that T-shirt. Physically he was at the beginning of being everything a man should be. So when Grady came up to me and said, *I'm going swimming. Want to come?,* well, let's just say he didn't have to ask me twice. Aside from all the obvious reasons, I also did not want to hang around for my mother's performance.

We had walked a little while, away from the people and noise of the social, down to the dock at McAdams's place. We sat on the edge of it, kind of like what I was doing right now, and just talked. I remember being surprised at how easy it was to be with him. We had never done that before. It felt different than I had expected . . . better. Like maybe there was more than just a superficial attraction between us. I don't remember what exactly it was that he said but he was suddenly in the water, and he grabbed my hands, pulling me in after him.

If I had to pick one moment when things started to go wrong, well, what happened next would be it.

I was wearing a summer dress, and it's hard to swim in a summer dress.

I *do* still remember what Grady had said as I tossed the heavy fabric on the dock.

Erica Bloom, I like the way you think.

And, boy oh boy, did I like the way he said that.

Before I knew it, his jeans and shirt were keeping my dress company on the dock.

For a long while after that, we just played around in the water.

Then it happened. First there was that smile, and then Grady said, *Truth or dare?*

Three little words.

I smiled. *Truth.*

When did you first realize you were madly in love with me?

I splashed water in his face.

That's not an answer.

Because I'm not in love with you.

Uh-huh, he had said, swimming in a circle around me.

Your turn. Truth or dare?

He scrunched up his face in an exaggerated thinking expression. *Dare . . . no, truth.*

I backed away from him, but he edged closer. *Why do you think every girl is in love with you?*

Not every girl, just you.

I'm pretty sure I rolled my eyes.

Truth or dare? he asked again, eyes serious.

Dare.

He swam closer still. *Let's skinny-dip for real.*

No way!

I'll go first. And before I knew it, Grady was tossing his boxers to the waiting pile of clothes.

Come on, Erica. You're a lot of things, but I know you're not a chicken.

A minute later the little I had left joined Grady's clothes on the dock.

We circled each other some more. I could barely stomach everything I was feeling, the excitement, the terror, and the stupid, stupid happiness.

One more dare, he had said.

But it's my turn!

He shrugged. *One more and you win.*

I didn't have time to answer; Grady was already over at the dock jumping out of the water.

What are you doing?

He turned. *Trust me!*

Trust me. Two little words.

You know what comes after two little words? One . . . one little word that describes the Erica from that night perfectly.

Idiot.

Gah!

Stupid memories.

Back in the present, I struck my foot forward, meaning to kick out a spray of water. Instead, my foot connected with something solid and fleshy.

"Ow!" a voice yelled.

I screamed and yanked my feet up.

"What was that for?"

I peered over the last wooden plank into the water.

"Grady! What are you doing?"

"Swimming."

"You're swimming by my place in the dark." I quickly covered my chest with my arms, suddenly remembering I was half-naked.

"I swim almost every night in the summer," he answered, resting his forearms on the dock. "It's good cardio."

"Huh, well, off you go," I said, making a shooing gesture. "Don't let me stop you."

"Always so anxious to get rid of me," he said. "Okay, fine, it isn't just about the cardio. I wanted to make sure everything was all right here after what happened last night."

"That's . . . nice." Suddenly I made a grab for my shirt. "Don't want to leave this lying around," I said with a chuckle. "Never know who might take it."

He wagged a finger at me and looked like he was about to say something, when I flung a hand up.

He nodded. "Right. You don't want to talk about the social."

I dropped my hand and looked up to the stars once more.

A moment of silence passed.

Grady broke first. "So, how is the insurance lady? I called but—" He suddenly stopped speaking. I rolled my gaze back down to his face. His eyes were moving up and down my barely covered body. I splashed some water at him. He smiled, then dragged his gaze back up to mine.

"She's fine," I said.

"Good. Good," he replied with a nod. "And you haven't been talking to anyone about anything, right?"

"Right. Sure. That would be a terrible idea," I said, mumbling over the corner of the thumbnail I was chewing.

"Erica," Grady said with warning.

"Seriously. It's all good. And my mother is trying to get a hold of my uncle."

He nodded. "Good."

Another moment passed. This *was* good. This was a normal conversation. So what if my heart was thudding painfully in my chest as I watched the play of moonlight on his face? At least I hadn't done anything that would lead anywhere embarrassing.

"Grady, why are you here?" I asked suddenly. Shoot. I knew I spoke, or rather, thought too soon. "I mean aside from investigating me for murder or seeing if I'm being murdered, why are you here?"

He smiled. "What? That's not enough?"

I shook my head. "No, I mean, I keep trying to avoid you, and you keep showing up . . . like . . . like . . . a stray cat that you feed just once and—"

"Please, no more animal metaphors," he interrupted.

"And, Erica, you might want to brace yourself for this, but it turns out that I don't want to avoid you. I've been trying to talk to you since you got home."

I crooked an eyebrow.

He dropped his head and sighed heavily, hands planted on either side of me on the dock. "Aren't you tired of all this dancing around?" he asked, looking up at me from under his brows.

"What are you talking about?"

He sighed again. "I always regretted waiting for the perfect moment with you . . . and then it was too late." Suddenly Grady shot up from the water and his arm wrapped around my waist, pulling me into the lake.

I flailed in the water, spluttering, trying to catch my breath.

When I could see again, I found myself pinned between the dock and Grady's chest. I had to grab his arms to stop myself from drowning.

I looked up into his face, inches above mine. He was still smiling. "Now, that's better. Perfect in fact."

"I'm thinking I'm having some déjà vu," I said, suddenly finding it difficult to remember all the mechanics of speaking.

"Me too."

A heavy moment passed.

Finally, even though I could feel my heart beating in my throat, I managed to say, "What is this? What are we doing?" I shook my head. "We barely know each other."

"Not true," he rebutted quickly. "I've known you most of my life."

"You know what I mean. It's been a long time. People change, and—"

"You're right. People do change. But I think I still have a pretty good idea of who you are . . . and I think you still know me, but"—I watched him lick his lips—"we could always stand to get to know one another better. Unless, of course, you are the killer. Then this is probably a bad idea."

I closed my eyes. "Grady . . ."

"Yes?"

"Why are you so . . . you're always so . . . why do you always have to be saying things?"

I could feel his body float even closer to mine. "What things am I saying, Erica?" he asked softly. I could also feel his eyes calling mine to look back into them, but I couldn't do it. I wouldn't do it. Too dangerous.

"You know, things . . . horrible things. Things that do other things to me."

He chuckled. "You have no idea how easy it would be for you to shut me up."

I peeked one eye open. His lips hovered inches from mine.

It occurred to me—and not for the first time—that I had never actually kissed Grady Forrester. Some part of my brain knew this was a terrible idea . . . nitro . . . glycerin . . . people issues . . . probably some trust ones too . . . but still I closed my eyes again, tilted my head, and—

—a boat engine roared behind us.

Grady looked over his shoulder and pivoted to tread water beside me.

I grabbed the dock with one hand and shielded my eyes against the lights of the boat with the other.

"Candace?" Grady called out. "What are you doing out here?"

Candace.

The name sounded like it should be four letters long.

"Oh, sugar!" she called out. "I thought I saw someone fall off the dock!"

Oh, sugar? My eyelids fluttered momentarily closed.

Candace killed the engine to her boat before settling her eyes on Grady. "I wanted to make sure you were okay. There have been enough accidents around here lately."

"Nope. We're fine. I was just asking Erica some questions and she, uh, tripped."

My eyes bugged. *I had done what now?*

"But what you doing here?" Grady asked again. I tried to read the expression on his face, looking for any signs of guilt, but he was giving nothing away.

"Bad day. Couldn't settle in, so I decided to go for a ride. Don't worry, Sheriff," she said, raising her hand cutely in the air. "I'm going slow. Don't want to hit any turtles."

Nobody said anything for a second.

Well, this was awkward.

I cleared my throat, trying to muster an interested voice, "Why such a bad day, Candace?"

"It's all these accidents!" she said. "I know I have no business feeling sorry for myself given what happened to Dickie, and now Harry, but there's this rumor going around the lake that we—the developers—have hired some sort of hit man to off citizens of Otter Lake so that we can buy up all their property."

I smiled. I couldn't help it. At least I wasn't the only suspect.

"I know! It's ridiculous! A hit man," she said, shaking her head. "All over some crazy accidents."

Grady and I exchanged a glance.

"Oh, no," she said. "No. No. No. Grady, tell me they're just accidents."

"I am not at liberty to answer that question."

"You're not at liberty?" she asked. "So they weren't accidents. Because if they were, you would be at liberty to say."

Wow. Cute and clever.

"First the snapping turtles, and now a murderer on the

loose," she said, shaking her blond head. "That will look great on the brochure."

"You look like you could use a drink," Grady said with his stupid smile. The stupid smile that I somehow thought was reserved just for me! What the hell was happening here?

"Or two," she said, smiling back. "Want to come?"

Oh . . . my . . . God! This was . . . this couldn't be . . .

"Might as well," he said, swimming over to her boat.

"What about you, Erica?" Candace asked. "You want to come along?"

"Um, no!" I said with a little too much incredulity. "I mean, I—"

"Nah, Erica doesn't want to come," he said, without looking at me. "I'm always saying horrible things to her."

What?!

I couldn't do anything but stupidly look back and forth between the two of them as Grady pulled himself up into her boat.

Was he trying to make me jealous?

Or was he trying to make Candace jealous?

Oh my God! He was probably trying to make both of us jealous!

"Okay then," Candace said, turning the key on the ignition. "See you, Erica."

Disbelief prevented me from moving or saying anything in return.

"Yup, later, Erica."

Waves smacked me once again in the face as the boat tore off into the moonlight.

"Freddie, I know who the murderer is . . . actually murderers," I corrected, putting emphasis on the plural. "I know who the murderers are."

"Erica?"

"Of course it's Erica. Who else are you solving murders with?" I had filled Freddie in on my find at Tommy's yesterday, but we hadn't spoken since.

"It's six forty-five in the morning."

"I know. I've been waiting the last two hours to call you."

"Um . . ."

"Don't worry about it," I said quickly. "You're welcome."

Part of me was aware that I might be sounding crazy, but I had been up most of the night thinking, and now I needed to share.

After Grady and Candace left the night before, I went back up to the retreat to face the women. Luckily, I found them discussing their favorite mystery novels, so I didn't have to contribute all that much. Then I went to bed and thought about Grady and Candace—all while keeping a close eye on my bedroom window.

And somewhere in those late-night, early-morning hours, everything had become very clear.

"Okay, I'll bite. Who are the murderers?"

"Grady and Candace," I said, really feeling the moment of gravity.

Silence.

"Freddie, you there?"

"Yup, yup, I'm still here." He paused. "Erica, are you okay?"

I yanked roughly at my sheets. "What? What does that have to do with anything?"

"Did something happen last night?"

"You mean other than my solving the case?" I pulled the phone back to look at it skeptically. Jeez, what was wrong with Freddie?

"I'm simply wondering if this is your emotionally stunted way of telling me that you need to talk about Grady again," Freddie said. "Not that I want to talk about Grady again because frankly—"

"Pfft."

"Oh, no, something did happen," Freddie said, suddenly sounding a little too much like Madame F for my liking.

"It all makes sense!"

"How? How does it all make sense? Tell me."

"Okay, well first, there were no murders in Otter Lake before Candace came to town, and now there are." The words came out really quickly. Was I talking quickly?

"Huh. You do realize, the same could be said about you."

"Yes, but I know I didn't do it," I said, slapping my chest. "God, Freddie, keep up."

"All right. What else do you got?"

"The development."

"Right. What about the development?"

"Developments are always evil."

"Always evil? Or just always evil in movies about the mafia?"

"I can't even begin to express how much you're disappointing me right now," I muttered.

"Well, I'm sorry," he said. "But you're sounding a little crazy. Whatever is happening around this lake is going to make Candace's job harder. I—"

"It's always poor Candace. 'You look like you could use a drink, Candace,'" I said in my most mature voice. "Why is everybody always so worried about her?"

"Actually, right now, I'm worried about you," he said. "What about Grady? Why would Grady kill his cousin's friends?"

"Because he's a sociopath."

"That's it?" Freddie paused a half second. "He's a sociopath?"

"Yes, a sociopath who likes dimples."

"Okay, now you're scaring me." Freddie paused before adding, "Grady is single. He's allowed to date."

"I know that," I snapped. "But he's not allowed to be confusing!"

"Okay . . . okay . . . I know *it*'s three days away, but . . . do you need me to come over? I was planning to come by after work because I have another idea for a lead, but if you need me to come now—"

"No," I said, suddenly feeling deflated. This wasn't how the conversation was supposed to go at all.

"Are you sure?"

"Yes." I lay down and rubbed at my grainy eyes. "What's your lead?"

"We've been so focused on Laurie, being Dickie's girlfriend and all, we forgot all about Tommy's girlfriend."

"Tommy has a girlfriend?"

"Shelley Michaels."

"Oh, no freaking way." I took a moment to try to picture it. I could see Tommy liking Shelley's badass personality, but for a commitment phobic guy, Shelley was a little on the possessive side. Like "smashing headlights with a baseball bat" possessive side.

"She'll know what's going on."

"That's a really good idea, Freddie." I sighed, then added, "I'm telling you, though, maybe it's a stretch to think Grady's involved, but there's something off about that Candace."

"Erica, everybody in Otter Lake has something a little off about them. So, really, she fits right in."

"Bah. Anyway, stay by the phone. I'm going to call you back in a little bit."

"Why? What are you g—"

I hung up.

A new plan had occurred to me while I was talking to Freddie. I just needed to find a way to ditch the *Murder She Wrote* Club staying in the cabins out back.

I got dressed in a hurry.

I'd decided my first course of action was to go to Tommy's. As the twins had pointed out, I should probably have tried to talk to him in the first place before breaking into his house. I wasn't about to beat myself up though. This detective thing had a learning curve.

I breathed in the cool, crisp morning air as I bounced across the water, closing my eyes briefly and turning my face to the sun.

Stupid Grady.

I didn't need him.

All I needed was to see the expression on his face when I solved this whole murder thing.

Just to be safe, though, I'd stay away from him until that happened. For realsies this time.

I cut the engine and drifted towards Tommy's property. He had two docks now—one tucked away, half-covered with trees, for his old boat, and a newer, longer one for his freshly bought monster. I was guessing he was still using his first boat for puttering around. His new speed demon had to be a gas-guzzler.

After a moment of indecision, I decided to tie off on the original dock. I didn't want to give my mother's little craft self-esteem issues.

The plan was to act like an old friend stopping by to see how Tommy was doing, but even I couldn't deny that it seemed risky—for a whole lot of reasons. First, Tommy could be the murderer. I had no idea what his motive could be, but his half-packed suitcase seemed to indicate that either he was scared or guilty . . . or going on a trip, but that was too reasonable for this crazy lake. Second, Tommy was probably the figure we had seen standing on the porch. That meant he most likely knew it had been me breaking into his place, which probably wouldn't make him happy. As a third and related point, he was, also, most likely, the person who had skewered my porch, as a warning to stay away. And now, here I was, walking up to his place, not following instructions at all.

I bit my lip.

Those were some pretty good reasons to go home and leave this to the police.

An image of Rhonda with her notepad flashed through my mind.

Yeah, I wasn't going to leave this to the police.

Still, I didn't have to be stupid about things. I pulled out my phone.

"What are you up to?" Freddie asked in his fake Southern accent. "I'm working."

"I know. I know," I said quickly, standing at the foot of the path leading up to Tommy's place. "I just want you to listen. I'm going to talk to Tommy. If he tries to kill me, I want you to call 911."

"What? No! First of all, you are not supposed to be investigating without me. I already missed cat-burglaring with the twins."

"Well, I'm calling you, aren't I? It's like you're here."

"And what if he does attack you? Help will arrive just in time to cart your dead body away."

I stepped over a rusted leg trap, giving it a grimace. "I don't think Tommy's the murderer. I just want—"

"Right, because Candace and Grady are the murderers."

"That's only one theory," I muttered. "Look. I didn't call for your input. Just keep your ears open for screaming."

I slid my phone into the blousy front pocket of my shirt. I heard all sorts of muffled complaining, but I clamped my hand over the pocket, and carefully treaded my way up to the back porch.

I peeked in a window before knocking. It looked much the same as it had the other night, but grimier in the light of day.

Maybe Tommy had already left town.

I raised my hand to knock, throat tight, when I heard something.

It was a strange sound, kind of like groaning.

Was that . . . ? No, couldn't be.

Oh, God!

Ewww.

I ducked down, so I wasn't visible from the windows.

"What's happening?" my pocket said.

"Shh," I replied softly. "I think Tommy's having sex."

Tinny laughter rippled up to my ears.

"I'm going to go," I whispered, already frog-walking my way to the stairs leading toward the dock.

"You can't go! It could be a clue!" Freddie cried before changing voices. "Oh, no, not you, honeybee. Actually, yes, you. The universe sends clues all the time, but are you listening?" Regular Freddie voice returned in an angry whisper. "See? This is why you should have waited for me to finish work!"

"Really, Freddie? A sex clue? That's how pornos start. Nope," I said, foot on the first step. "I have no desire to spy on Tommy and Shelley having sex."

"What if it isn't Shelley?"

I grimaced. Frick! I frog-walked my way back to the side of the porch that the noises seemed to be coming from and eased myself down to the ground.

"Yes! Yes! Yes! You nasty f—"

I shut my eyes. I did not just hear that.

"Did I just hear that?"

I clamped my hand again over my phone and inched my way toward the open window.

I thought I might have recognized the voice, but it was hard to tell through all the grunting and slapping sounds.

I stopped, back pinned against the wall, head right under the window frame. I wasn't tall enough to peek in, so I stood listening for a few minutes, hoping Tommy's partner would give herself away.

At first, the noises sounded fairly typical and slightly nauseating. Then the slapping sound got louder.

"Ow! What are you doing?"

Slap. Slap. SLAP!

"OW!"

I looked quickly around for something to step on.

A lot of junk lay scattered over the fine bed of pine needles, but there was nothing of much use. Finally my eyes settled on a case of beer, filled with empty bottles. It probably wasn't a good idea, but I didn't have a lot of options.

I ignored Freddie's pleas for information as I positioned the case under the window. I placed one foot on the soft cardboard, trying to distribute my weight evenly across the tiny round tops of three bottles. It felt okay. I gripped the window ledge and tested my stance before bringing up the other foot.

The slapping was coming rapid-fire now.

"What? Your girlfriend doesn't like to slap you around?"

So it wasn't Shelley in there!

It was now or never.

My hands pulled at the wood. I simply needed to peek over and—

"OW! Get off of me!"

Right before I could see who Tommy was yelling at, the window ledge gave way in my hands with a crack, and I fell backward in a loud clattering of glass.

A voice shouted from the window above me. "What the hell?"

I scrambled to get up, but suddenly Tommy's face appeared.

"Erica Bloom!"

My pocket said, "Uh-oh."

Chapter Nine

"Hey Tommy," I said, still on my butt.

"What are you doing?" he asked, before briefly looking behind him. I thought I heard a door slam.

"Um, I came by to see how you were doing." It sounded even lamer out loud. "You know, after Dickie? Harry?"

Tommy looked at me for a second, then jumped back from the window. I struggled to my feet.

Time to go.

I started to make a run for my boat when I heard the back screen door slam.

I quickly decided to go around the other way.

I sprinted to the front of the cottage, feet slipping on the uneven ground, hoping Tommy would follow me—then I would have a head start back around to the lake.

I didn't make it even to the front driveway before I felt Tommy's hand clamp down on my arm.

I screamed.

"Oh my God, Erica!" my phone screamed back. "Is he killing you?"

Tommy yanked me around to face him.

"What are you doing here?" he shouted, eyes flashing.

"Tommy, seriously, I was just coming by to check on you," I said, watching the growing beads of sweat on his upper lip. "And then I heard that . . . that you were busy."

"So you spied on me?" he asked, face contorting in disbelief. "Like some sort of pervert?"

I chuckled slightly before gulping it back down.

"What's so funny?"

I shrugged. "Well, I mean, of the two of us, one is definitely a pervert, but I'm not the one standing in my boxers." I laughed, but he didn't join me. Instead, he grabbed my arms, making me yelp.

"Why are you back in town?"

"Huh?"

"Why are you back in town?" he repeated, eyes darting around my face.

Suddenly, I was having trouble finding my voice. "To . . . uh . . . see my mother."

His eyes were still frantically searching mine. "Why now? Right before the Raspberry Social? You hate the Raspberry Social."

"Yeah, tell me about it." I was trying to sound glib, but I couldn't hide my fear. "My mother needed me to help out with her insurance."

Tommy's grip stayed tight.

"You work for the police, don't you?" He pulled me closer. "Back in Chicago."

I tilted my face away from his stale beer breath. "No. I'm a stenographer. I—"

"What do you know?" he demanded.

I froze.

He shook me again, hard enough for my teeth to clack together. "What do you know!"

Suddenly a voice came yelling from my pocket. "She doesn't know anything!"

Tommy dropped my arms and stared at my chest.

"If you don't let her go, I'm calling the police!" Freddie's muffled voice yelled.

Tommy's eyes widened. "You're wearing a wire?"

I waved my hands in front of my chest. "No. No. It's Freddie. You remember Freddie." I reached to take my phone out of my pocket, but Tommy wasn't looking at me anymore. His eyes darted in crazy jumps around the forest.

"Tommy?" I asked carefully.

"Get out of here," he said, backing up slowly toward the cottage.

He didn't need to tell me twice.

I moved as quickly as I could through the junkyard of a lawn. I was almost back to the boat when I heard Tommy yell, "If you know what's good for you, you'll stay out of this."

I gave a quick thumbs-up into the air and jumped into my boat.

"Erica, are you still there?"

"Yeah," I said breathlessly, "but I'm leaving now. I'm coming to your place." I ended the call, and wiped the sweat off my hands before gripping the pull cord on the motor. I gave it a good yank. Black smoke plumed around my hands.

"No. No. No," I muttered, yanking again. "Not today." Nothing.

"Argh!" I gave the motor a good kick, then fell backward on my butt.

Why? Did this many bad things happen to other people?

I took a breath and looked back up at Tommy's cottage.

For a split second, I thought I saw something move in the forest, but since it wasn't coming at me with a chain saw, I decided to pay it no mind. Then the sound of an approaching boat forced my gaze back to the water.

I squinted my eyes. I didn't recognize the boat, per se, but the police insignia on its side was pretty unmistakable.

Great. Maybe Freddie had called the police . . . or maybe I had just been a really bad person in a previous life . . . like Vlad the Impaler bad.

I yanked the cord again, but halfheartedly. I knew whose side it was on.

Grady cut his motor, allowing the boat to drift the last few feet toward mine.

No hint of a smile played across his lips today.

Well, two could play that game. Seriously, what business did he have being upset with me? I was the injured party . . . or, at least, the very confused party.

"Erica," he called out, tipping his hat back, "why are you here?"

"Why am I here?" I asked with a scoff. "Why are *you* here?"

"You want to know why I'm here?" he asked, making a smacking sound with his lips. "Let's see." He leaned forward on his hands, gripping the steering wheel—kind of looked like he was strangling it. Best not read too much into that. "We got a call. Mr. Connelly across the lake," he said with a jab of his thumb, "was stargazing with his telescope the other night when he saw three women—two older, one younger—creeping around Tommy's property in the middle of the night when Tommy wasn't home. You wouldn't know anything about that, would you?"

I looked skyward. "*Pfft.* No."

I glanced over to see Grady close his eyes and shake his head. "I'm getting a little tired of that *pfft*."

I planted my hands on my hips. "First, everybody knows Mr. Connelly wasn't stargazing. He was spying on people with his friend Jack Daniel's, hoping to catch couples having sex, so I don't see how you can take anything he says seriously."

"Erica, I don't think you get how *serious* this could be for you."

"No, no," I said quickly. "What I can't seem to get is how far all of this has gone. It's crazy, and the minute Harry wakes up—"

"It's not looking like Harry is going to wake up. At least not any time soon."

"Oh, no." All the breath escaped from my lungs. "That's terrible."

"Yeah, it is. Now do you see why you can't be snooping around Tommy's—" Suddenly Grady's brow creased. "Wait . . . you're not . . . you're not *seeing* Tommy, are you?"

I felt like I had been slapped in the face with a cold washcloth. I stared at Grady. For half a second, he actually looked vulnerable, like he was pretty upset by the idea. Suddenly my brain felt really hot. Thoughts spun so quickly, it was hard for me to catch just one. Like he had any business caring about who I was *seeing*? When he was out having drinks with Candace? And wait . . . Tommy? He actually thought I'd *see* Tommy? This was all too ridiculous. "No, I'm not sleeping with your cousin! Not that it's any of your business."

A flash of relief crossed his face. "Okay, I get that we should probably talk about last night, but first, if you're not seeing Tommy, what *are* you doing here?"

"Not that I'm admitting I was here the other night, but if I was, it might be because your cousin knows something about what happened with Dickie and Harry. In fact, he's acting a little crazy. Right now, he's probably hiding in a corner surrounded by guns."

He crossed his arms over his chest, making his fore-arms ripple. "Tommy has never worried about anything in his entire life."

"Exactly!" I yelled before grabbing the pull cord to the boat's motor, giving it another pull. More black smoke rose into the air.

"Stop that," Grady said, moving to tie our boats to-gether. "There's obviously something wrong with your engine. Let me take a look at it already."

"It's fine," I said, yanking again. It gave me nothing in return but smoke. I stayed bent over, hand on the cord. I turned to look at Grady again, blowing a piece of hair out of my face. "And did you know your cousin is planning a little vacation? Tell me, when has Tommy ever left the lake?"

Grady stopped working on the knot to look at me.

Ha! Satisfied tingles ran over my arms. There's some-thing you didn't know, Sheriff!

"Erica, I can't even begin to explain what a bad idea it is for you—a current person of interest—to be investigat-ing this case," he said, trying to pin me with his eyes. "And seriously, would you stop yanking that damn cord! Let me look at it!"

I ignored him and kept yanking.

Suddenly he was behind me trying to get at the engine. I turned so that we were standing chest to chest and gave him a solid push back.

"Hey!" he shouted, stumbling a mere step backward be-fore moving even closer. I could feel the heat from his body wash over mine. We stared furiously at each other.

He broke first. "You know what?" he said, throwing up his hands. "I give up! I give up trying to apologize. I give up trying to stop you from being arrested. Erica Bloom listens to no one! Especially not me! You win."

Emotions battled in my head. It was hard to think with him standing so close.

I barely managed a scowl before I turned back to the engine.

I felt his hand on my shoulder. "But I will not let you pull that damn cord one more time until I check it out."

A lot of things happened pretty quickly after that.

Grady angled to get in between me and the motor, just as I yanked the cord one last time.

The engine roared to life.

Sparks flew around us, and then a *Whomph!* of flame shot into the air.

Grady's arm clamped around my waist and hauled me into the air.

Next thing I knew I was underwater.

Chapter Ten

BOOM!

I flailed my arms and legs, trying to find the surface.

I struggled into the air and blinked my eyes open. It took me a second to process all the flames and smoke.

"My boat."

I turned to see Grady treading water, his face frozen with shock.

"My boat," he said again slowly before looking at me. "You blew up my boat."

Uh-oh.

I swiveled my head back to the dock. Yup, both boats were on fire. Not raging fire, but definitely burning. Tommy's boats looked okay. "Grady, I'm—"

"They're not going to give me another one, you know," he said, voice getting louder. "I had to do a lot of things to get that boat—smile at a lot of people."

I kept my mouth firmly shut.

"And then you come along, and boom." He mimed a small explosion with his fingers. "It's all gone."

"Grady, I didn't mean to—"

I stopped talking because of the way he was shaking his head from side to side.

"No!" he said sharply, pointing a finger at me. "You were pulling the cord, and I was like, Erica, don't pull it, let me help, and you were all like, pull, pull, PULL!" He slapped the water with his hand.

"Grady, I think you might be in shock."

"I loved that boat," he said sadly.

"But . . . it's just a boat?"

His eyes flashed wildly. "You know, my life was fine before you came back to the lake. More than fine. Then you arrive, and it's nothing but trouble!"

Now it was my turn to be shocked. "Seriously." I said the word quietly, but the volume was going up fast. "I cause *you* trouble?"

"Look around, Erica," he said, gesturing at the flames. "You're not even supposed to be here. Tommy? Really? You think you're some master detective, and you're investigating Tommy?"

"Hey!" I shouted. "Tommy knows something!"

"My cousin *is* stubborn and reckless and at times immature, but that doesn't make a person a killer, now does it, Erica? You of all people should know because you'd already be in jail."

I gasped.

A look of horror spread over his face. "I didn't mean—"

"Oh ho ho," I said, flexing my jaw. "That was nice, Grady. Real nice."

I heard sirens in the distance.

"Wait," he said, reaching out to me. "I'm sorry."

I started to swim in the opposite direction, away from the burning mess and Grady, toward the shore.

"Erica!" he called. "It's just . . . my boat . . ."

My feet found sandy bottom and I stood up, refusing to look back at Grady.

"Hey! I just saved your life, you know!" he shouted at my back.

I grumbled and kept stomping.

"What? No thank you?" he shouted. "No kiss on the cheek for the paper?"

"You want a kiss?" I shouted back. "Oh, sure. You can just go ahead and kiss my—"

I hitched a ride with the fire department back into town. Luckily, I didn't have to give much of a statement. Grady handled it. I couldn't help but notice that Tommy was long gone by the time anyone bothered to look for him.

I found Red lounging at the boat fill-up station, and he agreed to take me back to the island. The best part about Red was that he never talked, just spat occasionally. Well, except for when he was working as an electrician and shocked himself. Then he could swear a blue streak. But even if that were to happen today, I wouldn't be able to hear it. My ears were still ringing from the explosion.

I walked up the steps to the lodge, feeling like a drowned rat. I needed to call Freddie. He'd be wondering where I was, but first I wanted to shower and wash off the smell of smoke and gasoline.

I should have known it wouldn't be that easy.

"Erica!" my mother cried. "What happened?"

Two steps in the door, I was surrounded by clucking women. They led me to the couch en masse and huddled around. I could feel everyone's gaze on me, but my eyes fell flat.

They all expected me to say something. But my brain was like one of those giant buckets at a water park. Ever since I had arrived home, it had been filling with water. Filling. Filling. Filling. Until the boat explosion filled it right up . . . and tipped it over.

Now my brain was empty.

"She looks like she's in shock."

"She smells like a tire fire."

"Quick, someone get her some water."

I felt a mug pressed into my hand. I didn't move.

"Help her."

Before I knew it, water was poured into my mouth . . . water that burned like acid!

Alcohol sprayed from my lips.

"What did you give her?" I heard my mother ask as convulsions ripped through my throat.

"Moonshine. Hundred proof."

I gave Kit Kat a filthy look through the tears in my eyes.

"New hobby," she said, shrugging.

All the women resumed staring at me as my coughs settled. I mentally grumbled, before saying, "Look, ladies, I really would like to take a shower and eat a sandwich, a big sandwich. Then maybe we could—"

"No!" they all shouted in unison.

"Fine. If you must know," I began, "I blew up a boat today . . . two boats actually."

Silence fell on the room as they processed this information.

Then identical, phlegm-crackled laughs started up.

"Are you all right?" my mother asked quickly.

"Fine."

"Do you think we should call Homeland Security?" I heard someone whisper.

I looked up to see a thin birdlike woman with her hand over her mouth. I couldn't remember her story, but I was suddenly on her ex-husband's side.

"I'm not a terrorist," I said, ignoring the twins' growing laughter. "It was an accident."

"Are you sure?" one of the women asked with a knowing tone. "Given all that's been happening around here lately?"

I considered this for half a second before I said, "The engine's been giving off smoke lately."

My mother nodded.

"Don't say any more. We'll get started on the claim right away," Lydia Morgan said, jumping in. "Did you call the police. Is there a report?"

"I'm sure there will be. I—"

"You said two boats?" Maria Franelli asked. "I assume one of them was yours. Who did the other boat belong to?"

I didn't want to answer, but I was flanked on all sides.

I licked my lips, and met Maria Franelli's eyes, generously painted peacock blue.

"Grady's."

The room erupted.

The twins were now wiping tears away while at least half a dozen women gave high fives.

"Why? Why are you doing that?" I asked, looking about the room.

"He deserved it," somebody shouted.

"You go, girl!"

"I blew up two boats," I said, trying to figure out exactly what was going on here. "By accident."

"There are no accidents."

"Take your power back!" yelled another woman, shaking her fist.

"None of that even makes sense," I said, shaking my head and turning to my mother.

She shrugged her shoulders. "We're practicing unconditional positive reinforcement."

I looked back at the women.

Lydia made a noise indicating she wanted the floor. I half expected her to go into the details of my mother's policy, but instead she said, "What did it feel like?"

"I'm sorry?"

"I always wanted to blow up my husband's Mustang," she said. "What was the expression on his face like?"

The memory of Grady in the water looking at his burning boat appeared before my mind's eye. I felt the corner of my mouth twitch.

"There it is!" the woman with the porn-addicted ex yelled, pointing at my lips.

The smile spread even further.

"Was he all like, *My boat! My beautiful boat!*"

"He was actually," I said, nodding my head maybe a little too vigorously. "He really was."

I watched two women smile at each other and clasp their hands to their chests.

"Erica Bloom, you are my hero," someone shouted.

"Thank you," I said, getting to my feet. "Thank all of you. I mean I never intended to blow up his boat, but I guess that it was something I needed to do, like—"

"Stop. Stop right there," Maria said, holding out her bejewelled hand. "You had me at 'blow up his boat.'"

Before I knew it, I was clasped to her large chest. Then I was once again surrounded by all the women . . . and it actually felt kind of good.

Maybe my mother had been on to something all along. Maybe I did need more than fake Facebook profiles as friends.

"You know," I mumbled through the tangle of arms, "you ladies are all right."

They erupted in friendly laughter.

Then I did the unthinkable.

"Now who wants to help me solve this murder for real?"

*   *   *

I'm not going to lie. After the initial euphoria of all that
unconditional woman power wore off, I was a little uneasy
about having invited the ladies into the investigation. But
it was too late. I had opened the door, and now I had no
idea how to close it.

On the bright side, they agreed with me that Candace
was the most likely suspect. I had to like that about them
even if I was slightly alarmed by how quickly they were
willing to jump on that particular bandwagon. I suspected
it had more to do with their choosing sides in the Grady-
versus-Erica war than, say, impartial evidence, but, really,
I already had enough to worry about. I could explore the
state of my conscience back in Chicago.

Over the course of the afternoon, the ladies ate vegan
cookies and came up with a plan. First, they would all go
into town. Then our newly assembled Alpha Team would
go to the library before it closed and use the computers to
research Candace and the development company, while our
Beta Team canvassed the town, asking pertinent questions.

I'll admit, the Beta Team's mission had me a little worried. The citizens of Otter Lake didn't exactly trust people
from out of town. They especially didn't trust the kind of
people my mother's retreat attracted. I tried to explain
this to them, and they had promised in return to keep the
investigation low-key, but there was an excited gleam in
their collective eye that made me about as comfortable as
a wool sweater on bare skin.

I stood on the porch and watched my personal army of
detectives cross the lake in Red's pontoon, brow furrowed.
Both teams seemed to think I should stay under the radar
during the investigation, so I told them I was going to have
dinner with Freddie at the Salty Dawg if they needed me. I

figured no good could come of sharing my plans beyond that.

I was still furrowing when Freddie struggled up the last few stairs to join me on the porch.

"What's the problem?" he asked, trying to catch his breath.

"Nothing," I said, watching the departing boat disappear into the glare of the setting sun. A moment passed before I added, "Freddie?"

"Hmm?"

I turned my head to study his serious, *I'm deeply considering the sunset* profile. "Should I be concerned?"

"About so much," he replied, nodding sagely into the dying light. "But are you referring to something specific?"

I pointedly looked over his blue T-shirt, Hawaiian shorts, and flip-flops. "Well, you appear to be dressed somewhat normally. No Madame F today? No Sherlock?"

He waggled his eyebrows.

"I got something better."

"That frightens me just a little."

He nodded. "So I heard you blew up some boats today. Didn't bother to mention that on the phone."

I didn't answer.

"Was it in a fit of jealous rage?"

"No. The engine was old. And I'm not sure what the deal is with Candace, but I'm starting to think Grady might actually like me."

"And that's a bad thing," Freddie said half as a statement, half as a question.

"Terrible!"

"Right."

"I live in Chicago! He lives here!"

"Right."

"He likes Otter Lake Erica for some strange reason, and I like Chicago Erica!"

"Right."

"And God only knows how many Candaces he's dating."

"Uh-huh."

I planted my hands on my hips and shook my head. "I mean, I don't even want to open that door a little bit. He's investigating me for murder! And I accidentally destroyed his beloved boat."

"I hear you."

"I mean it's totally unworkable." I turned to read Freddie's expression. "Right?"

He said nothing.

"Well? Freddie? What do you think?"

He had already shuffled back toward the steps. "Right now I'm thinking that whoever the murderer is, I hope they kill me next."

I sighed and trotted after him. "Good one."

He skipped a little in the air. "I've been saving it all day."

Not long after, we were walking down Main Street. I couldn't help but wish the sun would set a little faster, so I'd feel less conspicuous. It was the first time I had set foot in town since the social eight years ago. Maybe only a few hundred of Otter Lake's total population lived in town, but right now, it felt like every single one of them had eyes on me.

Freddie and I crossed the street toward the Salty Dawg. Tommy's girlfriend Shelley waitressed there and lived in the apartment above it. Her family had owned the Dawg since it had opened, which was lucky for someone with a temperament like Shelley's, as it meant she always had a job.

It had been a hot day, but the temperature was dropping

quickly and the colossal raspberry looming over the town blocked the warmth from the last rays of sunshine.

I caught Freddie looking at it too.

"I can't help but think," I said cautiously, "every time I see that thing, that it's going to come to life—kind of like the marshmallow man in *Ghostbusters*—and destroy the town."

"I know!" Freddie exclaimed, slowly peeling his eyes away from the giant piece of fruit. "And just wait until you see it lit up."

We walked in silence for a little bit before I asked, "So whatever happened to Julie Mahone?" I couldn't help but wonder who we might run into tonight, and that got me thinking about all the people I used to know. "She was cool." Freddie and I used to hang out with Julie sometimes. She was the only person ever brave enough to dress goth in Otter Lake. I had to respect her for that.

"Last I heard, she's finishing up her residency as a pediatrician in New York."

"Really?"

He nodded.

"What about Matthew Masterson?" Matthew was from one of the oldest families in the area. They owned a beautiful historical estate on the other side of the lake, which they had somehow managed to keep even though most of their money was gone.

Freddie furrowed his brow. "Architect. Somewhere or other."

"What about Kate Turney? She was nice." Her family owned the local hardware store.

"Gone too. First grade teacher in Portsmouth."

I wrapped my sweater more tightly around my body. "Wow. Everybody we hung out with is gone."

"Oh, don't worry," Freddie said with a dismissive wave.

"They'll be back. Just like you. Otter Lake is kind of like a black hole, or—oh! Or the Hotel California."

"I'm not back, Freddie."

"We'll see."

I opened the door to the Dawg, washing us both in the warm smell of grease and stale beer. We picked a table and sat ourselves down.

"So," I said, putting my elbows on the surface before quickly pulling them back. Sticky. "Do you see Shelley?"

"Ah . . . nope," Freddie said, looking around. He pushed back his chair. "But I'll go find out if she's here."

I tapped at the table with an uneven rhythm, glancing around. Everything in the bar was made from wood except for the alcohol and the people. I quickly skimmed over all the once familiar faces. They were all looking back at me with uneasy expressions. Word must be out that I was a suspect in Dickie's murder. Either that, or they had heard about the boats. Suddenly a server I didn't recognize walked by with a tray full of shots. Without thinking I swiped one and downed it.

"I'm sorry," I said with a gasp. "Whoever those belong to, I'll buy them another. Two. I'll buy them two. It was an emergency."

The server walked away with a look on her face that I was doing my best to ignore.

"Erica Bloom!"

I turned to see a bear of man coming up to my table to pull out the chair across from me.

"Coach Waters!" I couldn't help the excitement in my voice. Of all the people I could have run into, this man was probably my first choice. Coach Waters ran the athletics department at the high school, such as it was, and headed up all the teams. He was built like a giant but was a softie through and through.

He hiked up the fabric of his jeans as he eased himself into the chair. "I saw you come in and I thought I'd say hello."

I scanned his face, taking in all the years that had passed. A few more wrinkles. Definitely grayer on top. But thankfully, he still had the same warm smile. "I'm glad you did."

"People treating you all right?"

I shrugged. "Haven't really been out much since I got home."

He patted my hand. "Well now, that needs to be remedied. Otter Lake is your home, and everyone's glad you're back."

"I'm not staying," I said with a quick shake of my head. "I'm just—"

He waved a hand, indicating that I didn't need to explain. "Doesn't matter how long you're staying. You're one of us. This will always be your home."

"I don't know if everyone agrees with you."

"I think you'd be surprised," he said with a smile that deepened the crow's feet at the corners of his eyes. "People just like a good story. Nobody really believes that bonfire—" He cut himself off and paused a moment before continuing. "Just don't let the rumors get to you."

I cocked my head. "Bonfire?"

"It's nothing. All nonsense." I could tell by the look on his face that he regretted mentioning it. "The important thing is that you don't let it get to you. People are happy to have you home. I, for one, know the athletics department misses you. The field hockey team fell apart after you graduated."

I chuckled lightly. I wanted to press him further, but I was so happy to see him I didn't want to ruin the moment.

Besides, I'd probably hear about this bonfire sooner than later, whether I wanted to or not.

"You know, we haven't won a championship since you left." Coach moved to get to his feet just as Freddie walked up behind him.

"Hi, Coach," he said, looking a little like an eager puppy.

"Freddie Ng," he boomed. "Where have you been? Hiding in that castle of yours again?"

Freddie shrugged.

"Have you been working on your jump shot like I told you?"

Freddie nodded quickly.

"Good. Good," he said, clapping Freddie on the back. "I'll leave you kids to your fun."

Coach walked away and Freddie sat in the vacated chair. "I love Coach. He always believed in my untapped athletic potential."

I nodded then asked, "Have you heard anything about me and a bonfire?"

Freddie's eyebrows jumped. "No. Why?"

I slumped back into my chair. "Just something Coach said."

"What's the matter with you?" Freddie asked, scanning my face.

"I don't know." I sighed. "He was just all nice, and now I feel all weird and emotional."

"Well, get it together," Freddie snapped. "We have work to do."

"Okay, okay. Jeez," I said, straightening up again. "So, is Shelley here?"

Freddie pushed one of the two beers he'd brought in my direction. "Her shift starts in a couple of minutes."

I took a big gulp. Then another.

"Easy, tiger," he said, watching me wipe my mouth with the back of my hand. "Oh, crap, that gives me an idea." He held up his index finger in a "wait one second" gesture. He then pulled out his phone, poked the screen a few times and brought it to his mouth. "I should have known this case wouldn't be a cakewalk. I was saddled with a partner—a dame no less—and she was a drinker to boot."

I blinked my eyes a few times, slowly. "Um, what was that?"

"I'm writing a book," he replied, squeezing his shoulders in across his chest in a self-hug.

"A book?"

"Yeah, don't get me wrong. The Madame F thing is great. Keeps me busy, and would pay the bills if I had any. But I don't think it's my calling," he said, wagging his finger in the air. "I was pretty upset when my Sherlock hat took that bullet, but then I realized something. Sherlock's not me. I'm more the gumshoe detective type."

"Right," I said, probably not trying hard enough to keep the judgmental tone from my voice.

He tipped his chair back onto the rear legs. "Then it was like BAM!" His chair skidded, and he had to grab the table to steady himself. He took a self-conscious look around, giving one woman an awkward wink before continuing. "A book! You coming back to town . . . it's all part of a bigger picture. It's the universe telling me I should write a book. A detective novel."

I blinked a few more times.

"So, what do you think?"

"I'm speechless."

"Oh, you're just jealous," he said, waving his hand dismissively. "That's what *you* need, by the way. A passion. A life's dream. A—"

"What I need is to not be charged with murder," I said,

taking another reckless swig of beer. A few drops spilled down my chin. "What I need is a mother who isn't hell-bent on ruining her livelihood. What I need is to get out of this town. Once I do all of that, maybe I can give your life dream and mine—whatever it might be—a little more focus."

Freddie slowly blew some air out of his lips. "That's fair."

Just then I heard a not-so-subtle tapping sound on glass.

The front of the bar consisted of two big picture windows on either side of the door. A group of women—my women—stood outside of those windows peering in. A few waved.

I glanced around the bar. The locals all stared at the women. Some with confusion. Some with just plain annoyance.

I looked back at the ladies, casually tucking my hair behind my ear with one hand while making a frantic shooing gesture, under the table, with the other.

Yup, bringing the ladies in was definitely not one of my better ideas.

It was silly to think anyone was going to talk to them, and now they probably wouldn't talk to me either.

Maybe if they left now nobody would figure out they were with me.

Tap. Tap. Tap.

The bird lady held up a stack of papers and pointed at me. I felt everyone's eyes turn. Well, ignoring them wasn't working. I gave the bird lady a pained smile and a thumbs-up. That seemed to satisfy them, and they drifted away from the window.

"What was that?" Freddie asked.

"Nothing," I said, rubbing a hand over my face. "They're helping."

"I thought I was your partner."

"You are." I swallowed some more beer. "I don't know exactly how it happened, but they're working with us now. Doing research. That kind of thing."

"Um, you should have discussed this with me first."

My eyelid began to twitch. "Freddie . . ."

"This isn't some Red Hat Society Murder Club, you know."

"Uh-huh," I said while mentally counting to ten. I seemed to be doing that a lot lately.

"It's gumshoe."

"Got it."

"Seriously—"

"Freddie!" Time to switch gears. "Okay, so let's get back to Shelley," I said, trying to keep my tone even. "You're telling me she's as bad as she was back in high school?"

"Maybe worse."

"How can that be possible?" I glanced over to the darkened door by the bar that led to the second floor. "Remember that Sadie Hawkins dance? Hey, did . . . did . . . what was her name again?"

"Nicole," Freddie replied, knowing exactly where I was headed.

"Yeah, Nicole," I said with a smile before remembering what we were talking about. "Did that patch of hair ever grow back?"

Freddie's eyebrows went up as he gave a small shake of his head to indicate no.

"Wow."

The beer was making my thighs feel a little weak, but my thoughts were racing. Maybe Shelley killed Dickie. She was crazy enough to do it. But then again there seemed to be a lot of people in this town crazy enough to do a lot of things . . . myself included. And while I didn't have much of a motive for any of my suspects, I had even less of one for Shelley. Besides, Freddie was probably exaggerating. Shelley had to have matured at least a little.

"YOU!"

I flinched. Then quickly looked over to the bar. Shelley stood in the door frame gripping the sides. She looked mad . . . crazy mad. Boy, somebody was in trouble.

"I should have known!" she yelled. "You're the one who's been sleeping with Tommy!"

I looked around the bar to see who was in trouble.

Funny thing was, everybody was looking at me.

"Freddie," I whispered without taking my eyes off Shelley. "Is she . . . talking to me?"

"Looks that way," he replied.

With a battle cry, Shelley launched herself forward.

I hit the ground and scrambled underneath the table.

I wasn't a coward—at least I didn't think I was—but I had seen Shelley fight. She was willing to go places normal people wouldn't go.

My eyes widened in horror as chairs seemed to magically fly off the ground, making way for Shelley's charging feet.

To the side, I heard Freddie scramble to get up.

"Freddie!" I yelled, making a grab for the loose fabric of his shorts rushing by.

"Don't worry! I've got your back!"

Unfortunately, it was my front I was worried about.

Shelley's tanned legs suddenly filled my view.

"Come out of there," she ordered with a bit of a growl. Her fingers gripped the edge of the table.

Oh my God. She was going to flip it.

She was going to flip the table like some crazed housewife on TV!

I wrapped my arms and legs around the post. Shelley gave it a good yank, but she couldn't flip my entire weight.

I needed to get this conversation under control . . . now.

"Shelley," I said in a loud but calm voice. "You've got it all wrong."

I tried to peer out from underneath the table to see her face, but all I could see was her bare midriff above her shorts. Tommy's name was tattooed across her belly with a little heart at the end.

"You would say that, Boobsie Bloom!"

Okay, so maybe it was the beer in me, but on some level, this was starting to get really annoying. "Seriously, Shelley, I'm not sleeping with Tommy!"

She pulled at the table in hard, frantic bursts, rattling my brain.

"Don't try to deny it. I know it was you!"

She bent and suddenly her face was inches from mine. I scrambled backward, finally allowing her to flip the poor piece of furniture on end.

Freddie helped me to my feet, pinning me by the arms in front of him.

"We can help each other, Shelley." I held my hands up between us. "I know Tommy's been cheating. Maybe together we can figure out with who."

She clenched her fists but seemed to be listening.

"We have history," I tried. "We went to school together. I wouldn't do that to you. I'm not crazy."

Chuckling broke out around the bar.

It was only one or two people at first, but then more joined in.

Then it seemed like everyone was laughing.

"What is going on?" I asked, looking back at Shelley.

She smiled and folded her arms across her chest. "After

last night, I think everybody here knows just how crazy you are."

"Last night? What are you t—"

I might have finished the question, but Shelley launched herself at me. Freddie and I stumbled backward and fell hard like dominoes.

Enough was enough.

They all thought I was crazy? I'd show them crazy.

I jumped to my feet and made a grab for the nearest chair. Before Shelley knew what was happening, I had her trapped in its legs and was pushing her back toward the wall.

All four posts of the chair hit the wood paneling with a solid *thunk!*

A few framed pictures shuddered on the wall. One smashed on the floor.

Shelley's crazy eyes settled on mine. I saw a little doubt flicker there . . . and I liked it.

"You and I are going to talk like grown women."

Shelley's gaze flashed to the bar. I knew her brother was pouring the drinks. I looked at him out of the corner of my eye. He took a step toward us.

"Stay!" I yelled, pointing a finger at him. He froze, along with everybody else in the bar.

"Now, Shelley," I said, lowering my voice. "A lot of crazy stuff has been happening at the lake this past week. A lot of stuff I wanted nothing to do with." I licked my lips. "And I'm not going to lie. It's stressing me out a little."

I heard someone shuffling up behind me.

"Uh, Erica," Freddie whispered. "Are you okay?"

"Fine."

"Maybe you want to put—"

I made a harsh shushing sound at Freddie even as I was having a brief moment of self-realization. Sure, Shelley had attacked me first, but pinning her up against the wall with a chair probably wasn't going to help my case.

I never did this kind of thing back in Chicago.

It was this freaking town.

This lake made people crazy.

I took a deep breath.

"Shelley?"

She nodded.

"I'm going to put the chair down, and we are going to have a conversation."

She nodded again.

"You are not going to attack me."

I saw doubt flicker in her eyes.

"Shelley!"

She grudgingly nodded again.

I brought the chair down slowly. We stared at each other a good minute before she moved to the nearest table and sat down. I joined her.

"Okay!" Freddie shouted, clapping his hands. "Show's over!" He smiled and whispered over his shoulder, "I've always wanted to say that." Then his voice grew big again. "You can all get back to your beers!"

Low murmuring resumed around the bar, and Freddie joined us at the table. "So . . . that was exciting," he said.

We both shot him a look before resuming our death stare at one another.

I broke first. "Shelley, you need to believe me. I have never slept with Tommy."

She looked me over slowly before letting her eyes drop.

"I didn't think so," she said gruffly. "Not really. You were always *so* hung up on Grady."

She shook her head. "I hate to say it, but it was kind of pathetic." Her eyes rolled to the ceiling. "But you just kept after him."

Leftover adrenaline and beer still had my brain feeling a little hot. "Okay, I think we're getting off t—"

"Then what you did at the social to get his attention?" Her eyes got big. "And dragging poor Betsy into it? I mean . . . wow."

"What I did?" I said, tilting my head. "What I did?" I repeated, leaning in. "You think I did that on p—"

Freddie put his hand on my arm. "How about I take over, hmm?"

I exhaled slowly and leaned back in my chair.

"So Shelley, we all know that Erica has . . . well, a reputation," he began. I gripped a piece of silverware on the table. It just happened to be a knife. Freddie cleared his throat. "But how do you even know for sure that Tommy is cheating? And why were you so convinced just now it was with Erica?"

I had to admit. That was smart. We both knew that Tommy was cheating, but if Shelley had to explain herself, it might give us some details that could be useful.

"I always know when Tommy's cheating," she said, disgust flaring her nose. "He's a dumbass."

"Then why do you stay with him?" I asked, jumping in.

Her eyes darted away from me. "We all make mistakes."

Huh. I couldn't help but wonder what mistakes Shelley had made.

"Anyway, I thought it might be Erica because it started up this week," she said. "I'm pretty sure I've got all the girls in town too scared to touch him. I thought maybe Erica forgot who he belonged to."

I flashed a look at Freddie.

"I'm not the only new girl in town," I said.

Shelley raised her eyebrows in question.

Right then the front door opened with a jingle.

"Hi, everybody!" a voice called out.

The entire bar answered the call.

"Candace!"

Chapter Eleven

That did not just happen . . .

I whipped around.

. . . everybody in the bar did not just shout Candace's name . . . in unison.

I waited for Freddie to stop beaming his welcome. When he didn't, I slapped him on the arm.

What? he mouthed.

I mouthed back, *You know what.*

She's nice. See? He motioned around the bar, showcasing how much everybody loved Candace.

I rolled my eyes.

You're a mean drunk.

"What are you guys doing?" Shelley asked.

We both snapped our silent mouths shut.

"Nothing."

I needed my beer. Where was my beer?

I looked back at the original table we had been sitting at, only to see Candace, in a pink sundress, picking her way over the downed chairs and tables to get to us.

Great.

"Hey, guys!" she called out, dimples winking at me.

Freddie, and even Shelley, returned the brightness of her greeting while I mumbled something that sounded like hello.

"Mind if I join you?"

Freddie eagerly nodded and moved to get her a chair while I silently mimicked her, *Mind if I join you?*

I noticed Shelley looking at me strangely, but then, a second later, she turned that stare to Candace.

Ha! Now she was getting it. One point, Erica.

Then Shelley stood up abruptly, chair screeching against the floor.

Uh-oh. While I wanted to cast doubt on Candace's apparently stellar reputation, I didn't want her to get beat up because of me. Again, that probably wouldn't help my case.

Luckily, Shelley simply said, "I've got to get to work," and walked away.

"Is she okay?" Candace asked.

"Fine," Freddie said, waving dismissively. "She and Erica got into a bar fight."

"What?" Candace asked, taking another look around at the furniture strewn about.

"It was nothing," Freddie said.

"Yeah . . . nothing," I added in my most menacing voice. I didn't exactly have a game plan when it came to proving Candace was the murderer, but if it was her, that meant she was trying to frame me with that weenie skewer. I figured it wouldn't hurt to let her know I was on to her.

"Don't mind Erica," Freddie said quickly. "She's still ringing with adrenaline." He shot me a warning look.

"Really, Freddie?" The words were out before I could stop them.

"What?"

I said nothing. Instead I looked away and crossed my arms over my chest.

"Did you guys want me to leave?" Candace said with a *blink blink* of her eyelashes.

"No," Freddie said. "Erica, here, sometimes, well, making friends isn't . . . she had a difficult childhood."

I was about to yell something when Candace said, "Oh, that can't be true. I liked Erica the first moment I met her."

"Really?" both Freddie and I replied.

"Of course," she said, looking at me. "You're so funny. But hold that thought. I'm going to go get us some beers."

"Aw. You don't have to do that," Freddie said sweetly.

She pulled a card out of her purse and waved it in the air. "I'm not. Just doing my job."

Freddie waited until she was a few feet away before he hunched over the table and whispered, "You really need to get a hold of yourself."

I rolled my eyes.

"Has it occurred to you that if she and Grady are seeing each other that she's not the other woman? You are."

I felt like somebody had just dumped the entire lake over my head.

It hadn't occurred to me. Not even a little bit.

"Oh my God, Freddie!"

He nodded. "I know!"

"It is just like Darwin said! I'm devolving. Soon I'll grow hair on my knuckles!"

"Wait . . . Darwin said what?"

Thoughts were racing. "I've been . . . not very nice to Candace!"

"I know!"

What *was* happening to me? The other woman? Oh no, no, no.

Freddie leaned forward. "You might want to think about

signing up for a retreat," he said with a knowing look in his eye.

My jaw dropped.

He leaned back again. "I'm just saying."

This was all too much. I looked around the bar, I guess looking for answers, but, again, the looks the other patrons were giving me were not reassuring. "Freddie, this can't be . . . I can't be . . ."

"Human?" he asked. "Just admit you're jealous. You'll feel better. And maybe then you won't have to go to your crazy place."

I shook my head for a bit, not knowing what to say. Finally I muttered, "Well, this is terrible."

Freddie nodded. "Very terrible . . . wait, why?" he asked with suspicious eyebrows.

"Well, you've put me in a very awkward position."

He looked at me sideways. "I've put you in a what now?"

"Awkward position!" I shouted. "Now I have to be friends with a murderer."

That earned me a few stares, but Freddie narrowed his eyes. "What are you going on about?"

"I can't be that mean girl," I said, shaking my head. "So I have to befriend Candace. Although . . . it's going to be really hard taking down a friend with murder charges." I took another sip of beer. "I now see what Rhonda has been going through."

Freddie turned his head even farther sideways. "Again, I'm really starting to worry about you."

"Me too," I said, nodding big. "Because of you I have to cozy up to a murderer!"

Freddie then leaned forward while looking side to side. "Keep your voice down. Dating Grady does not make her a murderer. It makes her . . . female."

I leaned forward to join him in whispering. "I should

know, right? But you heard Shelley. Tommy just starting sleeping with someone. No one in town would touch Shelley's man. It has to be Candace."

"So she's sleeping with Grady *and* Tommy?"

"Obviously. As her friend, I'll need to have a talk with her about that."

"Erica . . ." Freddie began but then stopped and took another approach. "Okay, are you sure this isn't all just because you're jealous?"

"And the hugging. I'll have to have a talk with her about the hugging . . . Wait! What did you say?" I snapped my focus back to Freddie. "No! It's not just because I'm jealous."

"So you admit it! You are jealous!" he said. Suddenly an enormous smile spread over his face. "Did you see what I did just there? I got you to confess. I'm starting to think I really am good at this." He rubbed his arms. "Tingles are running all over my body."

I slapped the table with my hand. Freddie jolted.

"For the record," I said, biting out the words, "Candace gave me a bad feeling before I knew she was dating Grady."

"That's because she doesn't have people issues."

I buried my face into my hands and mumbled, "People issues aside, I still think she might be the murderer."

"Based on what?"

I glanced back at the bar. Candace had a pitcher and glasses in her hands.

"Based on the fact that she just came to town," I whispered furiously. "That people who work for corporations are always evil, and—"

"Here we go, guys," Candace said, putting everything on the table.

"Thank you, Candace," Freddie said, carefully pronouncing every word. "You are so nice."

I reslumped in my chair, letting my arms dangle over

the sides. I was so confused. And suddenly my brain felt warm and thick.

She waved off his compliment before turning her attention to me. "Erica, I'm so glad I ran into you. I've been wanting to talk to you."

I perked up. "And I've been so wanting to talk to you," I said with a big smile.

"Um . . ." Candace looked to Freddie.

Freddie laughed nervously. Okay, maybe the smile was too big. I needed to practice.

"Of course. No, actually, I completely understand," she said. "I know things have been hard for you lately." She paused as I narrowed my eyes. "I want to help."

I covered my surprise by raising the glass of beer she had poured me. "Help how?"

"You're looking into Dickie's death, aren't you?"

"Maybe."

"Well, I want to help."

I struggled to sit up in an adult position. "Wait . . . what?"

"I want to help," she said, nodding her head. Her blond waves rippled. "I've got a lot at stake. This development is the biggest opportunity of my career, and if the police don't catch whoever killed Dickie and hurt Harry, well, everything I have worked for will be gone."

I said nothing. I simply searched her eyes. I looked hard for the lie but couldn't find it . . . yet.

"So I was thinking we could work together on this . . . like partners," she said, smiling back and forth between Freddie and me.

Freddie laughed, covering a spray of beer from his mouth with his palm.

"I mean, I know I'm not a detective or anything, but—"

"It's very kind of you to offer," I said, cutting her off. I know I had just resolved to befriend her, but I couldn't investigate my new friend for murder with my new friend as my partner. "But I already have a partner . . . Freddie."

"No, no," Freddie said, clearing his throat. "I think it's a great idea. You know, when I'm working, Candace can be the Cagney to your Lacey. The Starsky to your Hutch. The Barney to your Andy Griffith. I'll let you two decide who's Barney, but I think it's kind of a no-brainer."

"We get it, Freddie," I said. "Again, thanks, Candace, really. But I think I work better on my own."

"I don't think so," Freddie jumped in. "I mean you've got all the women at the camp working on the case. What's one more?"

Candace, again, looked back and forth between the two of us. "If Erica doesn't want to . . ."

It was then a thought occurred to me. "Wait . . . you know, maybe it is a good idea."

"Really?"

My brain was working fast now, beer-slicked fast. Maybe with my getting close to Candace, I could get into the cottage she was staying at—do one of those covert searches you see on TV when the suspect is in the other room.

"Really," I said, ignoring the concerned look on Freddie's face. "Great idea. Freddie's right. I could use another friend."

"Cool," Candace said, once again giving her dimples a workout. "So what's our first move?"

"Hmm, I'm not exactly sure," I said, the alcohol telling me it was a good idea to scratch my chin to make it look like my brilliant plan had just now occurred to me. "Maybe we should meet at your place in the morning to discuss it."

"Okay, but—"

The bar doors burst open.

Alpha Team moved in quickly, followed by Beta.

"Erica! Time to go!"

"Huh?"

"You've got to get out of here!" a woman I was pretty sure I had never seen before yelled. She waved like she was trying to roll me out the door with her hand.

I got to my feet.

"Your mother's getting Red to fire up the pontoon."

I didn't move.

"Quickly! The heat is on!"

I took a few steps forward. Obviously it was time for another discussion about the need for subtlety in a small town. But before I could get a word out, Maria Franelli had grabbed me by one arm while Lydia Morgan grabbed the other.

The beer was making it hard to resist.

"I'll come to your place in the morning," I called back to Candace.

She nodded.

"And I'll talk to *you* later," I shouted at Freddie.

Then the women dragged me out of the bar and into the night.

Chapter Twelve

It was hard to make any sense of what the women were saying on the way back to the retreat given the beer, their excited chatter, and the pontoon's motor, but the ancient-looking cop boat tied under the retreat's dock light gave me some idea that it wasn't good.

"What do we do?" one of the ladies yelled.

"Do you want to make a run for it, Erica?" Lydia asked, grabbing my arm. "I know people."

I raised an eyebrow. "What people, exactly, do you know?"

"People," she said gravely.

"You're an insurance agent."

"Exactly."

I slowly turned my head to break the intense gaze we had going on, in order to look to someone else for answers. "I still don't understand what's happened."

Red cut the pontoon's engine, and we drifted toward the dock. Two figures stood waiting. The distinctive silhouettes of Rhonda and Grady.

"Say nothing, Erica," my mother said sharply, pushing her way through the crowd. "Your uncle said to say nothing."

"You actually got a hold of him?" I asked.

My mother's eyes flashed to mine. "Of course. Why wouldn't I?"

"Because the last time you two spoke you called him a soulless money maggot?"

"I don't see what that matters," she replied. "He's family. Anyway, he can't get away right now, but he'll come out if he needs to."

Something big had obviously happened, but despite their constant talking, none of the women seemed particularly keen to fill me in on what had transpired.

I stood and elbowed my way through the women to jump from the pontoon onto the dock.

"Rhonda, Grady," I said, making eye contact with each. "Can one of you tell me what is going on?"

Grady crossed his arms over his chest and nodded for Rhonda to go ahead.

"Erica Bloom, we'd like to ask you a few questions."

I took a deep breath through my nose. Playing good suspect to Rhonda's cop seemed the fastest way to find out what was happening.

"Go for it," I said, ignoring the women filling up the dock around me.

"Perhaps we could do this somewhere more private," Grady suggested.

"No. Let's do it here." I turned to look at the women. "Why don't you all go on ahead. I'm sure this won't take long."

The women looked at me like I had canceled Christmas, but I guess the expression on my face said I wasn't negotiating. They slowly made their way to the steps—all of them, except my mother.

"Grady Forrester, haven't you caused enough trouble for my daughter in one lifetime?"

Grady smiled. "Yes, ma'am. That has been pointed out to me before."

My mother planted her hands on her hips and flashed her eyes to his boat in invitation for him to leave.

"I'm sorry, ma'am, but it's either here or at the station." She snorted.

"We'll be happy to leave just as soon as Erica answers a few questions."

"Well, none of it is on the record," my mother said, stepping behind me, placing her hands on my shoulders.

"Right," Rhonda said, snapping her notebook shut.

Grady gave Rhonda a quick swat on the arm. She started, then reopened her book. "We're not reporters," Grady said, angling his face in a way that suggested he was ducking and weaving my mother's glare. "Saying it's off the record doesn't . . . that's not questioning . . . that's . . . never mind."

"And just so we're all clear," my mother said. "If Erica did murder someone, it's all your fault." She ended with a vicious point at Grady.

"Mom, thanks, but I don't think that's helping," I said, suddenly feeling tired. "I didn't kill anyone, so I'm not afraid to answer a few questions." I looked to Rhonda. "Maybe we could just get on with this?"

She nodded. "Okay, Ms. Bloom, let's start with something easy. Where were you tonight?"

"I was having drinks at the Dawg with friends." As the words came out of my mouth, I realized how wrong, wrong, wrong, they were, but my brain was too slow to stop them.

Hurt filled Rhonda's eyes.

"Right," she said. "The Dawg." She made a note in her

book, pressing the pen with a lot more force than necessary.

"Rhonda, it was a spur-of-the-moment thing. I—"

She held up a hand.

I was a terrible person.

"Why don't we move on to the real reason we're here, Rhonda." Grady put a hand on her shoulder, flashing me a look reserved only for the worst sort of people.

Rhonda cleared her throat. "Okay, Ms. Bloom, where were you *last* night?"

"Here," I said stiffly. "Remember, Grady? I was right here." I pointed at the dock. "And then we were in there." I pointed to the water. "And then you were all—"

"I remember," Grady said, cutting me off with a lazy smile before snapping his face back to that of a law enforcement professional. "But that was early in the evening. What about after?"

"I joined the ladies for some therapy, and then I went to bed."

"Have you ever seen this flyer?" Rhonda cut in, handing me the same Raspberry Social leaflet she had the last time.

I smacked my lips together sharply before saying, "Yes, Rhonda, you showed it to me the other day."

"Interesting," she said, narrowing her eyes on my face. "Ms. Bloom, what do you know about the illegal bonfire set in the middle of town square last night?"

I looked from her to Grady as alarm bells sounded in my head. "Nothing. I mean, Coach Waters said there was some sort of rumor about me and a bonfire, but he didn't go into detail."

Rhonda's face tilted down toward her notebook, but her eyes peered up at me from underneath her brow bone. "Would it surprise you to know that we have several reports of a woman, matching your description, starting a bonfire last night at approximately three A.M. with stacks of these flyers." She rattled the paper. "The arsonist then proceeded to run through the square, naked, shouting . . ." She paused to flip back through her notepad. " 'I'll show you raspberries! Come see the raspberries!' "

I looked at my mother. Her dropped jaw said everything I was feeling.

"Yes, it would surprise me," I said, trying not to stammer. "It would surprise me very much. Who said it was me?"

"Aaron Cummings for one."

"Seriously? Mr. Cummings?" Mr. Cummings ran the local bait and tackle shop, was about sixty years old, and had been nearly blind since birth. "You're taking Mr. Cummings's word for it?"

"The witness considers himself to be an expert in female anatomy and reported that . . . that, quote, the cans were not as nice as he remembered from the social, but they did bear a certain resemblance to Boobsie Bloom's. He went further to say that if you were willing to put them in a lineup, he's sure he could identify them clearly." Rhonda looked up from her notes again. "So?"

"So what?"

"Are you willing?"

"To do what?

"Be in a lineup?"

"No, I will not be in a boobs lineup!" I felt something like pain explode deep in my brain. It was probably an aneurysm. It was this lake. The lake was the real killer.

Rhonda made a tsking sound, and clicked her pen again. "Note, suspect was uncooperative when asked to appear in a voluntary lineup."

I looked at Grady. The barest hint of a smile touched his lips.

"I think we've probably got all we need for now, Rhonda," he said, directing her by the shoulders toward the boat. Then he added, "I'll be right there. I want a word alone with Erica."

Grady watched Rhonda step into the creaky vessel, then turned back to face me. He brought a hand up to his forehead and massaged it a few times before he spoke.

"So, you were at the Dawg minding your own business?"

"I was." I said it firmly but found it difficult to meet his eyes.

"We also have reports of two gangs of women, from this resort, asking a lot of questions around town. I don't suppose you would know anything about that?"

"Hey, this is America," I said, throwing my arms wide. "No law against asking questions."

He took a quick step toward me. I tried to back up, but my mother wasn't moving. "I don't think you get how much worse you are making this for yourself."

I held his gaze this time, even though the intensity of it was making me sweat.

"I did it!" my mother suddenly screamed.

Grady and I jumped. He recovered first. "Thank you . . . but that really isn't necessary, Ms. Bloom," he said, looking to my mother. "Do you think I could have a moment alone with Erica?"

"What for?"

I put a hand on hers. "Mom, it's fine."

I felt her mouth move close to my ear. "Okay, but remember, honey, I love you," she whispered. "Even if you are going to be the death of me."

She then turned and stomped toward the stairs, managing to look like an angry butterfly.

My eyes moved back to Grady. Maybe it was the fact that my brain still felt a little buzzy, but before I could stop myself, I said, "So . . . I was thinking that maybe we should talk."

What was I doing? I hated talking. But there was the whole last-night thing. Then the boat thing. The Candace thing. That was a big thing. There was even the social thing, but we could strike that from the list if there wasn't time. In fact, all the things were just starting to build up . . . and soon they might tumble down.

"Seriously?" he said, closing his eyes and shaking his head. "Now you want to talk?"

"Yeah . . . why?" I asked, furrowing my brow.

He tossed his hands in the air. "Now's not exactly a good time."

Wait. What? My eyes bugged. That wasn't the way this was supposed to go. "I'm sorry?"

"Well, I'm kind of on the job here."

I planted my hands on my hips. "And since when are you the big professional?"

"I was always the big professional! I—" He snapped his mouth shut and growled slightly. "Listen. Whether you or your mother or any of those ladies up there in the retreat believe it or not, I'm on your side. Things are getting a little out of control. I shouldn't have come here last night. *That* probably wasn't professional. But . . . listen. I didn't want your mother to hear this. I know she can be . . . dramatic, and that might not help this situation, but the boats blowing up—"

"What about the boats blowing up?" I asked, a cold flash running over my arms.

"That explosion might not have been an accident."

The words *not an accident* tumbled around my brain.

"I don't have the report yet, but it looks like an explosive device might have—"

"What! No. The engine's old. I—"

"Actually the fact that the engine wasn't working properly may have saved your life. I'll know more when I get the report."

I ran a hand over my face. "I don't believe this." Suddenly my eyes jerked over to my mother. "Grady, don't tell my mom this until you're sure, okay?"

He sighed.

"You know how she is. All her cluelessness aside, if she thinks I'm in some sort of mortal danger, there's no telling what she'll do."

He nodded. "But you have to do something for me."

I raised my brow in question.

"No more detective games."

My lips moved to say something, but my brain couldn't figure out what it was. I didn't want to lie to Grady, but I didn't think he'd like the truth.

"Whoever is behind all this isn't stable. First, Laurie Day goes missing and now—"

"Yeah, I'm not entirely sure she's missing," I said over the thumbnail I was chewing. "I might have stopped by her trailer the other day, and I may have seen a half-packed bag."

Grady rolled his jaw. "Don't suppose you'd know where Tommy is?' "

I dropped my hand. "Wait, you can't find him?" I asked.

Grady shook his head no.

"You don't think he and Laurie . . . maybe they're together? I may have seen a bag packed for Tommy too." I paused, trying to think it all through. "Oh my God, you don't think something's happened to Tommy?"

"Honestly, I'm not sure what to think, but we are working on some theories. We, as in the police, are working on some theories," he said, patting his chest before pointing back to Rhonda.

"Wait. Are you okay?" I reached out to touch his arm. "After Dickie, then Harry, your family must be going crazy! What about your aunt? She must be worried sick. I—"

"We're not going there yet. Tommy could be anywhere." He said the words without emotion, but his face tensed. "I'm going to get a forensics team over to his place tonight. Are we going to find evidence of you being there?"

I pinched my lips together. Just my fingerprints, probably some hair, and . . . oh God, when was the last time I had seen the screwdriver? "Maybe."

"You need to get this. I believe somebody was trying to frame you with that skewer. Now they might be trying to kill you. I'm waiting on forensics on the boat to be sure, but my guess is that this person is in panic mode, and if you push them at the wrong time . . ."

I nodded.

Grady took a few backward steps toward the police boat. "I mean it, Erica. I'll throw you in jail for obstructing justice if I have to." He then stepped into the boat to join Rhonda. "I don't care who your uncle is."

I walked in a daze to meet my mother waiting for me at the foot of the stairs.

A horrible grinding sound echoed over the lake as Grady and Rhonda left.

My mother linked her arm with mine. "They should really get him a better boat."

I elbowed her lightly in the ribs.

"Oh! Right. Maybe after you leave town."

I spent the night tossing and turning.

Instead of the princess and the pea, I was the princess with the six-inch carving knife under her mattress.

I wasn't surprised that I was so scared. But I *was* kind of surprised that my feelings were so hurt.

Somebody wanted me dead . . . like actually dead.

The faces of Tommy, Laurie, and Candace drifted around the ceiling of my darkened room. I couldn't rule out any of them, missing or not. But to be honest, I couldn't imagine any of them killing me either. It seemed almost . . . unneighborly? I was used to seeing criminals in court, but they all wore nice identifiable orange jumpsuits. It was easy to picture them doing bad things. I guess that's the whole thing about criminals; if you could tell they were criminals just by looking at them, you could simply lock them up before they did anything.

And then there was the whole Grady situation.

I didn't like thinking about Grady, but I couldn't seem to stop thinking about him either.

And that whole situation just left me feeling . . .

Vulnerable.

Vulnerable . . . like a girl standing half naked in front of her entire town.

Grady.

I could feel the memory pressing against my thoughts. I didn't try stop it from coming this time.

Chapter Thirteen

Where are you going?

I watched Grady plant his hands on the dock and push himself out of the water.

It's a surprise, he said, quickly yanking on his jeans and scooping up all the clothes, mine included.

Why are you taking my clothes?

So that I know you'll still be here when I get back!

Grady!

He ran toward the end of the dock.

I'll be right back!

Grady!

I did trust him.

For about twenty minutes, I really, really trusted him.

I gripped the dock with my hands and treaded water. All the while, trusting him.

Then I got cold. Really cold.

It's hard to trust someone when your teeth are chattering.

So even though I really didn't want to, I got out of the water and sat at the edge of the dock. I hugged my knees to my chest and stared pure death at the break in the trees where I thought Grady would come out . . . at any moment. I truly believed at any moment Grady would come out.

I would have sat there all night, but then I heard the music echoing over the lake.

The band stopped, and a voice rang out over a loudspeaker. *Welcome, everyone. I hope you are enjoying the social so far!*

Cheers sounded in the distance.

Well, the fun's not over. We have a special performance for you tonight from Earth, Moon, and Stars.

I remember thinking, *Great, I'm not going to miss my mother's performance after all.* I would get to hear everyone's reaction. Even Tommy, Dickie, and Harry's. Grady had mentioned to me that even his cousin and his friends were making a point of going. It hadn't meant anything to me at the time, but . . .

Tommy, Dickie, and Harry.

Why would they make a point of going to my mother's performance?

And that's when I knew. I knew it in the core of my being.

They were planning something.

I jumped up and scurried down that dock, trying to cover myself.

I needed clothes. My eyes darted to the McAdams's home. I scooted up the stairs and yanked on the door to the cottage. Thankfully the mudroom wasn't locked. I looked frantically around in the gloom. A pair of men's rubber fishing overalls hung on a hook. They were way too big, but they'd have to do. I yanked them on and had just hiked the straps over my shoulders when a light flicked on.

I cringed, then turned slowly to the door that went into the cottage.

Mrs. McAdams stood on the other side, staring at me with very round eyes.

We both screamed, and I bolted, grabbing what I thought was a sweater off a hook on the way out.

I stumbled down the stairs.

The thing in my hand wasn't a sweater. It was a winter hat. I shoved it on my head anyway.

My eyes darted around.

I could hear the music for my mother's performance start up.

I needed to go!

I couldn't feel any pain in my feet anymore. I was running as fast as any person could in rubber pants.

Luckily I didn't have to go into the crowd. The back of the stage faced the water. And yup, sure enough, I could just barely make out three hazy figures skulking up the back stairs, shielded from the audience by a curtain.

Hey! I shouted.

The figures froze.

I ran-waddled toward them.

Erica? Harry called out.

I skidded to a stop a few feet away from them, hands holding the overall bib in place.

Dickie's eyes bugged. *What are you doing?*

What I am doing? I shouted. *What are you doing?*

All three stared back at me. No one answered.

Watching the three guys mount the stairs to the back of the stage, I realized Tommy was carrying something. *Is that Betsy?* I shouted. *Why do you have Betsy? And what is she wearing? Is that a leotard . . . and a tutu?*

Betsy. Beloved town mascot. Ancient at twenty-five years old. Toothless.

Beaver.

Somebody had rescued her after a run-in with a boat

motor, and taken her to the wildlife sanctuary. After that the whole town seemed to just fall in love with her.

A smile slid over Tommy's face. *We thought your mother might be lonely up there dancing all by herself.*

Before my brain could even process the words my head was shaking no. *Tommy, I'm warning you—*

What are you going to do, Erica? Give me another love bite? He turned his shoulder in my direction.

I took a few steps toward them. *Guys. Look. I know my mother is a little out there. But she's really proud of this dance, and the town already thinks she's a bit of a joke, and . . .* I didn't know what else to say. I looked at each of their faces. Dickie and Harry started to show a little uncertainty, but not Tommy. In fact, he stepped closer to the spot where the two sides of the curtain overlapped.

Tommy, I warned.

He chuckled. *Look out, boys! She's going to blow!*

I don't remember how I got up onto the back of the stage, but suddenly I was there wrestling for Betsy with Tommy.

Give me the beaver, Tommy, I growled through my teeth.

Not going to happen.

I wedged my arm in between Tommy's chest and Betsy's body and gave her a good yank. Poor Betsy groaned.

Tommy! You're going to hurt her!

You're going to hurt her!

Suddenly, without thinking, I raised my foot and stomped it down on Tommy's.

Ow! He let go of his grip, and began hopping backward on one foot, the other cradled in his hands. I hugged Betsy to my chest.

Ha! I shouted. *When are you going to get it, Tommy? These stupid pranks just never work out the w—*

Then the horror of what was about to happen stole the words right from my mouth. Tommy was still hopping. Hopping backward and reaching for the curtain for balance.

I reached toward him with one hand, but it was too late.

Tommy grasped at the curtain. The thick fabric fell to the ground with a heavy thump.

I felt the heat of the spotlight on my bare shoulders as the sound of the crowd's collective gasp ran over me.

I stood frozen to the spot. Betsy still clasped to my chest.

Out of the corner of my eye, I could see my mother. She was frozen too, mid-dance.

Silence filled the stage, the town, the entire lake for what seemed like an eternity before someone shouted, *What is she doing?*

Then, *It must be some weird Wiccan thing.*

She's half naked! And in a knit hat!

Is that . . . is that Betsy?

The crowd's tone turned from confused to horrified.

She's got Betsy!

Not Betsy!

New exclamations of horror ran through the crowd.

Don't hurt her!

My head was already shaking no.

Look, there's raspberry tart crumbs on her pelt!

You can't feed her! She's on a special diet!

Suddenly I saw Grady pushing his way past people to the front of the stage.

Thoughts ran wild through my head. Had he been in on it? Is that why he took my clothes? He knew what the guys were planning and he was the distraction? I glanced at his face. He looked genuinely shocked. But then again I was still supposed to be back in the water.

He stepped toward me with his palms in the air.

Erica, you had better drop the beaver.

Either way, he was right. I needed to drop the beaver. The crowd was turning ugly.

I nodded at Grady, then began to lower the ancient animal gently down my body . . . and with her went the bib of my overalls.

My eyes flashed up to Grady's already wide ones.

I didn't look down. Maybe what I thought had happened hadn't happened. Maybe—

I watched Grady gulp, right before he said, *Heavens to Betsy.*

I managed to get a few hours' sleep after my trip down memory lane, but I woke up with a brutal headache and an uneasy feeling in my gut.

Two days.

Two days left until the social.

Coffee. I needed coffee.

I swung my legs out of bed, knocking my feet against something furry.

Caesar scuttled away hissing. He then turned to give me a filthy look.

"You'll be happy to know that someone is trying to kill me," I said.

He considered me for a moment before rolling back on his butt to give his crotch a lick.

"Nice."

Gray light filled the common area and kitchen, perfectly suiting my mood.

I filled my mother's old kettle and lit the gas burner on the stove. Then I grabbed the jar of instant coffee I had stolen from Freddie's.

Someone was trying to kill me.

There it was again.

Seriously, how was I supposed to have a normal morning with someone trying to kill me?

At least I knew one thing for sure; I was shutting down all of my ongoing investigations.

This had all gone too far.

A few days ago, I was worried about when I was going to get out of Otter Lake. Now that question started with an *if*.

I screwed off the lid to the coffee right as a hand appeared on the other side of the kitchen window, rapping on the glass.

"Wah!"

Coffee grounds sprayed everywhere.

Candace's face appeared, evil dimples twisting.

"Oh, sugar! I'm so sorry," she said, voice muffled by the glass. "I brought you coffee." She lifted a to-go cup from the Dawg into view. She then pointed to the front door and disappeared.

Oh, crap! What had happened last night? Oh, God, had I agreed to be Candace's new partner? Had I befriended a murderer after all?

I looked frantically around the kitchen clutching my scalp.

It was too late to hide.

I could jump out the window like I had that day with Grady . . . but then she might kill my mother in her bed.

Could I ignore her?

No, that might make her mad . . . homicidally mad.

I heard the front doorknob rattle.

A weapon!

I needed a weapon.

I grabbed a knife from the counter and tried to shove it in the waistband of my shorts. After I poked myself in the butt, I realized that wouldn't work. Too obvious. I didn't want Candace to know I suspected her of murder. It might be the push over the edge Grady was talking about.

The kettle on the stove began to whistle.

That was it! The scalding water.

I grabbed the hot handle of the kettle and instantly dropped it. Too hot. Okay, not scalding water.

I would have to go in unarmed.

I rolled my shoulders. She was a little bit of a thing. As long as she was unarmed, I was pretty sure I could take her in a fight.

I walked over to the door, took an empty gulp, and swung it open.

"Hi!" Candace said with a brightness that matched her yellow rain slicker. "Did you get lost on your way to the door?"

I tried to laugh, but the sound came out stumbling and tripping.

"Are you okay?"

"Uh-huh," I said. "Come in."

As I pulled the door back, I wrapped my hand around something leaning against the wall.

Candace took a quick step toward me, only to stop with a jerk when she realized she had the tip of an umbrella stuck in her belly.

She looked up at me, confused expression on her face.

"Um, poke, poke," I said in a cutesy voice. "Is it raining?"

God, when had I become Mr. Bean?

"Drizzling," she replied, cautiously reaching out toward me with the coffee in her hand.

I put the umbrella down and leaned on it, trying to look casual.

I needed to get a hold of myself.

Freddie was right. Other than the timing, I had no good reason to believe Candace was the killer. Laurie or Tommy could have done it. Or somebody else entirely. I had zero concrete evidence to link anyone to any crime. This all needed to stop, or I really was going to land myself in jail.

I gave Candace my best attempt at a smile. "I'm really sorry, Candace. I didn't get much sleep."

"No, it's my fault," she replied, holding up a hand. "You said you'd call in the morning, and here I am showing up on your doorstep. I have been told that at times I can be a little too eager." She pulled her face down into an *uh-oh* expression and rocked her body back and forth.

I took a breath. I really *did* want to be a good person.

"That's okay," I said, trying to take pointers from her effortless ability to be so . . . nice. "But listen, Grady came by last night and warned me to stay away from doing any kind of investigating."

"I know," she said, before taking a sip of coffee. "He told me."

Time stopped for a second.

Be a good person.

"Well, I think I'm going to take his advice, and let the whole thing drop."

"Really? That's too bad. I mean you're probably right. I don't know why I even suggested it. This could mean real trouble for you," she said as though I didn't already know that. "I guess I just thought it could be kind of fun. Girl detectives on the case, you know?"

"Uh-huh."

"I mean I totally respect Grady's ability to get the job done. But Rhonda? Love the girl to death. I have a beer with her at least once a week, but it's just . . . I don't know," she said, searching my eyes. When I gave her nothing, she opted for another track. "You know what? I'm going to be quiet now. I just hope the police are doing their jobs."

I had no idea what to say, so I settled for a nod.

She nodded back. "But look, there's something else I wanted to talk to you about."

"Okay."

"Grady." She gave me a small smile that could only be described as smitten. "We've been spending some time together. I wouldn't call it dating necessarily, but, well, this is a small town. People talk. And I wanted to make sure I wasn't stepping on anybody's toes."

Her eyes flicked down to my feet and stayed there a moment before she flicked them back up, lower lip trapped sweetly between her teeth.

Oh, God, why couldn't she be the killer and just end this now?

"Nope," I said carefully. "My toes are great."

Now if I could only stop my face from twitching.

"What a relief! I mean Grady is so sweet."

"Sweet? Really?"

"Oh, yeah, he's such a big puppy dog. And I get the feeling that he doesn't have a disloyal bone in his body."

"Huh."

She paused. "Oh, great. I've done it again. You're probably thinking about the social. He told me all about it."

Heat rolled up my neck to my face. "Did he now?"

"Can I just say," she said, placing her hand over her heart. "Actually forget *say* . . . I'd like to give you a hug. Can I give you a hug?" she asked, stepping forward.

"No."

Candace froze mid-step, arms hovering straight out in front of her.

"I mean, I think I'm getting sick." I really was. Positively nauseous in fact.

"You do look flushed." She let her arms drop. "Well, Grady feels terrible about that night. He'd really like to apologize to you, but he's not sure you're ready to hear it."

I tried to focus on what she was saying, but it was hard to hear over the person screaming in my head.

"It all happened a long time ago," I said. "I don't blame Grady."

"That's what I said!" she exclaimed, throwing her hands up in the air before dropping them dramatically like a broken puppet. "I mean, don't get me wrong, it sounds horrifying. And what were you, eighteen? Nineteen? But the moment I met you, I knew you were a pretty cool chick. There's no way you'd be wallowing in some teenage prank. I mean give her a little credit, Grady."

"Yeah, give me a little credit, please," I said, chuckling.

A moment of awkward silence passed.

"You know what?" I said suddenly. "I think maybe we should keep on investigating."

I was a terrible person.

"Really?" Candace asked. "Are you sure?"

"Absolutely!" I clapped my hands together with a loud crack. "Let's go to your place and discuss. Any minute, the retreat will be crawling with women."

"Oh, I don't think we should go to my place," she said, looking down at her coffee, giving it a swirl. "That's why I came here. I was out late last night, and the place is a mess. Plus I don't have any snacks! I hate having guests over without snacks. Why don't we have breakfast at the Dawg?"

Three things. First, nobody has breakfast at the Dawg unless they want a coronary at forty. Second, I did not miss the *I was out late* comment, but I absolutely could not go there right now. And third, it seemed awfully suspicious that Candace didn't want me in her place.

Time to put the screws to her.

"Oh, don't be silly," I said, suddenly overflowing with warmth and enthusiasm. "I don't mind. I'd love to see what's been done to the Millers' old place. That's where you're renting, right?"

"Right, but—"

"Well, come on! Let's go!"

"You're still in your pajamas."

"Right," I said, pointing at her. "I'll change quickly."

"I still don't think—" Suddenly Candace's phone began to trill the song "Zip-a-Dee-Doo-Dah." "I've got to take this."

I'll go get dressed, I mouthed. I casually walked around the corner of the hallway before I flattened my back against the wall to listen.

A few moments passed before I heard Candace say, "Yes, sir. No, everything is on track."

If I wasn't mistaken, she sounded nervous.

"Absolutely, I look forward to your coming to the social. And yes, I am aware of how much the Raspberry cost." She paused. "But these people, sir, when you meet them, you'll understand. Everyone in Otter Lake is so nice and welcoming."

Images of Kit Kat, Tweety, Grandpa Day, among others, flitted through my mind. This girl certainly had an interesting way of looking at the world.

"Yes, sir. I am aware of the stakes. Good-bye."

Crap! I needed to get dressed. I ran as quickly and quietly as I could down the hall and pulled on the first pair of jeans I could find, along with a T-shirt.

A moment later I was shuffling back down the hall still fastening the top button of my jeans.

"Everything all right?" I asked.

"Oh, fine," she said, but her voice didn't sound fine.

"Just work, you know. Change is always hard for small towns, and the company has a lot invested in this development."

Hmm, invested enough to kill?

"Are you okay?"

I realized during my inner monologue my eyebrow had gone up quite high with my suspicions. "Fine. Fine. Ready to go?"

"Oh, I can't now."

"Really?" I asked, working hard to keep my eyebrow down.

"My boss suddenly wants all of the financials for the last couple of months, and I have a million things to do before the social. I shouldn't even be here now," she said with a sad shake of her head. "But I figured all work and no play . . ."

"Oh, that's too bad."

"And to top it off, one of the properties we purchased—a hunting cabin just outside of town—something tripped the alarm." She poked at her phone. "It happens all the time. Seriously, like once a week. There's a family of raccoons living under the floor, but we have to have alarms at all of our properties, and I have to go check them out when they go off. Due diligence, insurance, and all that."

"Which cabin?"

"The one off the dirt road near Hunter's Corners."

"That's not too far from Freddie's place," I said, suddenly feeling very savvy. Missing people. Cabin outside of town. It could be nothing . . . or . . . it could be something. "We could check it out for you."

"Really?"

"Sure."

"No, you shouldn't. What if it's not a raccoon? I mean

it probably is, but . . . oh, that's why you're going," she said, shoulders slumping in disappointment. "You're investigating. I want to come."

I pouted my lower lip. "But you're so busy."

"I am," she said with sad eyes.

"And it's probably raccoons."

"It is," she said with resignation. "But, you know what? This is a bad idea. Just in case something happens, I don't want to put you in any danger, and I don't want to get myself fired."

I began walking to the door. "You're probably right."

"You agreed to that very quickly," she said, taking a step toward me, unable to resist the polite pressure of being shown out. "You're still planning on going, aren't you?"

I put up my fingers in what I thought was a scout's promise, but it might have been the Vulcan "Live Long and Prosper" sign.

"I would probably do the same thing." Candace sighed. "But don't break an ankle or anything. And while the alarm should be off now, if you trip it, call me."

I nodded.

"I still have to head over there myself once I take care of some paperwork just so I can say that I did." She looked like the saddest little yellow duckling ever as she made her way to the door. "And call Grady if anyone is there. Don't be a hero."

"Your concern has been noted," I said, nodding sharply.

She smiled, popping her dimples back into place. "You're pretty funny, you know that?"

"I'm glad somebody thinks so."

For a second, I thought I saw what Freddie liked so much about her, but they do say that sociopaths are often charming.

I shut the door behind Candace and made a beeline for my mother's old flip phone. Mine was still a little wet from the boat explosion.

"Freddie, I got us a hot lead."

Chapter Fourteen

"Why'd you have to pick today to go traipsing through the woods?"

Freddie's overcoat flapped in front of me. Underneath he wore a T-shirt, basketball shorts, and the same Doc Martens he used to wear back in high school. "It's cold, rainy, and the mosquitoes are brutal."

"I didn't pick it," I said, stepping over a tree root. "We're following a lead."

"A stupid lead."

I had filled Freddie in on everything that had happened since I left him at the bar the night before. He had listened, but without much enthusiasm.

"Are you okay?"

He made a huffing sound. "Finally, she asks about me."

I stopped walking and flipped a piece of hair out of my face. "Okay. What's wrong?"

"It's the book," he said, still walking, swatting away branches with limp arms.

"What's wrong with the book?"

Finally he stopped. "Writing is hard! I have writer's block!"

"You only started yesterday," I reasoned. "How can you have writer's block?"

"You don't understand," he said, resuming his steps. "You're not an artist."

I scrambled over a slippery log trying to catch up. "Well, maybe today will inspire you."

"Madame F doesn't think so."

"Freddie, you're Madame F."

"Exactly."

We walked the final bit in silence. Obviously, I did not know how to feed Freddie's artistic soul, but at least he was here, grumpy or not. Then something else occurred to me. Maybe the book thing wasn't the only problem.

"Um, I feel like it's possible I owe you an apology for last night." I hated apologizing, but given my behavior at the Dawg, maybe it was warranted.

"Forget it. Blowups are bound to happen between us," Freddie replied, waving the thought off. "The way I see it, there are some really good people in the world, and then there's people like us. You're a mean and very cheap drunk, and I hide behind friends in bar fights. It's part of what makes us work."

We came to the edge of the clearing. The rundown cabin stood a few feet ahead. I slowed down, but Freddie kept plowing forward.

"What are you doing?" I shout-whispered.

He turned. "I'm going up to the cabin."

I was still hidden behind a tree while Freddie stood on what I imagined was supposed to be the front lawn. "What if somebody's in there?"

"I am so not in the mood for this today," he said, planting his hands on his hips. "I'm going up there and knocking, like any normal person would do when greeting a family of raccoons."

"Don't you think we should watch it for a bit?"

"If somebody's in there, they've already heard us," he said, raising his voice nearly to a shout. "Now come on."

I moved out from behind the tree. This still didn't feel right, but Freddie was already knocking on the door.

"Hello? Mr. Raccoon? We're here to have a few words with you about an alarm?"

Suddenly I noticed a smile on Freddie's face.

"Are you having fun now?" I asked, joining him on the shaky porch.

"Okay, maybe this is better than being at home with my artistic demons." He chuckled. "*Hello? Mr. Raccoon?* Good times."

I rolled my eyes. "Glad you think so. I—WAH!"

A loud thump sounded inside.

I clutched Freddie's arm. "What was that?"

"I don't know," he whispered, eyes wide. "Somebody might be inside after all."

"What do we do?" I asked, but I was already subconsciously pulling Freddie back with me toward the forest.

"We're going to look in the window," he said with the slightest quaver in his voice.

"You're nuts!" I let go of his arm and jumped off the porch. "Come on!"

"We are never going to figure out what's going on if we run away every time we actually run into someone!" He looked at the window but didn't actually move toward it.

"You're forgetting Grandpa Day nearly shot you in the head!"

"Stop it!" he spat. "You're freaking me out!"

"Good!"

He brushed me off with a hand then took a step toward the window.

"Freddie," I said, running up the porch stairs before deciding against it and running back down. "Think about it. If they're friendly, why haven't they come to the door? They have to have heard everything we've been saying. Now get away from there."

He swatted again in my direction.

I was wringing my hands. Literally wringing my hands. I didn't want to die. I didn't want Freddie to die. Grady was right all along. I should have list—

"Raccoons."

"I'm sorry?"

"A whole family of them. I think they were sleeping, and we woke them up."

As the adrenaline seeped away, I was surprised to find that I was actually a little disappointed. I really thought we might have been on to something.

"Wait a minute," Freddie called out, still peering in the window. "There might be something going on here after all."

"What do you mean?" I ran up the stairs to stand beside Freddie.

"That sleeping bag over there on that scary old couch." He pointed at the glass. "That looks kind of new. And . . . is that a laptop I see peeking out underneath it?"

"Holy crap! I'm going in." I scurried over to the door and turned the knob. It didn't open, but it felt loose. I gave it a shove with my shoulder.

"Now who's the reckless one?" Freddie asked, but he joined me at the door, and we pushed it together. It gave.

Five angry raccoons turned on us and hissed.

"Uh-oh," I said, once again grabbing Freddie's arm.

"Don't be afraid," he said slowly. "Raccoons can smell fear."

"All that does is make me more afraid."

"And they can smell it."

We huddled together for a moment.

"What do we do?" I whispered.

"I don't know. It's your turn," Freddie said, giving me a small slap on the arm. "Raccoons freak me out with their masks and creepy little human hands."

"I'm not feeling it," I said.

Freddie gave me a push forward. "Fake it until you make it."

All the raccoons hissed again. One of them got up on its hindquarters.

"Begone!" I shouted, waving my arms in a circle. "Begone!"

The raccoons started.

"Begone?" Freddie barked. "Really? Begone? You're too much."

Freddie's delight in my raccoon-whispering proved distressing for the furry beasts. They scattered through a side door leading toward the back of the cabin.

"Well, that takes care of that," I said, slapping my hands together. "Do you think we triggered the alarm again?" I looked around, trying to spot it.

Freddie pointed to a bashed-up keypad, dangling from the wall. "I think we're good."

I walked over to the laptop and pulled it out from underneath the sleeping bag.

Both Freddie and I sat on the couch.

"Can you even get Internet out here?"

"Yup, another perk from the development company," Freddie said. "Free wireless for six months."

As we waited for the computer to load up, I asked, "So

are people really upset about the development or are they just looking for something to talk about?"

"Oh, they pretty much believe Satan is behind it," he answered, shuffling around, trying to stay afloat on the sinking sofa. "Everybody loves Candace, but nobody wants the type of change her company's bringing in."

"I figured as much."

"It's hard to stop progress though," Freddie added. "There are a lot of seniors on the lake, and taxes are going up. They need to sell, and nobody's going to beat the development company's prices. It's already started happening. Of course, there's a few holdouts, but even they're starting to reconsider. The lake isn't what it used to be."

"How so, wise one?"

He gave me an unimpressed slow blink with his eyes, but answered anyway. "Their way of life is dying. The younger generation around here is full of bums. Myself probably included." Freddie suddenly looked puzzled like he had never considered this before. "It's like nobody wants to work or grow up. They just want to buzz around the lake and act like idiots. If anything, it's getting worse as they get older. It's kind of sad. Grady's like the most mature person of our generation."

"Wow," I said, stunned. "That is sad."

Freddie sighed. "Now I'm sad."

"I'm sorry."

"You should be."

We both turned back to the computer.

"Jackpot!"

The screensaver was a picture of Tommy pretending to do something to his boat that was probably illegal in at least a few states.

"I've got to call Grady and tell him," I said, reaching for my phone. "His family's been going crazy."

"Whoa, whoa, whoa. Slow your roll there, missy," Freddie said, placing his hand on my arm. "I saw Tommy's mother this morning when I docked at the marina. She looked just fine. Chatting up a storm, in fact, with Mr. Armstrong about the new line of snowmobiles he has coming in for fall. So really, if Grady's worried, he might want to try talking to his family, because I'm guessing Tommy let his mom know he's okay."

"But Grady said . . ." I was trying to remember what Grady had said. Actually, he hadn't said much. I had just assumed. "It still doesn't seem right. I think—"

"Listen. We're the ones who have being doing all the work. We deserve the first look." Freddie put one finger on the laptop's touchpad and slowly dragged the arrow over to the e-mail icon.

"I don't know, Freddie."

"Besides," he said with a small shrug, "I think we've already established that Grady's not exactly telling you everything about everything these days."

Dimples flashed before my eyes. "Open it."

Freddie double-tapped the pad. "I doubt he left anything incriminating around anyway. But, then again, it is Tommy we're talking about."

We scanned the messages in his in-box. There looked to be about five thousand from Shelley. All in caps. All with an overuse of exclamation marks.

"Wait, what's that one," Freddie said, pointing at the screen. "James Jones? That's a fake name if I ever heard one."

This is the last e-mail you will be receiving from me.
I assure you our business arrangement is concluded.
Should you go to the police with your wild, unfounded
accusations, or mention our involvement to anyone,

you will regret it. I look forward to never hearing from you again.

"Now, that's interesting," Freddie said, leaning back. "What do you think it means?"

He blew a thin ribbon of air through his lips before answering. "Well, this is most likely the person that Tommy got the money from, right?"

"Right. But what do we do?" I asked. "Now do we call Grady? Should I tell Candace Tommy's squatting here?"

"No and no," Freddie said, eyes suddenly flashing. He whipped his phone out of his pocket. "Lucy, do I have an idea for you."

"You're judging me again."

"I didn't say anything!" I protested.

"I can feel it in your eyes," Freddie said without removing his own from the computer screen. "And I'm doing all this to save your butt!"

"I'm sorry," I said, walking over to his beer fridge to see what might be hiding inside. "It's just kind of creepy that you know how to do this."

"I told you. I have never done this before. I looked into it, so I that I'd know how to protect myself," he said, tapping the adhesive tape over his Webcam. "I don't want anyone spying on me . . . unless I want them spying on me."

"This has to be illegal."

"I think we crossed that bridge with the break and enter."

"Candace knew we were going to the cabin," I said. "Oh, shoot, that reminds me." I grabbed my own cell and called up a number. "Voice mail . . . Hey Candace. Just so you know, there's really no reason for you to go out to the cabin. Nobody was there except for the raccoons. An entire family is now living inside, and they have these creepy little hands, and there's at least—"

Freddie distracted me with frantic waving.

"Too much detail is a dead giveaway for lying," he whispered.

"Um." I bit my lip. "So don't go to the cabin."

I almost hung up, but again Freddie waved his hand in the air.

"Oh! But I wouldn't turn the alarm back on either because of all the raccoons . . . you don't need to know how many. Bye."

Freddie sighed. "Well, that didn't sound at all suspicious."

I said nothing, just plopped myself down on the edge of the computer desk.

"We should practice in advance next time."

I shook my head. "I really am starting to wonder if we're bad people."

"Well, stop it. No good can come from wondering. Plus your *wondering* is getting loud, and it's making it hard for me to hack into Tommy's computer so that we can spy on him with his Webcam." He squinted at the computer, typed a few more keys, and then said, "Bingo!"

"It could not have been that easy."

"Oh, but it was."

Back when we were at the cabin, Freddie used his phone to send an e-mail to Tommy. An e-mail with an attachment program that we then opened. The program linked Tommy's laptop to Freddie's home computer, allowing us to spy on Tommy through his Webcam without his ever knowing. We then put the laptop back exactly where we found it under the sleeping bag. We figured that eventually Tommy would come back to the cabin and turn on his computer, allowing us to see what he was up to. If Candace discovered the laptop before Tommy returned, everything would be ruined.

I stared at the screen. "Why is it all black though?"

"I'm going to give you a moment to think that through."

"Oh, his laptop isn't on," I said, then slapped Freddie on the shoulder. "Stop being so snarky."

"Sorry, the brilliance of my plan is going to my head. I feel like a James Bond villain."

We both looked back to the blank screen.

"This is a bit of a letdown," Freddie said, biting off the edge of a fingernail.

I went back to rummage in the fridge. "I guess there's nothing to do but wait."

"Not exactly. I have to work," Freddie said. "But I'll leave the window open."

"Do you want me to go?"

"Nah . . . actually no," he said, snapping his fingers. "You can help me."

"Help you!" I shouted, popping up from the fridge. "Did you not hear me on the phone? I'm a terrible liar. I think fortune-telling is out for me."

Freddie pulled his Madame F turban down on his head. "Listen. It's hard to keep things fresh, and you owe me. It'll be great." He grabbed me by the shoulders and plunked me into a chair in front of the computer. "Now don't say anything, and try to look like you're in a vegetative state."

Two hours and seventeen minutes later, I didn't have to try anymore to look like I was in a vegetative state.

At first, it was pretty interesting being Madame F's ward, Katianna. Freddie kind of pulled together a story as he went along. Apparently I had suffered a traumatic head injury after jumping off a bridge with my star-crossed lover, who, sadly, didn't survive. I was now brain-dead, which made me the perfect conduit to the other side. But now my butt hurt, and I wanted a drink of water.

"I sense your great-aunt," Freddie said, voice now sounding half Southern, half Hungarian. "She is near. Bring her to me, Katianna."

I tried to keep my eyes dead and forward, but I noticed the black box in the lower corner of the computer screen come to life.

Tommy's computer!

Freddie hadn't noticed it. He was swaying back and forth, summoning someone's great-aunt, which probably meant his eyes were closed. I didn't want to ruin his gig, but this was important.

"Freddie," I murmured out of the corner of my mouth.

"Great-aunt Sonya," he called out, voice swelling. "Where did you put the Christmas turkey platter?"

Oh, for God's sake.

The computer chimed. Freddie's client had written something. I looked at him sideways. He was peeking through one eye.

"The large turkey platter," he added, face tilted to the ceiling. "Not the small one!"

I kicked him with the side of my shoe. He kicked me back.

The computer chimed again.

Freddie once more peeked at the computer then added, "The one with the woodland fruit motif!"

My eyes shot to the lower screen.

Tommy's face!

All right, enough was enough.

Besides, Freddie's Eastern European ghost voice was getting to me.

I cleared my throat.

"Yes, Aunt Sonya, use this vessel to speak your truth."

"Um, Freddie."

"Yes, Aunt Sonya," he said with warning. "You had better know where the platter is or get back to the other side."

I motioned to the lower corner of the screen with my eyes.

"Oh!" Freddie jumped. "We have to go!"

The computer chimed again.

"Try the cupboard in the basement." Freddie fumbled to close the psychic chat window. Silence fell over us as Tommy's unsuspecting face filled the screen. He looked tired, and maybe a little scared.

"Oh, this feels wrong, wrong, wrong," I whispered, pinning my hands between my legs.

"You don't have to whisper," Freddie said, but he was kind of whispering too. "Do you want to turn it off?"

"No," I said. "I still care about me, and me not going to prison, but I wanted to say that out loud, so the universe knows, that I know, this is bad."

" 'Cause that makes you a less bad person?"

"Exactly."

"I'm not sure it works that way," Freddie answered. "Wait. Why is he looking like that?" he asked with a point.

Tommy's eyes weren't focused on his screen, but to the side of it, at something in the cabin. Then he pushed the computer off his legs, and we were left with a view of the battered couch.

"Turn up the volume," I said, waving at the keyboard.

Freddie fiddled with some speakers, and we both leaned forward.

"You shouldn't be here," I heard Tommy's distant voice say.

Silence.

"Who's he talking to?" I whispered.

Freddie shushed me, but then whispered, "I can't tell, but the voice is definitely female."

We turned back to the computer.

"She's going to kill us."

Tommy's voice was barely audible. I stopped breathing to hear better.

"She killed Dickie. Then tried to kill Harry. We're next. She doesn't want anyone knowing about the money."

Freddie and I exchanged *Oh my God* eyes.

"This is all Dickie's fault. He probably tried to black-mail her for more money. Did he tell you anything?"

Hairs stood up on the back of my neck. There was only one person Dickie would have been talking to outside of the boys. I mouthed the name *Laurie*.

Freddie nodded.

"She has to suspect I'm running from her. This is the last place she'll look for me."

I knew it! There was only one female in town that I knew who had boat money. I turned to Freddie and mouthed, *Candace*.

Freddie didn't nod this time, but I knew by the look on his face, he was thinking the same thing.

"I'll get the rest of the money tomorrow. Then we should both get out of town."

Silence.

We jumped as Tommy's face suddenly appeared back in front of us.

"I need to calm the hell down," Tommy muttered.

"What's he doing?" I asked, still whispering.

Freddie shook his head.

Then Tommy slid the laptop away from him, down his legs. Then he grabbed the waistband of his pants with one hand, and slid the other hand—

"Oh my God!" My hands flew to cover my eyes. "Turn it off! Turn it off! Turn it off!"

Freddie made a grab for the mouse.

I hit the floor, sending my wheeled office chair spinning.

"No!" Freddie screamed.

"Freddie? Freddie? Are you okay?"

Silence.

"Freddie! Did you get out in time?"

I looked up to his face. The heels of his hands were pressed deeply into his eye sockets. "I'll never unsee it. Never." He then pushed away from the desk, still in his chair, and rolled toward the fridge. "Move!"

I shuffled out of the way.

He opened the little door and pulled out a beer.

I struggled to get off the floor and back into my chair. My legs felt wobbly from all the adrenaline.

"I can't believe that just happened," Freddie said, twisting off the cap of the beer.

"Now do you believe me?"

He took a long sip then said in a shaky voice, "That doesn't mean it was Candace."

"We know, now, it's not Laurie because that had to be who Tommy was talking to! And whatever this is," I said with emphasis, "it has to do with money and blackmail. Candace is the only person who makes even a little bit of sense."

"Why? Why would she have given money to those three?"

Thoughts shuffled quickly through my mind.

"You said that the guys were being more obnoxious than usual?" I asked, speaking my half-formed thought.

"Yeah."

"What if they were doing that—not because they're immature jerks, but because Candace was paying them."

"And why would Candace pay them to do that? She wants the lake to be attractive to potential customers. She—"

Freddie stopped talking and looked at me. "You think she's trying to get the old-timers to move out. Sell their properties."

I nodded. "It kind of makes sense. And you heard Tommy say that Dickie was probably blackmailing her for more money, hence the murder."

"I'm not sure *hence the murder* is something anyone should ever say. It's like saying *therefore* I kicked the puppy or *understandably* the old lady was cross-checked."

"Stop it. You know what I mean."

"I'm really having trouble with this," Freddie said, shaking his head. "Candace is a nice person, and I can't help but think your feelings for Grady are pushing you to the wrong conclusion."

"Swear to God," I said, slapping one hand over my heart and putting the other in the air. "This has nothing to do with me being jealous."

"Are you sure? The universe is listening." Freddie rolled his eyes up to the ceiling. I fought the urge to look up too.

"Okay, then," I said, "who do you think Tommy was talking about?"

"I don't know, but this evidence is circumstantial at best."

I loudly blew some air out of my lips.

"And," Freddie said, "at the risk of not having my pitchfork ready for the lynch mob party to Candace's, we didn't actually see who Tommy was talking to."

I threw my hands up. "Haven't you ever heard of . . . that . . . razor thingy?"

"Occam's?"

I snapped my fingers. "Yes."

"Never heard of it."

I ignored Freddie as he laughed at his own joke.

"This looks like a duck," I said, counting off my fingers. "Quacks like a duck, and . . . does something else like a duck."

"Please stop trying to explain this to me. It's painful." Freddie tapped the desk with the top of his beer bottle. "I hear what you're saying. I'm just not ready to convict Candace based on what we saw tonight."

I slumped back into my chair. "You used to be more fun," I said halfheartedly.

He was right. I knew he was right. The evidence was circumstantial at best. And accusing someone of being a murderer was a pretty big deal. Chicago Erica wouldn't do it. We needed to be responsible about this. We needed to be levelheaded. We needed to put our petty jealousies aside and—

"What we need is a trap!" Freddie suddenly shouted.

I smiled as a little tear came to my eye.

"Freddie, you are the absolute best friend a girl could ever have."

Chapter Fifteen

After our initial enthusiasm wore off, we discovered devising a trap was harder than it had first seemed. We knew we were in trouble when we found ourselves discussing the merits of moving our deliberations to a cave outfitted with one of those swiveling blackboards and our Internet search for the Acme Corporation resulted in nothing useful.

After an hour or two, we decided to call it a day.

As I drove Freddie's extra boat back to the retreat, I went over the next steps in my mind. Even if we didn't have a plan, at the very least, we had a direction. And while Freddie wasn't convinced of Candace's guilt, I was. There had always been something just a little off about those dimples.

I felt a surprising calm come over me.

Maybe it was the night wind brushing the hair from my face. Maybe it was being at the helm of a speedboat that cost more than a house. But, whatever it was, I was a woman on a mission. And it was time to take my life back.

I slowed the engine as I approached the retreat. With the twinkling lights of the lodge peeking through the trees, it actually felt kind of homey. For once, I didn't feel like my shoulders were hunched so high my head was at risk of disappearing. And that too was good because my first job was to face the women and shut them down.

I pulled the boat in and tied it to the dock.

I stood for a moment taking in the lodge above.

My mother was right. They were good women. They had lent me support, and it had felt good.

I breathed in the cool night air, tinged with the scent of campfire smoke.

Yes, I was growing as a person. In a short period of time, they had taught me a great deal . . . but now it was time to get serious. When Freddie and I came up with a trap—which I had no doubt we would—I couldn't risk the women mucking it up with their good intentions and thirst for cozy adventure.

I trucked up the stairs full of purpose. I would be kind but firm. Grateful but resolved. Apologetic but uncompromising.

I rested my hand on the heavy handle of the lodge's door.

I was captain of my own ship.

I pushed into the entryway, and my jaw dropped.

I was captain of a dinghy.

The women, however, they . . . they had rebuilt the *Titanic*.

Pushpins and string traced complicated patterns over maps covering one wall of the common room. Another wall showcased black-and-white photos of people, only half of whom I recognized.

The women, meanwhile, buzzed around stacks of papers teetering on chairs and tables, each in turn holding out a mug to be refilled from the pitcher that sloshed with iced tea in my mother's grip.

She was the one who spotted me first and rushed over.

"What's . . . what's going on?" I asked.

"Isn't it wonderful?" she replied. "Everyone has been working so hard on your case. You'll be cleared in no time."

I walked slowly toward the hub of action, picking just that moment to remember the Acme Corporation discussion I had had with Freddie.

"She's here!"

The women swept toward me en masse then ushered me to a spot on the sofa.

"We have so much to tell you," Susan Anderson, the crying cat lady, said.

One of the other women squeezed her on the shoulder. "Well, we can't prove anything yet, but we're getting close to figuring out who's behind all this."

"Okay." My eyes flitted over the stacks of evidence. "What have you found out?"

I saw a number of eager little grins, but no one was talking.

The excitement generated by their enthusiasm was starting to get to me. "Come on! Don't leave me in suspense."

Finally, Lydia Morgan spoke. "The development company."

"Ha!" I shouted, clapping my hands in the air. "Finally."

"Listen, we've been doing a lot of digging," she said, rushing over to one of the walls. She pointed at a photo of a polished-looking man, handsome in a plastic, too-good-to-be-true kind of way. "This man here, Bryson Maxwell, is head of PR for Lakeside Living, a subsidiary of MRG Properties, one of the largest real estate developers in the world. The MRG stands for MacDonnel, Richmond, and Goldstein, but it is colloquially known as Many Rich Guys."

"I'm with you," I said, bouncing on the sofa cushion. "I like it. Keep going."

"We've been looking into some of the previous developments he's been involved with, and it took some digging, but . . ."

"Yeah, yeah." I nodded eagerly.

"There's been some shady doings."

"Excellent," I said. "Well, not excellent, but I like that I'm looking less guilty all the time."

"Now," she said, passing me a newspaper article printout. "Nothing's been substantiated, and there have never been any charges, but Lakeside Living has had a number of complaints filed against them. It seems that after they target a property, acts of vandalism and other misdemeanor crimes tend to rise in areas where the owners are reluctant to sell."

"I knew it!" I jumped to my feet and walked around the walls eyeing the women's handiwork. "It was Candace all along."

"Oh! We don't have any proof that she knows of her company's doings."

The urge to tell them everything that Freddie and I had discovered was strong, but I knew he would not be impressed if I shared our potentially illegal investigating with anyone else. I did, however, allow myself to say, "How could she not know?"

Suddenly a zebra spoke. "That's what I've been trying to tell them." It was Maria Franelli dressed in another pair of jungle-themed pajamas.

"Regardless," Lydia said, giving her a look. "We were thinking that the three young men . . . the ones with the distasteful name . . . that, perhaps, they were paid to cause similar trouble around Otter Lake and that Laurie knew about it."

I pulled my lips in and gave her a big nod. "I am so picking up what you're putting down."

She smiled and cocked an eyebrow. "Then something went wrong."

Or someone went wrong. Someone with dimples.

"We think maybe Laurie's in hiding."

"The alternative is too horrible to even think about," Lydia said, nodding.

Suddenly another woman in pink flannel cut in. "But I'm telling you . . . the police must have looked into this already."

I scoffed . . . loudly.

The woman's cheeks flushed.

"I'm sorry . . . you." I really needed to learn their names. I think this one had a husband into sexting his junk. "But the police," I said, making big air quotes on that last word, "would probably do a better job investigating the corporation, if the police," air quotes once again, "weren't dating Candace."

The collective gasp the women made, I have to admit, was very satisfying.

"Now," I said, pausing for dramatic effect, "what do you have to say for the so-called innocent Candace?" I crossed my arms over my chest, soaking in the women's horrified looks.

"Oh, you poor thing."

"I'm sorry?" I blinked my eyes a few times. "Wait . . . no!"

"She's jealous."

"That's why she's always had it in for Candace."

"No. No. No! You guys are supposed to be on my side!"

"Oh, that's terrible. She's so cute too, that Candace. Those dimples? How do you compete with that?"

"I'm not competing," I yelled.

"I'll tell you how you compete," one lady said, pointing to my chest. "Those. Nobody can compete with those."

She's lucky she wasn't standing any closer, or I would have snapped that finger off. Instead I said, "You guys thought Candace was suspicious too . . . like two days ago."

"Yeah, but we've had a session on the damage women do to one another," Maria said, albeit somewhat dryly. "You should have been there. It might have helped."

"That's right, ladies," my mother shouted above the din. "Let's not turn against our sister Candace. Let's focus on the real problem. Grady Forrester."

The women quieted down, obviously interested in this developing angle.

My mother's caftan wings soared as she opened her arms wide to capture their collective attention. "You all saw the way he looked at Erica on the ropes course."

The women began murmuring again. A few nodded their heads.

I stood speechless.

She dropped her arms and balled her hands into fists. "That he would even dare to show his face after what happened all those years ago."

"And the audacity he had of standing on that dock in those tight cop pants," one lady interjected. "No man should look that good."

"Exactly!" my mother said, pointing to her. "Can you blame my daughter for being jealous?"

"Hey!" I shouted, trying to interrupt the wave of interpretation.

"He's been torturing her mind for years!"

"Amen!" someone shouted. "They all do."

"It's never the mistress to blame . . ."

The tone of the women's ongoing murmuring turned a little skeptical at that.

"It's the man!"

The murmuring exploded to a roar.

A knock interrupted the rising clamor.

We all looked over to the front hall.

Heavy footsteps sounded on the wood floor.

A voice called out, "Ladies, did I come at a bad time?"

Grady.

Chapter Sixteen

I scooted over to the door before the women could rush him and pushed Grady back outside.

"Hey! What are you doing?"

"I don't think the ladies want to see you right now," I said, slamming the door behind us.

He smiled. "What are you talking about? Those ladies love me."

"Not right now they don't."

I'm not going to lie. Part of me might have enjoyed seeing the ladies take Grady down a notch or two, but I couldn't see that happening without it becoming glaringly obvious that I was the motivation behind the lynch mob. Hey, maybe I was a little jealous, maybe even a little hurt, especially that Grady had told Candace all about our history, but he certainly didn't need to know that. He also didn't need to know what was going on behind that closed door. I had come to accept that I couldn't control the women or their detecting activities, but I doubted Grady would see it that way.

"It never fails," he said, shaking his head.

"What?"

"You! Every time I talk to you, I know you're up to something crazy, and there is absolutely nothing I can do about it."

My mind flashed to his threat of arresting me for obstruction, but there was no need to help him out in this.

"Sometimes . . . this job . . ." He pushed his hat back and scratched his hairline.

"It's a lot of responsibility, isn't it?"

He looked me in the eye as though surprised I would say that. "It is."

I nodded. "I bet when you were growing up, you never thought you'd be the person responsible for keeping everybody in line."

He chuckled. "No, I guess I didn't."

I backhanded him on the chest, hard. "Well, get over it! People's lives are at stake!"

He pointed a finger at me, pressing his lips together in an angry line.

I planted my hands on my hips. "Well, seriously. And you wonder why people of interest look into their own cases?"

Grady grabbed my elbow. "That's it. You're coming with me."

Uh-oh.

"You're not arresting me, are you? I'm sorry I lost it like that. It's the stress. I—"

He led me firmly to the porch steps.

I skidded to a halt. "I'm not going anywhere with you."

He stopped, let go of my elbow, and spun on me. He looked mad.

"Um, Grady?" I asked cautiously. "Did you growl? I swear I just heard—"

"If you're not careful, I might bite too."

I swallowed.

"Can I at least ask where you're taking me?"

His upper lip twitched almost into a snarl. "Somewhere we can talk in private."

"This is private."

He jabbed a finger back at the retreat. I turned. About fifteen women had their faces pressed up against the glass.

"Point taken."

He stomped away from me, but instead of walking toward the steps that led down to the dock, he headed to the back of the retreat, toward the ropes course.

"Grady?" I called out, scampering after him.

He didn't stop.

"Grady!"

This time he stopped, but he didn't turn.

I moved quickly to catch up to him.

I stopped a foot or two away. He still hadn't turned. "Can you at least tell me what we're going to talk about? Because this is feeling a little like the part of the movie where I get murdered in the woods."

"So I'm the murderer now?"

"No, I—"

He spun quickly toward me. His face hovered inches from mine. I tried to breathe, but that much Grady up close made it difficult.

"This ends tonight."

I stayed quiet.

"You are going to hear my side of the story."

I started to make a sound, but Grady's finger shot up toward my lips in warning.

"Don't you *pfft* me one more time, Erica Bloom."

I pressed my lips together before saying, "I told you, Grady, I don't care about the social! I wish everyone would stop bringing it up. Because I don't care. We have other things to talk about, like Cand—"

"Oh, you care," he said. He paused for a beat then said, "I mean, I get it. It was embarrassing—"

"Ha!" I shouted, folding my arms across my chest. "I'm so not embarrassed."

"Oh, yes you are," he shot back. "Anyone would be! It was embarrassing! And part of it was my fault," he said, lightly hitting his chest with his palm. "But not in the way you think."

I furrowed my brow. "I think nothing . . . nothing at all . . . not ever." Wait, that didn't sound right. "I mean I don't think about anything . . . ever." That wasn't much better.

Grady ignored me. "I'm pretty sure that's why you're not listening to anything I say about staying out of what is so obviously a police matter." He flexed his jaw. "But tonight you are going to listen. Listen to the whole thing. I will be heard."

We stared at each other for a moment, surrounded by the chirping of frogs and insects. Then Grady spun away again and resumed his stomp into the woods.

All sorts of emotions tumbled through me. After a moment, I chased after him. He was waiting for me in the moonlit clearing of the ropes course. His back was still to me, but it looked as though he were holding something.

I cleared my throat to let him know I was there.

He looked over his shoulder, and tossed something to me.

"Put this on."

I didn't have to pick it up to know what it was.

"No way." I planted my feet and crossed my arms over my chest. "No freaking way."

He turned to face me, full-on.

"Put it on."

"There's no way I'm putting that on."

Grady scooped down to pick up the climbing harness and crossed the distance between us in a few long strides. "You're going to put it on. You want to know the reason why?" His eyes flashed in the moonlight. "Because deep down you know you want to hear what I have to say."

I rolled my eyes.

"More than that, I think even deeper down you want to be proven wrong about me, but you're afraid."

I huffed air out my nose. "What exactly are you going on about?"

He stepped even closer. The butterflies in my belly fainted.

"You, Erica Bloom, are deathly afraid that I'm not the bad guy." He leaned in, slowly licking his lips. "And if I'm not the bad guy, then you're in serious trouble."

"I have no—" I had to stop for a moment because my voice cracked. "I have no idea what you're talking about."

"Then put on the harness and find out."

He pushed it toward me. The rough fabric brushed against my stomach.

"Why not just tell me?" I asked, flicking my eyes down to the hand that was nearly at my waist. "Why the harness?"

"Because I'm getting through this story tonight. No more running away. No more blowing up boats that mean the world to people."

"You said that wasn't my fault," I said quickly. "That someone tried to blow up the boat."

He closed his eyes and whispered, "Pull. Pull. Pull. *Erica, stop. Let me help.* Pull. Pull. Pull." Then he made the sound of an explosion.

"Fine, but I'm still not putting that on," I said with a point.

"This is your last chance to hear, straight from the horse's mouth, what happened that night." He let the harness drop. "Take it . . . or leave it."

Chapter Seventeen

Ten minutes later, I was fully harnessed and stepping out onto a thick rope, twenty to thirty feet above Grady.

"I hope you're happy," I shouted down.

"Best I've felt in days," he called back.

I moved both feet onto the lower rope while gripping the upper tightly with both hands. "Okay, well, let's hear it."

"Move out to the center of the course."

"Seriously?" I shouted.

"Seriously."

I grumbled and shuffled toward the center of the ropes. I wasn't terrified of heights, but I wasn't exactly a big fan either. This had better be one good story.

When I made it, I looked down and saw Grady's teeth practically glowing in the moonlight. "Satisfied?"

"Not hardly," Grady shot back, "but you can stop there."

I waited a few moments, but he didn't speak.

"Hello? Anytime now."

"I'm trying to figure out the best place to start."

"How about you start at the part where I'm naked in the

water, like an idiot, and you leave, telling me to trust you?"
I asked loudly . . . really loudly.

"No, I think we should back up a little."

I groaned.

"Well, you're skipping over all the good parts," he said.

I tightened my grip on the rope, imagining it was
Grady's neck. "I don't remember any good parts."

His laughter floated up to my ears. "Oh, I remember all
sorts of good parts."

I said nothing and stared up at the sky. Stars.

"I remember talking," he said.

I shook my head.

"I remember splashing with you in the water."

I still said nothing.

"I definitely remember you suggesting we skinny-dip."

"Grady! That's not what hap—"

"Joking! I'm joking!" he called up. I could practically
feel him willing me to look down and meet his eyes, but I
couldn't. "It was a great night before everything happened.
One of the best."

"So what the hell happened!" Hmm, that came out a
little shouty too. I guess maybe I did care a little bit.

I heard him take a breath. "I never intended to leave you
there."

"So where did you go?"

"My grandmother's place."

"Grady, please." I took a few steps toward the platform.
"I'm not sticking around to hear some story about a sick
grand—"

Grady gave a few quick pulls on the ropes that attached
to my harness.

"Hey!" I yelled.

"Would you listen?"

I stopped moving.

"I wanted to go to my grandmother's place because, first, it was close. Second, I knew she and my grandfather were at the social, which meant, third, I could get us some . . . supplies."

"Supplies?"

"Blankets. Food. A candle or two." He almost sounded shy. "I didn't want our date to end. I thought maybe we could keep talking . . . until the sun came up."

"You're lying."

He pulled the rope again in warning.

"Fine. So what happened? Why didn't you bring the supplies?"

"Do you remember my saying that Tommy, Dickie, and Harry were making a point of watching your mother dance?"

I nodded.

"Well, it didn't hit me at first, but when I heard the music for your mother's dance, I just knew they were up to something."

I let this information sink in before saying, "And?"

"I ran straight there"—he paused for a moment—"but I was too late."

I huffed loudly. "That's a pretty convenient story."

Suddenly, with a big yank, my body flew into the air. My arms flailed, hands grasping for the ropes, but Grady was in control now.

I spun uselessly in the air.

"Did you hear the first part of that story at all?"

I didn't answer, just made another sudden grab for the ropes.

Grady yanked me again.

"Did you?"

"Yes, I heard you."

"What did I say?"

"Why?" I asked, spinning in another circle. "Is there going to be a test after?"

"I would like to know, once and for all, for my own peace of mind, that you heard me. Now what did I say?"

I grumbled something nasty before saying, "You said that you were planning something . . . nice."

Strangely my body lowered a few inches. I looked down at Grady.

"Go on," he said.

"That you were gathering blankets, food, and candles for us."

My body eased a few feet lower this time.

"And why did I do that, Erica?"

"Supposedly because you wanted to spend some more time with me."

"Supposedly?"

"I'm sorry," I said, shaking my head. "I'm keeping my *supposedly*."

The rope lowered me further down. My feet dangled inches away from Grady's head.

"And why, Erica?" he asked, voice much lower. "Why did I want to spend more time with you?"

I paused, chewing on my lip.

"Erica?"

"Because it was a good night," I mumbled.

"I'm sorry, I couldn't hear that."

I resisted the urge to kick the hat off his head.

"One of the best!"

The rope lowered me the rest of the way down, and I landed, body mere inches away from Grady.

"You were listening," he said.

I looked up into his blue, blue eyes. My heart beat painfully in my chest.

"I really mean that, you know."

Then his face lowered toward mine.

The deafening hum of insects filled my ears.

It was finally going to happen. I was going to kiss Grady Forrester.

He licked his lips and whispered, "And I am sorry. It was stupid and immature and wrong to take your clothes."

My lips were feeling the magnetic pull of his, but I knew I had to say something first.

I owed it to him.

"I'm sorry too. I guess . . . I never really thought you were in on it."

I closed my eyes and inhaled deeply. Oh, that felt good. I really needed to say that. Now, I could enjoy this kiss. I leaned forward with my lips puckered . . . and hit nothing but air.

My eyes flew open.

Grady had pulled back. "What did you say?"

"I . . . I never really thought you were in on it," I said, scanning his face. "Well, maybe at first. But then I wasn't sure."

Grady walked back a few more steps. "Then why wouldn't you talk to me after?"

"I was leaving," I stammered. "And it all just felt like too much."

"Too much," he repeated, planting his hands on his hips.

I stared at him, trying to figure out what exactly was happening here. "Yes. You, my mother, this place. The social. It was all too much."

Thick silence fell between us for a moment.

"And you didn't think I'd want to know that?" Grady was nodding, but the nod was increasing in speed.

"I, uh . . ."

"I've been feeling guilty all this time!" He had gone

from nodding his head to shaking it back and forth. "Thanks a lot, Erica."

"Wait—what?" I tilted my head.

"Oh, yeah," he said, head back to nodding. "You know, just because I'm a guy, it doesn't mean I don't have feelings."

"What are you even talking about?" I shouted. But I was suddenly feeling a little guilty. I never did really stop to think about how Grady felt that night. Given that I was feeling that way, it was pretty funny that the next thing I said was, "Freddie was right. You do have issues."

Grady let out a shout. "Me! I have issues?" he exclaimed, eyes bugging. "Look. I understand growing up at the retreat, it might leave you with some . . . it might leave you weird. And I kind of like your weird . . . but even so . . . you . . . you can be pretty hard on people."

I scoffed.

"Yeah," he said, nodding. "Do you know how bad people felt about that night? About the way they overreacted about the whole Betsy thing? That's why they keep bringing it up. Not because they feel sorry for you."

I planted my hands on my hips. "Now you're just talking crazy."

"Yeah. They put it all together pretty quickly, but did you give anyone the chance to apologize? Nooo."

"I—"

"No," he said, putting up a finger. "I'm not done. While we're on the subject, did you ever stop to think that maybe you have some responsibility in what happened?"

"What!"

He was still nodding. "Your mother is a big girl. And while you haven't come to terms with who she is, the rest of the town, well, they have," he said, spreading his hands wide. "You . . . we both should have just let those three pull their stunt."

My jaw dropped. I struggled to pull it back up enough to say, "Are you being serious right now?"

His eyebrows shot skyward, and he nodded quickly.

Suddenly I spun and blazed a path toward the forest.

"Erica!"

I whirled around for a brief second, and before I even realized what I wanted to say, I shouted, "What about Candace?"

"What about Candace?" he shouted back.

I stomped back over to him. "Why are you having all of these touchy-feely conversations with me, when you are dating her?"

"I'm not dating Candace."

"Oh, please. She thinks you are," I said, folding my arms over my chest. "And you left me in the water—again, I might add—to have drinks with her!"

"That wasn't. I wasn't . . ."

Grady looked nervous, but not in a cheating-guy kind of way.

Then it hit me.

"Oh my God," I said, covering my mouth with my hand.

Everything was tumbling together. It was all so clear. It all made sense. I pointed a shaky finger at him. "You . . . you think she did it too!"

Grady's eyes got very wide.

All my angry feelings started to boil off into happy rainbow bubbles.

"You do! You think she killed Dickie!"

Grady's jaw flexed. "I have no idea what you are talking about."

"Oh, but you so do," I said, jumping, still pointing at

his chest. "I knew it! Well, I didn't know that you knew it! But—"

"Erica, stop," Grady said, holding out a hand. "You have no idea what you are talking about."

"No, really, this is great," I said, laughing. It really was. I knew I wasn't crazy. Or at least not supercrazy. "I mean, it's not. It's still terrible. But it's also a little bit terrific. That's why you were spending all that time with her. We should totally pool resources. If you show me your evidence, I'll show you mine. Ha!"

He pointed a finger at me. "Erica, I'm not going to tell you again . . ."

I stopped jumping for a moment. "Stay out of it. I know. I know," I said as seriously as I could. "But this is so exciting!"

"I'm leaving."

Grady brushed past me headed back to the retreat.

"Grady, wait!" I shouted to his back. "Don't go! I have to apologize!"

He didn't bother to turn around. "I don't want your apology."

"But I was wrong!"

He didn't stop walking, but he did call out, "About the social?"

"Not the social! Well, maybe the social. I don't know. Jeez. But no! About you!" I shouted to his departing form.

"What about me?"

"You're an awesome sheriff!"

I woke up with a start. Last night had changed everything.

I hadn't realized just how much it had been bothering me that jealousy might be the reason behind my suspecting Candace. But no, Grady had proven it. My instincts about Candace had been spot-on.

I had to get going. There was lots to do.

I was on the right track. And I needed to hurry.

One more day.

Coming up with a plan to trap Candace into confessing to murder was proving difficult. Maybe Freddie was having better luck. I had to tell him about Grady anyway.

I reached for my phone, but let my hand drop midway.

He had been pretty snarky the last time I called him in the morning. I looked over at my clock. The fishing frog was pointing to seven.

I couldn't wait any longer! I had to do something.

Maybe Candace confessing wasn't the only way out of this mess. There was still Tommy. Maybe I could reason with him. He was in danger. The best thing he could do would be to come forward . . . if he hadn't been in contact with Grady already. Either way, I needed answers.

Right then my dried-out phone croaked like it had a cold. At least it was working. I glanced at the number.

Candace.

Crap, she was on to me. I just knew it. But I couldn't let her know, that I knew, that she knew, I was on to her. I sighed. My life was a Monty Python skit. But hopefully it was one that didn't end with me getting murdered.

"Hey Candace," I said as brightly as I could.

My forced glow was immediately dwarfed by the cheeriness of the sun. "Erica! How are you? I got your message. Thanks for that."

It took a second for my brain to catch up. Oh, yeah, the cabin. Nope, I still didn't want her going there. "No problem," I said, rubbing my brow.

"I'll still have to run over there today to check it out, but you bought me some time."

"No," I practically shouted. "Don't do that!"

She paused. "I'm sorry?"

"I mean, you're still so busy with the social, and I've got nothing but time." I needed caffeine. I couldn't think quickly enough. "If you're worried, I'll go over there again today. In fact, I'm heading out right now!"

"Oh my goodness," she said slowly. "You found something there yesterday, didn't you?"

"No!" I shot back. Dammit, sociopaths were smart.

"Erica, no. You need to stop." I could practically see her blond curls shaking back and forth with fake concern. "It's one thing to go around town asking a few questions, but I talked to Grady last night. He told me how serious this could all be for you."

She had talked to Grady last night? Man, he was really on the case. "I swear, Candace, I didn't find anyone."

"Anyone?" she practically shrieked. "Shut the front door, you found Tommy, didn't you?"

"No!"

"Don't go back there, Erica," she said firmly. So firmly, she didn't quite sound like herself. "It could be danger-ous."

This was bad, bad, bad. I had just told Candace, aka the killer who wanted Tommy dead, where he was hiding out. Tommy could get killed because of me!

"I gotta go." I hung up quickly and threw my phone onto the bed like it was hot.

I wrestled my way out from the bedsheets.

I had to warn Tommy!

"Damn it, Freddie!" I yelled into my phone. "Call me back!"

Branches whipped against my body as I ran the trail to the cabin. I nearly broke the speed barrier crossing the lake, thanks to Freddie's boat, but I still wasn't sure if I'd make it in time. Candace was already on this side of the lake.

My chest heaved trying to suck in more air. My body didn't seem to get the fact that this was life or death. I stopped and rested against a tree, blinking my eyes a few times to clear the spots.

I could do this. Tommy was a jerk, but he wasn't going to die because of me.

"Go! Go! Go!" I shouted, launching myself forward.

I spotted the cabin through the trees. I slowed my run until I stopped completely at the edge of the clearing. I thought about calling Grady, but I didn't have his number. I then thought about Rhonda, but I had lost the card she had given me. I was a terrible person. I had already debated calling 911, but they would ask, *What is your emergency?*, and I couldn't figure out how I could answer that without sounding crazy. I didn't think 911 sent out emergency vehicles for well-founded hunches.

I looked over the abandoned-looking cabin as the soft hum of insects filled my ears.

All still.

There was nothing to do but go forward.

My feet took slippery steps over the muddy ground as I crept forward. Suddenly I stopped.

Dammit! Why did I always forget to bring a weapon?

I searched the forest floor and decided on a good-sized stick.

Armies of invisible chipmunks scurried around me, setting my nerves even more on edge.

I padded up the cabin steps, and peeked in the window. My eyes went straight for the couch. No Tommy, just a crumpled-up sleeping bag. But something looked wrong about the whole scene. It took me a second to piece it together. An old TV tray now stood by the couch and from what I could see, a single piece of white paper lay waiting on top of it.

Crap.

I should probably just leave it and go home. Tommy obviously wasn't here, and Candace could show up at any time . . . with more than a stick!

But there was a piece of paper.

A piece of paper that might have something written on it.

Waiting for me.

I placed my hand on the wood of the cabin door and gave it a small push. It swung right open. Well, that settled it. I was going in.

I stepped over the threshold, my eyes scanning the room for hostile raccoons.

Nothing.

I took a step forward, and then another, cringing at the sound of my own footsteps. I made it halfway across the room before I noticed the blood.

My eyes focused on the paper, spotted it there first. The page was smeared with something red. I then looked to the floor. It was hard to see with all the dirt, but there were smears on it too, and fat red droplets.

My heart thudded painfully in my chest.

I palmed my phone as I crept toward the piece of paper.

Yup, definitely a bloody smear, vaguely in the shape of a handprint. I tiptoed around the table to read the handwritten scrawl. Even I knew better than to touch the paper.

I squinted at the blood-covered words.

Screw all y'all. I'm out.

What?

What the heck did that mean?

A racket of noise rushed me from behind.

"Erica Bloom!" a voice shouted. "Drop the stick, and put your hands in the air!"

Chapter Eighteen

"Where's Grady?"

Rhonda hooked her thumbs into her belt and rocked on her heels. "Why do you ask?"

"Because . . . I . . . look, Rhonda, Grady kind of let something out of the bag last night. And I don't want to get him in trouble, but it would kind of explain why I'm here."

Rhonda narrowed her eyes. "Is there something wrong with your eyebrows?"

"Why?" I asked with a nervous chuckle.

"They just jumped in the air, twice, really quickly."

Law enforcement officials of all kinds swarmed around us in the tiny cabin. Their numbers had grown since Dickie's death. Outside powers must have started taking notice.

I leaned toward Rhonda. "I was trying to . . . you know . . . give you a *wink wink, nudge nudge*."

Rhonda considered me for a moment then asked, "Ms. Bloom, have you taken any drugs within the last twenty-four hours?"

I leaned back and threw my hands in the air. "No, Rhonda."

" 'Cause you're acting kind of funny," she said, rocking a little on her feet.

"No drugs."

"Ms. Bloom, I believe you were told to stay out of this investigation."

"Okay, but Rhonda. I'm kind of on the inside now." I glanced about the room to see if anyone was listening to our conversation. "And I was worried about Tommy."

"And how exactly did you know that Tommy was here? And what exactly had you so worried about Tommy that you had to rush over here at . . ." She looked at her watch. "Quarter to eight in the morning?"

I smiled, but I felt a little sick to my stomach. "Maybe you should ask Candace that." If we had any hope left of finding Tommy alive, we needed to stop wasting time.

Rhonda crossed her arms over her chest. "All right Ms. Bloom, I'll play. Why would I ask Candace?"

A new thought suddenly hit me. "She called you, didn't she? Told you I was here?"

Rhonda turned silent.

"I knew it! She's setting me up, you know."

Her eyes narrowed. "What are you talking about?"

"What did she say to get you here?" I said, pacing a half circle around Rhonda. "That the alarm went off?"

Her eyes narrowed even more.

"She wanted you to find me here," I said, stopping suddenly and spreading my hands wide. "Surrounded with all this blood."

"Ms. Bl—"

"Rhonda! Call me Erica!" I shouted. "I'm sorry about the Dawg!"

She straightened up and rolled her shoulders back,

thumbs looped in her belt. "Ms. Bloom, I should warn you that I have been trained to do on-scene assessments of a person's mental stability."

I closed my eyes briefly before meeting her gaze once again.

Rhonda made a V with two fingers then pointed them at her eyes before swinging them around to me.

"I'm not crazy! Well, no more than anyone else around this lake."

"Okay then. So, let me get this straight. Candace is trying to frame you for whatever happened here," she said, scanning my face. "Except we have no evidence that Tommy . . . that something happened to Tommy except for that note."

"You and I both know that Tommy never would have resorted to suicide. He likes himself way too much for that."

Rhonda nodded her head a second before snapping back to her angry cop face. "Then why the note? If she did something to Tommy . . . why leave a suicide note?"

"I don't know." My hands flew in the air. "Maybe she was trying to make this look like a suicide, and things went wrong."

"And let's back up here, for a second." Rhonda paused to lick her lips. "Why exactly do you think Candace is the murderer in the first place? Everyone around here likes her . . . everyone but you."

Well, me *and* Grady. I couldn't help but wonder why Grady hadn't filled Rhonda in on his suspicions, but then again Rhonda wasn't exactly good at keeping her suspicions to herself. Maybe he didn't want to tip Candace off. "Well, Rhonda, I'm certainly not jealous if that's what you're implying." I said, willing an immediate stop of all blood flow to my face.

"Are you willing to come back to the station and take a polygraph on that, Ms. Bloom?"

"Rhonda, you don't have a lie detector machine," I countered.

"So that's a no?" she asked, scribbling away on her notepad.

I didn't bother answering.

"But if it's not jealousy, what is it?"

I opened my mouth, but no sound came out. How did I answer that question? I was starting to believe I should tell Rhonda everything I knew. What the ladies had discovered about the development company. Tommy paying for his boat in cash. Even the part about spying on Tommy through his Webcam. Sure, that last part might be illegal, but it couldn't be like superbad illegal. But again, it seemed Grady's call whether or not to bring Rhonda in.

"Rhonda—"

Suddenly a new voice entered the mix. "Stop!"

The cabin door banged open.

In it stood Freddie, once again wearing Doc Martens, Hawaiian shorts, a shirt, and an overcoat.

"Not another word, Erica!"

Rhonda's head whipped around.

"You get away from her, Rhonda Cooke."

"Freddie Ng, this is a potential crime scene," she said. "You need to leave. You're probably stepping on blood."

Freddie looked down. "Ew. Gross." He slid the bottom of his boot a few times against the arm of a worn-out chair before looking up again. "Fine. I'll leave, but unless you're going to arrest her, she's coming with me."

Rhonda met my eyes. She paused before saying, "I should detain you for questioning."

Freddie jumped in again. "Go ahead, Rhonda, but if

you do, know that I'm hiring her the best lawyer money can buy! Like right now."

She flicked a look at Freddie before turning back to me. "You'll need to give a statement sometime in the next twenty-four hours."

I nodded.

Neither one of us moved for a moment. She still had me pinned in her gaze.

"Erica! Come on!"

We both turned. Freddie was halfway out the door.

"We still on for beers next Tuesday?" Rhonda shouted to him.

"Wouldn't miss it!" he shouted back.

I took one last look then hurried past Rhonda to catch up with Freddie, who was already disappearing into the woods.

"Hey!" I called out to him. "Freddie! That was pretty badass!"

He raised one fist into the air and vanished behind a tree.

"So Grady didn't actually say that he thought Candace was guilty?"

I growled my frustration. "Freddie, I'm telling you! It was the look in his eyes."

"Uh-huh."

"No uh-huh. You should have been there!"

"If I wanted to watch a train wreck, I'd turn on *National Geographic*."

I furrowed my brow. "*National Geographic* shows train wrecks?"

"You weren't supposed to probe that too deeply."

"Sorry." I sighed and leaned back in my chair. I didn't know how to convince Freddie about Grady, so I decided to drop it, temporarily. "Okay, so what do you want to show me?"

Light rain hit against the windows of Freddie's office as thunder rumbled in the distance. Another dismal day. We had come straight back here, made a plate of bacon, and settled ourselves down in front of the computer.

"Are you sure you don't want to talk more about Grady?"

"Actually, you wouldn't believe the other things he said last night . . . Oh, you were being sarcastic." I should have picked up on it sooner given that Freddie's eyes had rolled so high up into his head that his eyelashes were flickering. "You go."

"Okay then. I found a way to record Tommy's Webcam," Freddie said with a satisfied smile. "So we don't miss anything."

"Seriously? You are a genius, but . . ." Thoughts raced through my mind.

"What?"

"I was trying to think if I saw the laptop at the cabin this morning." My mind's eye ran over the memory. "I think we're good. It's probably best the police don't know we are . . . or maybe were . . . spying on Tommy."

"Holy crap. Good thinking," Freddie said, smacking me on the shoulder. "You know, we're getting better and better at this. Maybe we should consider taking on some other cases."

"Yeah," I said, shaking my head. Wait . . . where the heck had that come from? Must have been all the happiness of bacon nitrates hitting my bloodstream. "How about for now, we just focus on keeping me out of jail . . . maybe by proving that Candace is a psychopath."

Freddie rolled his eyes and sighed. "I'll admit that what Tommy said to Laurie—if that even was Laurie he was talking to—could, *could* point to Candace. I'm telling you, though, my gut says she didn't do it."

"Let's agree to disagree," I muttered, all the while thinking, *until I'm proven right.* "But wait . . . so Tommy took his computer with him to commit suicide?"

Freddie looked at his own computer and opened the file manager window. "Well, he has been spending a lot of alone time with it from the footage I've seen, but it does seem unlikely."

"If the murderer, *i.e.*, Can—" Freddie put up his hand to stop me from saying her name. I huffed a breath, but let it drop. "If the *murderer* came to see him though, wouldn't he or she take the laptop, just in case?" Then something else occurred to me, sending shivers racing over my body. "You don't think the Webcam recorded what happened, do you?"

Freddie suddenly looked at his computer as though it might be dangerous. "I hadn't thought of that. It records a new movie file every time the laptop is turned on. I watched the first few, but this one," he said, moving the cursor over a file, "it's new."

We exchanged a questioning glance. A new round of thunder rolled its way toward the cottage.

"We should send this to Grady," he said.

I nodded.

"Should we watch it first though?"

I shrugged sharply. "I don't know."

"It's probably just Tommy watching more porn."

I nodded again.

Freddie's whole body suddenly jumped. "I clicked it! I didn't mean to!" A new screen popped up on the computer. "My finger! It did it by itself."

We watched a small hoop spin on the blank screen of the movie player as the video loaded.

"We could still turn it off," I whispered quickly, leaning in.

"We could," Freddie replied, eyes glued to the screen.

I waited, fully expecting Tommy's face to fill the view. That didn't happen. Somebody else appeared.

Freddie whispered, "Oh my God," right as I screamed, "I knew it!"

A loud crack of thunder shook the windows as Candace's adorably evil face filled our view.

"I told you! I told you all along it was Candace! And you were all like, *Oh, no, my gut says it's not Candace!* Well, take that, gut! It's Candace!"

"Sh! Sh! Sh!" Freddie said, frantically waving a hand at me.

I stopped screaming and leaned in again, trying to listen over the sound of blood rushing through my ears.

We both stared at Candace's concentrated face. It was beyond creepy. It didn't look like a recording. It felt live.

"What's she doing?" I whispered.

"I don't know, but, again, talk normally. She can't hear you, and you're creeping me out," Freddie said before saying, "I think she's snooping around Tommy's laptop."

Candace spoke, and we both jumped. *"Tommy,"* she mumbled. *"Yeah, figures Tommy would leave his e-mail open."* Then the expression on Candace's face changed. Her eyebrows gathered together, and her eyes suddenly looked abnormally sharp, almost shrewd.

"What the heck is this?" she muttered.

We watched her eyes travel the screen from side to side, reading. As she did, her expression changed even more. All the soft, cute curves of her face disappeared, leaving something much more hard and determined behind.

"That son of a bitch!"

I gripped Freddie's arm and shook him. "She swore! I knew it! Everybody swears!"

"Hush!"

I could barely control my heart rate. This was it.

Go on, I willed her. *Give me a little more.*

Candace peeled back her lips, showing her teeth.

She was going to say something.

Freddie and I gripped each other.

"I'm going to kill him."

The clip ended, freezing Candace's face in a crazed expression.

Freddie and I stayed unmoving for a second, hands still gripping one another.

Lightning flashed through the room.

"We have to send this to Grady," Freddie said quickly. "Like now." I was already nodding in agreement.

Surely this had to be enough. While Candace hadn't outright confessed to killing anyone, the clip proved she was at the cabin right before Tommy went missing. Not only that, I thought, eyes flicking back to Candace's demented expression, the video clearly showed she was a maniac.

Thunder cracked above us.

"Hurry, Freddie," I said, slapping him repeatedly on the shoulder. "Then I'll call him."

A bright flash of lightning exploded, making me blink.

Freddie's fingers flew over the keyboard as light and noise ripped through the room.

"Wait . . . what is happening?" he shouted.

The computer made a loud *ZAP!*

"No. No. NO!"

"What?" I asked, watching Freddie jab the power button trying to load the computer back up.

We waited, but nothing happened.

"No!" Freddie slammed his palms on the desk.

"What? What is it?"

Freddie swiveled slowly in his chair to face me. "She's dead," he said, flicking his eyes to his computer.

"What? No! She can't be dead! What happened?"

"Power surge . . . either that or Tommy gave her an STD."

An hour later, we were still sitting in front of the dead computer. Freddie had tried everything he could think of to resuscitate her, but nothing had worked.

"It just goes to show you," Freddie said, shaking his head. "You can't watch that much porn and get away with it."

I slumped even further into my chair. "I thought you said it was a power surge."

"No, my power bar should have protected against that." He kicked it with his toe. "I think someone up there," he said, jerking a thumb toward the ceiling, "has a sense of drama."

"But don't you have antivirus software?"

"I had to lower the protection on my computer to establish the link with Tommy's. I should have known." He gently caressed the side of the monitor. "I should have protected you better. I'm sorry."

"I can't believe this is happening."

Freddie's eyes rolled up as he shook his head. "Even though I hate the thought of all those filthy police hands on my baby, we could still bring the hard drive into Grady. Maybe they can still pull something off it."

"Yeah. I guess." I sighed. "But can I be honest with you about something?"

Freddie smiled and leaned in. "This sounds promising."

"I've kind of had this fantasy where I—I mean, we

solved the crime and slammed down a bunch of evidence on Grady's desk and then I tear out of town."

"Right. Right. Little crazy, but right." Freddie leaned back for a second with a faraway look on his face. Suddenly his eyes snapped to mine.

"What?"

"I just realized something," Freddie said.

"What?"

"You're happier. A little crazier too. But definitely happier."

"Of course I'm happier," I said, crossing my arms over my chest. "It's good to be right."

He shook his head. "No, that's not it."

"Then what is it?"

"You're finally letting your crazy out at a steady rate," he said. "You're flowing with the Otter Lake current instead of against it."

I made a face at him.

He chuckled. "You know it's true. Oh, and I guess maybe I should finally say something else." He paused dramatically. "You were right."

"I'm sorry?" I asked, raising an eyebrow. "I didn't catch that."

"You were right about Candace."

A small smile tugged at the corner of my mouth. "I'm not one to say I told you so."

"I believe you said exactly that . . . a few times . . . while jumping up and down."

"Can you blame me?"

"Nope."

"She did look murderous," I said, smile spreading all the way across my face. "Didn't she?"

"Oh, yeah."

A silence fell over us. It was a lot to process. At times

this had all felt like a game. Then I would remember Dickie and Harry . . . and now Tommy.

"Do you think she killed him?"

Freddie's smile faded with mine. "I don't want to go there yet."

"Me neither."

I got up and walked to the window overlooking the lake. The storm clouds had moved off, but light rain still pattered against the glass. Even on a gray day, the lake was beautiful. Still. Peaceful. Not a soul in sight . . . except for the gaggle of ladies driving by in Red's pontoon.

"Where are they going?" I asked out loud.

"Who?" Freddie replied, still giving his keyboard the occasional tap.

"I guess the women haven't given up investigating." The thought made me nervous, but then again, maybe they were having better luck than I was. That being said, I couldn't take another brainstorming session. I wanted to figure out how best to handle this situation with Freddie alone before I talked to anyone else. "Hey, Freddie?"

"Yeah."

"Do you mind if I spend the night here?"

"Going into hiding, are you?"

I nodded.

"That's cool. We can order pizza and come up with Plan B."

I walked over to the desk and picked up his spare boat keys. "I'm going to run over to the retreat and grab a few things while the ladies are out."

"Sure. If I'm not here when you get back, it's because I'm buying a new computer."

"I'm really sorry about that, by the way."

"Whatever. It will make a good story when I'm a best-selling author."

* * *

A few minutes later, I was speeding across the lake, squinting through the drizzle that didn't feel so drizzly anymore now that it was being driven into my face.

We had been so close!

Now we had nothing . . . and tomorrow was the Raspberry Social.

Right then, I noticed something out of the corner of my eye.

Ever since Laurie had gone missing, I had made it a habit to follow a route between the retreat and Freddie's place that went by Laurie's trailer. It had yet to pay off . . . until today.

I squinted harder through the rain. It was hard to be certain, but it looked as though a woman was running from Grandpa Day's cabin to the trailer. A woman who looked a lot like Laurie.

I cranked the wheel on the boat, fishtailing water.

Laurie was the key!

She knew the truth. If I could get her to come forward, this whole nightmare would be over.

I sped up to the dock, waiting until the last moment to cut the engine. I jumped out of the boat and rushed to tie it to the slippery dock.

She wasn't going to disappear this time.

I ran toward the camper, skidding a few times over the slick grass.

"Laurie!" I shouted, banging on the thin door. "It's Erica!"

I heard someone move inside, but she didn't come to the door.

"I know you're in there!"

The door whipped open, and I stumbled back.

Laurie stood before me. She had the door propped with

her foot and her muscular arms crossed over her chest. I watched her eyes flick around behind me as though she expected to see someone there.

"What are you doing here?" Her voice wasn't welcoming, but then again Laurie's voice was never welcoming.

"Everybody's been looking for you."

"What business is it of yours?"

I wiped the rainwater from my face with both hands. "Listen. Let's cut to the chase. I need you to come forward to the police and tell them what you know about the guys and their deal with Candace's company."

I could see the thoughts jumping behind Laurie's eyes.

She licked her lips, and then said, "How—"

"It doesn't matter. You could be in danger, but then you probably already know that, and that's why you're in hiding."

"Seriously, Erica," she said, taking one step down toward me. "What do you know?"

I wanted to say that I knew that Candace was the murderer, but accusing her out loud still somehow felt reckless. "Look . . . I know that Candace is losing it, and I know that she went after Tommy last night." I licked rainwater from my lips. "And I know that *you know* the guys accepted money from the company to cause trouble around the lake. Am I right?"

She nodded tightly.

"You have to tell Grady."

"No way in hell," she said, jaw flexing. "And listen carefully, Erica, if you're not careful, you're going to get yourself killed."

"Laurie, did you know I'm a suspect? I mean, they suspect Candace too, but—" I cut myself off. I didn't want to get Grady in trouble. He never actually said Candace was a suspect. But I had Laurie here, now! I couldn't lose this opportunity. She could disappear like Tommy! "Laurie, the cops aren't going to care that you guys accepted money from Candace. Not when there's a murderer on the loose. I'll call my uncle. He'll get them to cut you a deal. You tell them everything you know about Candace, and they won't charge you."

Laurie studied my face; then she moved to shut the door. "I'm sorry, but I've got bigger problems."

"Exactly. That's why you need to go to the police! If Candace knows that you know about the deal, what's to stop her from killing you?" I asked, reaching to keep the door open. "Or . . . or! What if Tommy makes a deal with the police first! Then . . . then you could be left with charges of withholding evidence or . . . aiding and abetting. I don't know exactly what charge, but do you want to take that chance?"

I searched Laurie's face to see if I had any hope of changing her mind. All I got back was steel.

"Fine," I said, reaching to my pocket for my phone. "If you won't go to Grady, I'll get Grady to come to you."

She slapped my hand, hard, sending my phone spinning.

"Listen, Erica. I talked to Tommy. He's leaving this rotten lake, and I plan to do the same thing. You may think you're the answer to all my problems, but—"

"I am!" I threw my hands into the air. "Well, not me, but the police!"

She laughed. It was an ugly sound. "The police aren't going to help me."

A voice called out behind us.

"Everything all right there, honey?"

I looked over my shoulder. Grandpa Day. And he had his gun.

"Fine," Laurie shouted back. "She's leaving."

Grandpa Day pushed the brim of his hat up with the point of the gun. Something about his stance looked more threatening today. Laurie had probably told him she was in trouble. I made a sound low in my throat but picked up my phone and turned back toward the dock.

I clenched my fists as I walked.

Fine. She was scared. But the police could help! Unless she had accepted money too. Maybe she was afraid she'd be charged. Or maybe she was just too afraid of being next.

I spun around one last time. I had to try, despite Grandpa Day's itching trigger finger.

"Laurie, please—"

"Forget it! Grandpa?"

I heard the cocking of a gun.

"Don't come back, Erica! I know all I need to know! You don't scare me!"

My shoulders slumped in defeat as I turned the key in the ignition and pulled away from the dock.

Suddenly this day kind of sucked, but I still believed Laurie was the key to clearing my name. Maybe I should still call Grady and get him out here to question her, but she'd probably just stonewall him the way she had me. Still—

A thin ray of sunlight peeked through the clouds.

Wait . . . maybe . . .

New thoughts tumbled through my mind.

Maybe I didn't need Laurie herself. Maybe I just needed the threat of Laurie.

Why hadn't I thought of this before!

I killed the engine and pulled out my phone.

"Freddie?" I said, taking a deep breath. "I think I've got us a trap."

Chapter Nineteen

Raspberries. Raspberries with beaver teeth. They were everywhere. Chasing me—

My eyes snapped open as I jerked up in bed.

"Stay back!" I flung my arms out toward the fifteen or so startled women hovering around my bed.

I slapped my hands over my face and fell back onto the mattress.

It took me a moment to sort everything out. I had planned to spend the night at Freddie's before I remembered his horrible snoring. Unfortunately, I didn't remember that until two in the morning when he woke me up with it. Moving to another floor hadn't helped, so I decided to come back to the retreat with the intention of getting up and out before the women. Apparently that plan had failed.

"Sorry. Sorry," I said, from between my fingers. "Bad dream."

"We understand," I heard my mother say. "It's *the* day."

The Raspberry Social.

Time had run out.

It was here.

I took a deep breath.

I didn't have time for this. I needed to rally. I had real problems, and now that I had come up with a way to trap Candace, I was going to solve those problems.

Time to focus.

Job one was to keep the women off my scent. While they had proven themselves to be terrifyingly useful in many ways, this trap would need subtlety. And I was fairly certain it was a mathematical impossibility for this many people to stay subtle at one time. I just had to figure out a way to separate myself from them without rousing suspicion.

"Honey, we were thinking that maybe you should lay low today," my mom said.

I peeked one eye through my fingers. "Huh?"

My mother's blue ones stared back at me, rounded like some baby animal's. "The entire town is going to be out today, and they'll all be talking . . . mainly about you." She patted my leg.

"Yes," Lydia Morgan added, "but we wanted you to know that we're still on the case."

The birdlike woman, whose name I still hadn't learned, piped up next. "Seeing as it's our last full day, we're going to give it our all. Don't you worry about a thing."

It just couldn't be this easy.

"We thought we might go interview that Shelley person at the Salty Dawg," Maria Franelli said, rolling her shoulders, then tilting her head back and forth. "She's been holding out on us."

While I knew that they were barking up the wrong tree with Shelley, at least that would keep them from barking up mine.

I swallowed and tried to smile away my lies. "That's a great idea, ladies."

The women all gave me pitying looks before turning to leave.

"Be careful though," I said, remembering my bar fight. "Shelley can get a little wild at times."

"No problem, Martha here," my mother said, pointing to a short, compact woman, "knows jujitsu."

The woman jumped into a fighting stance.

"Wow," I said, keeping my eyes on her. "Wow . . . and thank you. Really. Alpha Team, Beta, you guys have been great."

I meant it too. They had been great, but now it was time for the team that was higher than Alpha to take over . . . the Freddie and Erica Team . . . the Über-alpha Team.

Oh, that was good.

I made a mental note to tell Freddie. He might want it for his book.

Two hours later, Freddie and I were gliding across the lake on our way into town. The festivities got started early on social day. Local businesses had to set up their sample booths, covering everything from preserves to ammo; judging needed to get under way for the bake-off, and the speakers needed to be set up for the bands.

A few minutes later, we pulled into the town's tiny marina—if you could call a bunch of docks tied together a marina.

I stepped out of the boat and took in the beauty of the day. The sun beamed brightly, all traces of clouds long gone, and a slight breeze rippled through the cheery red banners lining the town's street.

It was beautiful . . . really. So freaking beautiful I wanted to peel all my skin off.

"Snap out of it, buttercup," Freddie said, in a voice that

sounded like something out of a black-and-white movie. "This investigation needs you."

My feet stayed rooted to the dock. "Freddie, it has been brought to my attention recently that I may have been a little embarrassed by what happened at the social eight years ago. In fact, I may still be a little embarrassed."

"What a truly startling discovery," Freddie said, without much shock at all.

"I know."

"Erica," Freddie said, moving to stand beside me. "Because I'm a really awesome friend, I'm going to give you three choices."

I said nothing.

"One: we can hug this out. You can cry. I'll cry. Then we can walk into town, holding hands while smiling at the haters, blinding them all with our positivity."

"Ew," I said, not taking my eyes off the scene ahead. "What's option two?"

"We turn around, go back to my place, eat a lot of pizza, and mess with people's fortunes on the Internet."

"Except your computer's dead."

Freddie gasped. "I had forgotten. Just for a moment. Now I have to feel the pain all over again." He heaved a sigh. "It's probably better this way. Leaving would mean no trap, and putting your future in the hands of the Otter Lake Police Department."

I sighed. "Okay. What's three?"

"We man up and do this thing!"

Freddie pushed me hard on the shoulder toward the town.

I spun and hit him on the chest.

"Yeah! That's it!" he shouted, pushing my other shoulder. "Hit me again!"

I did, harder this time.

"Yeah!"

I balled my hands into fists and struck out twice more, lightning fast.

"Okay, that's good."

I wound up to hit him again. His hands shot up. "Seriously, stop hitting me now."

"Right. Sorry."

We walked shoulder to shoulder, footsteps echoing underneath the dock, until we reached land.

"So, Freddie, Grady was saying that most of the townspeople felt bad about that night. That they understood what really happened. Is that true?"

"For some," he said with a nod. "In fact, it probably would have been everyone if Betsy hadn't died shortly thereafter."

"She did?"

Freddie nodded again. "Hard to say if it was the shock or the raspberry tart," he added, squinting his eyes.

"Or old age!"

He shrugged.

"But it's not like people talk about it anymore. I mean—"

Suddenly, a boy in a striped shirt, maybe eight or nine, zoomed by screaming and clutching his chest.

I pointed. "That wasn't supposed to be m—"

"And so it begins," Freddie murmured.

"Come on," I said, grabbing his arm. "Let's just get out of here before anyone else sees us."

A little while later, we were crouched in some bushes taking in the scene. We needed to do some surveillance before we launched our attack.

"Okay, so how do you want to play this?" I whispered to Freddie.

"Me?" Freddie asked, shuffling to make more room in the bushes. "How do I want to play this? It's your plan."

"Exactly," I said, pushing down a branch to peek through the greenery. "I'm the big-picture person. You're the details guy."

"I never agreed to that."

I muttered a few unpleasant things under my breath. "Fine. We can sort that out later, but in the meantime, what do we do?" I had been thinking my trap was beautiful in its simplicity, but now I was worried it was just simple.

Freddie didn't answer.

The plan had two parts, and if we couldn't get Part One off the ground, we'd never get to Part Two. And Part Two, well, Part Two was where all of our hard work paid off.

We both stared at Candace's back about twenty yards in front of us at the MRG booth. She was handing out gift bags to the happy citizens of Otter Lake. Beside her stood the man the ladies had shown me in the picture, Bryson Maxwell, head of PR, Candace's boss. He was as handsome as his photo, but I couldn't seem to get past the fact that he actually wore a pink sweater tied around his neck, draped over a white polo shirt.

"We're just going to have to go in," Freddie said suddenly, getting to his feet and brushing the dirt off his shorts.

"Just go in?"

He nodded while ducking from the flight path of a dragonfly. "It will be like we practiced. We'll say the lines loud enough so that she can hear, but not so loud that it looks like we want her to hear."

"What about her boss?" I asked, chewing the corner of my lip.

"That might help. She'll be even more on edge. She won't even see the trap coming. And if we stick to the script, PR Ken won't have any idea what we're talking about."

"Right," I said, getting to my feet. "Go team."

Freddie and I walked a long circle out from the bushes so that we ended up at the start of Main Street by the water. This way it would look like we were walking the strip and coming across Candace by chance.

Unfortunately, the small street was already filled with people, all of whom seemed to be either looking, pointing, or talking about me.

"Stop drawing attention to yourself," Freddie whispered. "You'll blow our chance!"

I stopped in my tracks and glared at him. "What would you have me do, Freddie?"

"Well, you could stop looking so freaked for one. It's like blood in the water," he mumbled out of the corner of his mouth. "Go offense."

"Offense?"

"Make them uncomfortable with their rudeness."

I looked at him blankly.

He sighed. "Here. Watch. I call this the old school." He took a few steps then stopped abruptly, fixing his narrowed eyes on two middle-aged men, who had, up until that moment, been staring at my chest, laughing. Freddie took a deep breath and boomed, "What are you looking at?"

The men started and turned away.

Freddie smiled and resumed walking.

"I also have what I call the George Takei phaser stare and the Corporal Klinger Section 8—I like retro TV—but you need to develop your own style."

I shook my head. "I don't know if I can do this."

"Where's the Erica Bloom who liked to bite first-graders on the shoulder? Pin people up against walls with bar chairs? Get mad!" he said, giving me a shake. "Where do they get off making you feel this way? Make them uncomfortable!"

I looked around at the many familiar faces of people

walking by . . . all looking at me. I took in the sight of teenaged girls snickering and clutching at one another, the men of all ages elbowing their friends' ribs as I walked past, and the church group glaring at me, disapprovingly, from their baked-goods stand. Suddenly, it was more than I could take.

I stopped and flung my arms out wide, accidentally smacking Freddie.

"What?" I screamed to the crowd, trying to look at everyone at once. "You want another look!"

Everybody on the street froze, then backed away slowly, giving me a circle of space.

"Is that it? 'Cause I'll do it!" I didn't even realize it at first, but my hands were pulling up the bottom of my shirt. "I'll—"

Freddie shuffled to my side and yanked my arm. "That's good, Erica. We're good."

"Too much?" I let go of the fabric clutched in my fingers.

Freddie nodded. "Let's keep going."

"I went offense."

He patted my hand. "I know. Remember: steady stream of crazy."

"They're just boobs."

"I know."

We resumed walking.

Luckily, it only took a few minutes before everyone was back about their business. Even better, no one was taking the chance to look at me again, helping Freddie and me appear to be two friends simply enjoying a small-town event.

"Okay, approaching target in less than a minute."

I glanced at the MRG stand. It was packed. Those must be some pretty awesome gift bags.

Candace, at first, looked her normal sunny self, leaning over the counter in her yellow sundress to tie a balloon to a stroller, but on closer inspection, I couldn't help but think her smile was a little strained, and I noticed slight bags underneath her eyes.

"Got your lines?" Freddie asked under his breath.

"Got 'em."

"Let's do this thing."

We strolled toward the booth.

"This is perfect," Freddie whispered to me. "She's talking to Dr. Reynolds now. Let's ease into position."

We edged our way through the crowd until we stood right at the counter beside the doctor. Candace spotted us and clearly wanted to end things with the good physician, but he was not one to be easily put off. The sound of his talk reached my ear. "So he's holding his sawed-off thumb in the other hand, and he says, I know I don't have an appointment, but . . ."

I tuned out of the doctor's conversation and looked at Freddie, who had the first line. Now was the perfect time. Why wasn't he speaking?

Go! Freddie mouthed.

You go, I mouthed back.

I noticed Candace staring at us, a confused look on her face. I held up a finger to her, and mouthed, *We'll be right back.*

Freddie and I hurried out of earshot.

"What are you doing?" Freddie whispered.

"Me? You were supposed to go first."

"No! We're doing version two!"

"No! We agreed version three was better!"

We argued for a few more seconds before coming to an agreement.

"Now are we ready?" Freddie asked.

"Let's go."

We casually strolled back to the booth for a second time.

"So we sewed the thumb back on right there in the office," Dr. Reynolds said to Candace, who was still nodding politely but pushing the gift bag at him. "He doesn't have any movement in it, but at least it didn't go gangrenous."

I looked at Freddie. "They're finishing. Go."

"So Laurie said she has evidence proving who the murderer is?" Freddie said, voice loud, but not too loud.

"Yeah, she said to meet her alone behind the giant raspberry tonight at nine." I snuck a glance at Candace. Her body still faced the departing Dr. Reynolds, but her posture was rigid. She was totally listening.

"Tonight at nine?" Freddie repeated.

"At nine."

"Behind the giant raspberry?"

"Behind the giant raspberry."

"All alon—"

I slapped Freddie in the belly. The speech had sounded more subtle last night over beers.

Candace made a move toward us, and was just about to say something, when her boss sidestepped her with large strides, hand outstretched to me.

"And you must be Erica Bloom."

I shot a confused look at Freddie, but accepted the handshake.

"I'm sorry," he said, putting his free palm over his gym-ready chest. "I'm Bryson Maxwell, head of PR for MRG Properties."

"It's nice to meet you," I said slowly. "But how do you know who I am?"

He was already nodding in a polished way before I even managed to finish the question. "Candace, here, provided me with a briefing package on this town's lovely event, and it included archival photos of the horrible practical joke that was played on you and your mother so many years ago."

I looked again to Freddie. "There are archive photos?"

"In the library," he said, shrugging. "Town history."

"May I say," Maxwell said, recapturing my attention, "that you are even more stunning today, and far more on the right side of legal consent."

My eyes widened at the handsome plastic face in front of me.

Candace jumped in. "He's joking, Erica," she said, placing a hand on Bryson's shoulder. He shrugged her off.

"When I'm making a joke, Ms. Bloom here will know it because of all the laughing she'll be doing."

Candace shrank back.

"Now, Ms. Bloom, I'm only in town for a short while, read one night, but I would love to spend this evening with you as my guide." He smiled and spread his hands wide. "What do y—"

"Well, hello there," a male voice interrupted. "I don't think we've met."

Suddenly I felt Grady brush against my shoulder. He reached out and offered his hand to Bryson. The head of PR grasped it, and the two men froze, mid-handshake . . . smiling at one another.

I looked back and forth between Grady's and Bryson's face. It was hard to tell what was going on exactly . . . or who was more beautiful. Then it hit me. They were trying to figure out the same thing. They were having a smile-off!

"Mirror, mirror on the wall," Freddie said quietly.

The men released their grip.

"Grady Forrester, Sheriff."

Bryson snapped his fingers. "I recognize that name too from the archives. You won Otter Lake's Most Beautiful Baby Contest three years in a row. Quite a feat, that. Must have been hard to figure out where to go after such an achievement."

Grady held his smile, but it twitched at the corners.

"And weren't you also there the night when poor Ms. Bloom was put on display?"

Grady stood as frozen as a statue.

"You'll have to clear this up for me," Bryson said with an exaggerated thinking expression. "Ever since I heard about that little story, something's been bothering me."

"And what's that?" Grady asked in a low voice.

"Why didn't any of the good men in this town rush forward to offer Erica a coat? A jacket? Shirt off their own backs? The poor girl had to run huddled off the stage in rubber pants."

I found myself nodding vigorously.

"It seems bizarre to me that no one came to her rescue."

Grady cleared his throat in a way that sounded an awful lot like a growl. "Erica was up there only for a moment."

I had to nod again . . . less vigorously.

Bryson nodded in agreement too for a few beats, before switching directions and shaking his head side to side. "I guess there's never a hero around when you need one."

I cleared my throat. "Um, I really don't need a hero."

"Of course," Bryson said, right as Grady said, "Exactly."

"And really, it wasn't a big deal," I said. "My chest is not a big deal."

Neither jumped to agreement that time. Jeez, you'd think I'd had nuclear weapons hidden in my bra.

A silence fell over our little group.

Someone needed to break the tension.

"Well, it's been great seeing everyone. I'm Freddie by the way," he said to Bryson with a filthy look. "Not that you cared to inquire." He then pulled at my arm. "Come on, Erica. Time to go."

I didn't move right away. I kind of wanted to see how this whole thing was going to play out.

Freddie leaned his mouth to my ear. "Our work here is done."

"But . . . but," I said, stumbling backward as Freddie pulled harder.

"Erica!" Bryson called out. "I certainly hope to see you this evening."

I faked a smile until I saw Grady make some pretty angry eyebrows at Bryson's words. Then I smiled for real.

I spun awkwardly on one foot to walk forward with Freddie.

"Why did we have to go?" I asked. "Things were just starting to get good."

"I know," Freddie replied. "Grady looked so jealous."

"So why did we have to leave?"

"Erica, haven't you figured it out by now? No matter how hard we try, we are always just one step away from ruining everything."

"Good point."

"Let the preparation for Phase Two begin!"

The preparation for Phase Two mainly involved taking a nap.

Freddie and I had been up late the night before planning, and we needed to be fresh. I thought for sure I wouldn't be able to sleep, but I was wrong. I woke up at seven, drool pooling on my pillow.

Showtime.

I had some trouble picking out an outfit. I didn't want to be too hot. My trap-a-murderer nerves were already making me sweaty but, at the same time, part of me felt there weren't enough clothes in the universe to protect me from walking into that damn social. I settled on jeans and a T-shirt—not too tight as to remind people of what was underneath, not too loose as to tempt the wind to blow it off. It could happen . . . especially to me.

An hour later, Freddie showed up, and we set off for town.

As we made the final turn toward the marina, I was nearly brought to my knees by the sight before me.

"My God," Freddie said. "I think Candace upped the wattage."

The giant raspberry looming over the town lit up the night sky like a fallen sun.

I found myself unable to peel my eyes away from the massive fruit god. "I didn't think Otter Lake had that kind of power."

"That is one epic berry."

"Pull in over there," I said, pointing to an abandoned dock covered with low tree branches. "I don't think I can walk through the crowd again. Let's go through the woods."

Freddie and I trudged through the bush toward the meeting point. We needed to get there early to set up. Despite the equipment we were carrying, and the ungodly amount of bugs, Freddie and I kept our complaining to a minimum.

Minutes later, we made it into the shadow of the festival's mascot. While the berry looked almost alive from the front, from the back, it was simply an enormous amount of scaffolding, with thick, wire cables anchoring it to the ground.

Freddie glanced at his watch. "Twenty minutes. Anything we need to go over?"

"I don't think so," I replied, chewing on a nail. "You don't think she'll bring a gun, do you?"

"She hasn't gone after anyone else that way. Why would she change her MO now? Besides, if she tries to shoot you, I'll call the police right away."

I swatted a mosquito buzzing at my ear. "Thanks."

"There's still time to back out."

"No. We're doing this thing."

I meant it too.

There was part of me that simply wanted to prove my innocence and fulfill my evidence-on-the-desk fantasy, but something else was pushing me on. Something I hadn't expected. It bothered me that someone was terrorizing Otter Lake. Sure, Tommy, Harry, and Dickie, God rest his soul, were . . . were something else, but they were Otter Lake's people, my people. Candace couldn't blow into town, hurt its citizens, and get away with it. She was going down.

"And you're sure that thing," I said, pointing to the cone listening device Freddie was pulling out of his backpack, "will be able to pick up the sound of our conversation from up there?" I flicked my eyes up to the scaffolding.

"Absolutely. This thing can pick up a conversation from a mile away." He waggled his eyebrows. "And it conveniently connects to my phone."

"Again, it really worries me that you just happen to have this equipment on hand."

"Stop judging me. I'm lonely." He gathered all his equipment in his arms and headed toward the scaffolding. "Speaking of which, in case you die tonight, I want you to know that it's been really great having you home."

"Thanks, Freddie. And in case you die, I want you to know that you're the best part of Otter Lake."

Freddie scoffed. "Who said anything about *me* dying?"

Nineteen minutes later, I stood alone in the gloom of the giant berry.

Every few seconds, I glanced up to the scaffolding to make sure Freddie was still perched on the same wooden platform with his equipment ready.

I could do this.

I didn't know how, exactly, I was going to get Candace to confess to being a murderer, but that wasn't going to stop me from trying. I did bring a prop that I hoped would get the ball rolling. I squeezed the empty manila envelope in my hand.

I glanced at my watch.

Five after nine.

I looked up at Freddie and shrugged with my hands out.

He made a dismissive, shooing motion. He probably didn't want me to give his position away.

A horrible thought suddenly occurred to me.

What if Candace hadn't heard our conversation? She looked like she had been listening, but what if she couldn't hear us over Dr. Reynolds's stories of backroom surgery?

Then, an even more horrible thought occurred to me.

What if she had heard and had come up with a counterplan? What if she was in the woods right now . . . watching me . . . waiting for the perfect moment to strike!

I jumped as a branch snapped behind me.

Oh, God! Candace!

Wait! I wanted it to be Candace . . . didn't I?

I spun to face the threat.

A small breeze chilled the sweat on my brow.

Yup, someone was in the woods. Walking toward me.

I clenched my manila envelope, suddenly wishing it were a nightstick or nunchuk. Why did I never think to bring a weapon?

I looked over my shoulder up at Freddie. His eyes were zoned in on the forest like some freaky cat.

I swiveled my head back.

Frick. Whoever it was, was getting closer.

Closer.

Closer.

"Grady?"

Chapter Twenty

"Erica, there you are."

Grady broke through the clearing. Seeing him in jeans and a T-shirt jarred me for a moment. I had gotten used to either seeing him in his sheriff's uniform or nearly naked in the water.

"What are you doing here?" I asked. "Shouldn't you be working?"

"I do get nights off," he said with a smile. "And I was looking for you."

"How did you know I was here?"

"One of your mom's guests tipped me off. She saw you and Freddie getting out of his boat and heading into the forest. Those women seem to have the entire town under surveillance." He tilted his head. "You wouldn't happen to know anything about that?"

"Not a thing."

He smiled again. "Anyway, that's not why I'm here."

"So why are you here?" I asked quickly. "And, more importantly, when are you leaving?"

His eyes narrowed. "Why exactly are *you* here?"

"Um . . . you helped me realize that I was, um, severely traumatized by the social, so Freddie and I decided to spend the night back here, watching from the wings." I gave myself a mental high five. That was some quick thinking on my part.

"Where is Freddie?"

"Getting beer." I was on a roll. "Now go. You're going to ruin it." I grabbed his arm and tried to lead him to the front of the berry. There was a makeshift dirt path he could take back to the tents. "You're part of the trauma."

"What's that in your hand?"

"Nothing. Stop it. You're horrible."

He looked at me, confused puppy-dog expression on his face. "Um . . ."

"What?" I asked, eyes searching the forest behind him. "What do you want?"

Grady moved his face inches in front of mine. "Okay, so listen. I feel bad about our conversation at the ropes course. I mean I get why you did what you did. She's your mom."

"She certainly is that," I muttered.

"And I could see how the whole thing might have been a bit much."

"Good. Good. Now good-bye," I said, giving him a gentle shove.

He planted his feet. "But I also realized something else."

"Ooookay," I said, suddenly suspicious of where this was going.

"I know what the problem is between the two of us."

I cocked my head. "And what's that?"

"This town."

"Wow . . . wow . . . Grady, that's deep," I said, trying once again to push him on his way. "But seriously . . ."

"No, hear me out. Otter Lake is a small town with a long memory. And you're right. What happened shouldn't be a big deal, but in small towns, small deals can become legendary. And it's hard to shake the past."

"Well . . . thank you for your concern," I said, trying to sound natural. "But don't worry. I am totally focused on the present. The here and now! Screw the past."

He lowered his hands onto my shoulders, his very warm hands. "Please stop and listen to me."

I made a frustrated noise, but forced myself to look him in the eye. Maybe if I listened, he'd say what he needed to say and get out.

"Subconsciously or consciously—"

"Suddenly everybody in this town is a freaking psychologist!" I couldn't help but shout, but he plowed on.

"—part of you associates me with that night. And I meant it when I said everybody, well, practically everybody, feels bad about how they reacted that night, but the problem is that it's still a good story. And that's embarrassing for you, *and* it puts distance between us."

Suddenly the frustration I was feeling fizzled out with the realization that he had really put a lot of thought into this. You could even say a sweet amount of thought.

"But I now know how to fix the awkwardness between us." He took a few steps back, and his fingers were moving to grasp the bottom of his shirt.

Suddenly my throat felt tight. "What exactly is happening here?"

Grady swept off his shirt in one smooth motion.

I glanced quickly up at Freddie. His eyes and mouth had widened to three shocked circles.

"Grady, what are you doing?"

"It's time Otter Lake had something else to talk about on social night," he said, tossing his shirt to the ground.

My eyes moved over his bare chest. "You can't be serious! You're not thinking of . . ."

His fingers moved to his belt buckle. "Oh, I am."

His jeans dropped to his feet.

"Really, Grady, it's—"

He interrupted me with a hand. "Where did I put . . . oh! There it is." Somewhere within the pile of clothes, he found a wool hat and put it on his head. "How do I look?"

Before me stood the most beautiful man in the universe wearing only boxers and a knit hat.

"Um . . . good," I said. "But I don't think this is really—"

"Now, I know what you're thinking." He hooked his thumbs around the waistband resting snug against his hips. "And I'm gonna lose them. I plan to cover the front, but the back? That will be for all to see."

"Isn't this illegal?" I stammered.

"Who's going to arrest me?"

"Grady, I'm not sure this . . . I mean, you don't have t—"

He stopped me again by holding up his hand. "Yes I do." He turned and headed for the path that led to the social. "Afterward, we'll talk."

"Um . . . okay." I scurried forward a few steps, but stopped when he reached the edge of the berry, his tall dark form haloed in light.

This couldn't be happening.

But it was.

I watched him straighten his shoulders and take a breath.

I swallowed, holding mine.

Then . . . his boxers hit the ground.

Chapter Twenty-one

"Erica."

I heard the voice but couldn't be bothered with it.

"Erica!"

The voice hissed at me again with enough venom to snap me out of my dream state.

I looked up to Freddie. "What?"

He jabbed a finger toward the other side of the berry. "Someone's coming!"

I heard the rev of an engine from the direction Freddie was pointing. Then I watched headlights illuminate the trees as a truck slowly angled its body around the outermost scaffolding.

I shielded my eyes from the harsh glare.

A second later, the engine died. I heard the truck door open and then shut.

I blinked my eyelids a few times.

Candace.

She hurried toward me, still wearing the yellow sundress from that afternoon, but she also had a purse. A big purse. Big enough to hold a gun.

"Erica, thank God."

"Candace," I said with what I thought was just the right amount of gravitas.

"I'm so glad you're okay." She moved her purse so that it hung down in front of her, making it easily accessible to both hands.

"Why wouldn't I be?"

"Listen, I heard you and Freddie talking today," she said, taking a step toward me. I took a step back. "Something about Laurie giving you evidence? I was worried you might be in danger."

"Might I, Candace?" I asked, raising a brow.

She turned her head to look at me sideways a moment before continuing. "You don't know everything that's going on. I would have told you earlier today, but my boss was right there."

"Tell me now, Candace," I said. "Tell me everything."

"Have you been drinking?"

"No! I . . . I'm just emotional." I shuffled my feet. This confronting a murderer was harder than it looked in the movies. I suddenly felt very awkward, like I had an extra arm or something, and I didn't know where to put it. "What with it being the social and everything." This social trauma everyone was so wedded to was really coming in handy.

She nodded. "Listen. Did Laurie come?"

Ah! Now I knew what to do with my body parts. I held out the envelope. "She did. She gave me this."

"Good."

My eyes narrowed. "Is it good?"

"You're doing it again," Candace said, squeezing her purse.

"Doing what?"

"Repeating back everything I say in the form of a question."

"Am I . . . I mean, I'm sorry." Heat flooded my cheeks. I obviously hadn't found my stride with this thing yet, but I was getting there.

"You're starting to freak me out," she said.

"I said I'm sorry!"

She gave me a look, then asked, "Have you opened it yet?"

Hmm, I hadn't prepared for that question. If I said yes, she might freak out and kill me. If I said no, she might not confess to anything, just make a grab for it. I didn't know what the right answer was, but I did know that Grady would be back soon, and I'd lose my chance to get this confession.

"Candace, the jig is up," I said, hoping I sounded tough.

She tilted her chin up and to the side while looking at me with big, confused eyes.

Oh, she was good. So very, very good. I pressed on. "I know it was you who killed Dickie."

"What?" Her hand flew to her chest.

"I know it was you who attacked Harry."

"Erica!"

I strode toward her. "And what have you done with Tommy?"

She stumbled back.

"Oh, stop it," I said. "You don't fool me."

"I . . . I thought we were friends."

"We are! I mean . . . it's all right here," I said, smacking the envelope against my palm. "In black-and-white."

Suddenly her lip quivered. "You are really starting to hurt my feelings."

"Ha!" I shouted. "You don't have feelings!"

"Erica, I'm going to call your mother," she said, reaching into her bag. "I think you're having some sort of stress-induced break with reality." She dug further into her purse. Oh, God, what if it wasn't a phone she was reaching for?

"Drop it!" I screamed, cowering a little. "Don't shoot me!"

Candace brought out her cell so that I could see it, while at the same time allowing her bag to fall to the dirt.

"Is this about Grady?" she asked, softly.

"Grady?" I straightened back up. "What? No!"

"I knew it the moment you said you were fine with us dating," she said with a sad nod. "You weren't fine."

Oh, God, this was about to get awkward. "This is not about Grady."

She crossed her arms over her chest and shook her head. "I should have been more sensitive. I thought we were good, but with Grady and I spending more and more time together, well, I don't think I really appreciated the effect it was having on you."

"This is not about Grady!"

"I should apologize," she said, pursing her lips with decision.

"Please, no. I don't want to feel sorry for you," I pleaded. "Not when I'm about to take you down."

She raised her hands in a defensive posture. "Easy, Erica."

No. No. No. This was going all wrong.

"Listen," I said, taking a breath. "I have evidence. I know that you were paying Tommy, Dickie, and Harry to cause trouble around the lake so that the townspeople would be more likely to sell."

She closed her eyes. "You're right."

"I am?" I flicked my gaze up to Freddie to make sure he was getting this. He gave me a thumbs-up.

"Not about me, personally, but about the company." She sighed heavily. "I just found out. I went to the cabin the other night. I know you said everything was fine, but I had to do my due diligence. I saw that someone had left a laptop there. I turned it on so that I could figure out who it belonged to and return it." She paused, inhaling deeply. "And when I opened the browser, the e-mail came up. It was Tommy's. I was going to shut it off, but I saw something in his in-box."

"What?"

"An e-mail from Bryson's secret account."

"If it's secret, how did you know it was from him?"

"It said it was from James Jones, but the e-mail address had the handle ThisGuy! She shook her head again. "He has the same thing on the license plates of his Porsche."

For the first time, an uneasy feeling began to grow in my belly. I think it might have been doubt, but I wasn't about to take a second look to be sure.

"Anyway, he basically admitted that he had paid them to cause trouble. He also threatened Tommy."

"You swore though!" I said, pointing at her. "You were mad, crazy mad!"

Thoughts traveled over Candace's face. "How do you know that?" she asked, furrowing her eyebrows.

"Not telling."

She narrowed her eyes. "I was mad. I've worked long and hard on this development. I love the people of this town. I couldn't believe he would do that. I wanted to kill him." She sucked back some air. "I've prayed about it since then, though, and I'm in a much better place."

I folded my arms over my chest. "Why didn't you go to Grady with this information?"

"I wanted to give Bryson the opportunity to turn himself in. It seemed the right thing to do. And then I heard you saying that Laurie might have evidence . . . and I'm still not sure who the killer is."

Suddenly, I wasn't sure if I did either. "You don't think it was Bryson?"

"No, he's greedy and mean," she said, shaking her head, "but those guys wouldn't be worth it to him. And Bryson isn't stupid. He wouldn't leave any traces behind for something as serious as a murder."

"No, no. I don't believe it." I put my fingers to my temples. "You didn't want me in your place! You went out of your way to stop me!"

"I told you, it was messy! And I didn't have snacks!" She was actually starting to sound a little angry herself.

"Seriously?" I asked, dropping my chin. "Come on now."

"I like to be a good hostess!"

"This can't be right." I had a real sinking feeling that I might be a bad person after all. "So then if you didn't do it, and he didn't do it. Then who did it?" I asked, still trying to think all of this through.

"I don't know," she said, looking at me carefully. "There's no chance you could—"

"No! I didn't do it!"

"Then who?"

A new voice joined the mix.

"I did it."

Chapter Twenty-two

Laurie Day.

I turned to see Laurie behind me, anger carving deep lines in her face. Had she always looked so crazy? Yes, yes, she had. But I had refused to see it, instead opting to lay the guilt on a cute pair of dimples.

My eyes flashed back to Candace. She looked even cuter scared, what with her big round eyes.

Then something caught the corner of my eye.

Freddie.

His mouth was moving frantically, mouthing something over and over. It looked a lot like *I told you so!,* but it was hard to be sure. Thankfully, he was also rummaging through his bag. I knew he was going for his cell.

All three of us had heard Laurie confess. Now, we just needed to live long enough to tell someone.

"Erica," Laurie ordered. "Go stand by Candace."

I licked my lips. "Laurie—"

"Save it, Erica. There's nothing you can say now." She pulled a gun out from the back of her jeans.

Maybe there wasn't anything left for me to say, but that wasn't about to stop me. I needed to stall.

"None of this makes any sense," I said, shuffling over to stand beside Candace with my hands up. "Why do you care about the guys taking money from the development company?"

"I don't," she said, motioning me closer to Candace with the point of her gun. "Other than the small fact that Dickie was supposed to use his cut of the money to buy me a ring. You know what he bought instead? Four paintball guns and a snowmobile with the Tasmanian Devil airbrushed on the hood."

"Then why would you want to kill all three of them?"

"I didn't want to kill *them*," she said as though I were an idiot. "I wanted to kill Dickie, and I did."

"Over a ring?" I asked.

The tendons in Laurie's neck rippled. "I wasted way too many years on that lying, *cheating* bastard."

I sucked some air through my clenched teeth. Ouch.

Laurie's eye twitched.

"I can't believe I didn't see it before. Here we were going all big picture, and it was you, staring me in the face the entire time." I paused to lick my lips. "You chopping that chicken should have tipped me off. Nonmurderers, they don't chop that way. Not with that kind of gusto."

Suddenly a female scream sounded in the distance. Oh man, Grady must have reached the tents. What had taken him so long? More importantly, how long would it take him to get back?

Laurie's eyes moved in the direction of the festival. She must have heard the scream, too.

Now was my chance to risk looking at Freddie again to see if he had gotten through to the police.

When my eyes found him, he was lying on his belly, straining his fingertips toward the platform below.

What the hell was he doing?

Was that his phone?

Oh my God! He had dropped his phone!

I let my gaze fall back to Laurie.

"Erica, move away from Candace."

My heartbeat thudded painfully in my ears. Stalling was still my best bet. "You told me to stand beside her."

"And now I'm telling you to move away."

I stood my ground. "Why?"

She planted her gun-free hand on her hip. "Remember how I told you the other day that if you weren't careful, you were going to get yourself killed? Well, you should have listened."

"Wait!" I shouted, dropping the envelope and putting my hands up. "I gotta know! Why Harry? What did he ever do to you?"

She smiled. "Don't you remember? He came to the retreat that night? Pretending to be sympathetic with his big bag of weed. He knew something. I could tell. Those three told each other everything." Her smile disappeared.

"Or he was trying to be sympathetic!" I shouted.

"But he wouldn't die," she continued, ignoring me. "That's why I had to be more careful with Tommy. Go big or go home."

"Oh!" I pointed at her with frantic speed. "That was you that day slapping Tommy around in the bedroom . . . and . . . and you blew up my boat!"

"I snuck around to the water while you and Tommy were in the front. I had actually planned to blow up Tommy's boat. "Made one of those nifty magnetic bombs you just snap on. Had it all ready to go. You see, I was going to blow up his old boat, so it would look like an accident, but I confused your old hunk of junk for his. Can you believe that? Too much hurrying, I guess."

I scoffed.

Candace placed a warning hand on my shoulder, but I ignored her. No way was I going to be led like a lamb to the slaughter. I had to keep stalling.

"That's when I got the idea of blaming it all on you. Poor, crazy Erica, coming back after all these years to exact her revenge. It was brilliant."

"Yeah, brilliant," I muttered. "Hey! That was you running around town naked burning all the flyers!"

"Enough. Stand over there." She motioned to a spot a few feet from Candace.

"No."

"Move!"

"Erica," Candace said softly, "don't make her any more angry."

"Forget it," I said, rubbing my feet into the ground. "She's staging a freaking crime scene! She's going to shoot you, and then shoot me in the head to make it look like some murder-suicide! And I say no! Move the freaking bodies yourself!"

"You don't have a choice!" Laurie shouted. "I have the gun!"

"You're going to kill me no matter what! Why would I make it easy for you?" Spittle hit my chin.

Laurie straightened her back and leveled the gun at my face. "Fine. I should have known you were useless . . . just like your mother."

"Really?" A familiar feeling churned in my belly. "You want to go there?"

She smiled.

Oh, yeah. It was time to go there. "It's on!"

I charged Laurie. She didn't shoot. The look of surprise

on her face told me she wasn't expecting me to launch a shoulder into her belly.

We hit the ground hard, stunning us both.

The gun! I had to get the gun!

Laurie stretched the weapon over her head while I clawed my way up her body.

A moment later, we were rolling. Rolling toward the scaffolding of the giant raspberry.

With each rotation, I scanned the structure for Freddie. Finally, I got a glimpse of him. He was scampering back and forth on the platform. We were headed straight for him, and I could tell he didn't want to make a run for the built-in ladder and leave us.

We stopped when we crashed into a two-by-four.

Laurie was pinned underneath me, but she still held the gun.

"Give it up, Laurie!" I yelled, between gritted teeth. "You can't stage a good enough crime scene to get away with this!"

She stared back at me with crazy eyes, all the whites showing. Then her forehead rocketed toward mine.

I pitched to the right to avoid the vicious head-butt, losing my leverage over her.

I scrambled back on my hands and feet until I hit a plank of wood.

Laurie was already getting to her feet, gun still pointed at me.

"You're done," she said.

Oh, God! This was it!

I squeezed my eyes shut.

But instead of a bang, I heard a battle cry from above.

I cracked an eye open to see Freddie's form sailing through the air, hands outstretched in giant claws.

Yes! He was going to take her down! She couldn't stand up to his weight! She'd be—

He missed.

Freddie hit the ground . . . a foot or two shy of Laurie.

"Freddie!" I screamed, scrambling over to him.

I put my hands on his back, which still, thankfully, was heaving up and down.

"You monster," I said, snapping my face over to Laurie.

She shook her head. "You two are something else." She leveled the gun again. "Bye, Erica."

"Erica!" a voice shouted out. "I really tried to go through with it, but I ran into Mrs. McAdams. Kind of startled her and—" Grady suddenly appeared from the path at the side of the berry. "What the hell is going on here?"

Chapter Twenty-three

All of us looked over to Grady, his lower regions barely covered by the hand clutching his boxers.

Laurie cursed and swung the gun toward him.

"I'm going to ask one more time," he said slowly. "What the hell is going on here?"

"We solved it," Freddie called out, gathering himself up into a seated position. "Laurie's the murderer."

"What?" Grady looked at Laurie, then Candace. "No, that's not right. Candace is the murderer."

"What?" Candace shrieked.

I looked over to Candace, but I couldn't quite meet her eye. I cleared my throat and said, "As your friend, I was going to tell you—"

"Oh, jeez," Grady said, eyes flashing to Candace as the wheels in his brain gave a turn. "I mean—"

"Yeah, Erica thought the same thing," Freddie said, jerking a thumb in my direction.

Candace charged our group, completely ignoring Laurie. "So the entire time we were dating, you thought I was the murderer?"

"Dating?" Grady's eyebrows shot up. "You thought we were dating? Oh, no. I am so sorry. I never meant to give you that impression."

Candace's eyes bugged. "How can you say that? We had lunch! We went out for drinks! You did all that smiling at me!"

Freddie nodded. "Yeah, he does that."

"I was investigating," Grady said, looking a little sheepish. "My smile always has been both a gift and a curse."

"This is happening," Candace said, clutching at her hair. "This is *really* happening."

"I thought you knew," Grady said, offering her an awkward pat on the shoulder. "All those things I told you about Erica? I kind of have this thing for her that I can't seem to shake."

"Aw," Freddie said, elbowing me in the ribs.

Laurie cleared her throat. "Well, now you can die with her."

Candace shook an angry finger at Grady. "No! No. I don't want to hear this from you right now."

"Is anyone even listening to me?" Laurie shouted. "The murderer with the gun?"

"I am," Freddie replied. "I have always found you fascinating."

A gunshot shattered the night.

Once she had our full attention, Laurie brought the gun down from the sky and swung it around at each one of us. "I've had it! I'm going to kill you all now, if for no other reason than to shut you all up!"

Freddie and I clutched one another.

"Laurie," Grady said, taking a careful step toward her with one hand up, the other still clutching his boxers. "You don't want to do this."

"No. I think I do. And I'm going to start with you," she

said, finally settling her aim on Grady. "It makes sense that Erica would kill you first."

I took a breath and pried Freddie's hands off me. I couldn't let this happen. I slowly got up to my feet. My first instinct was to tackle her, again, but I was afraid the hit would make the gun go off.

"You'll never get away with this," Grady persisted.

The muscles on Laurie's arm rippled. "You never know. I think I'll take my chances with your idiot police department."

"Put the gun down!" a new voice called out.

All eyes shot to the woods. Now who was here?

A figure marched through the break in the trees, gun drawn, aim focused on Laurie.

Rhonda! Where had Rhonda come from?

"It's over, Laurie," Rhonda said. "Backup's on the way. You're done."

Laurie spun to point the gun at her. "You're not going to shoot me."

"Oh, really?" Rhonda's tongue darted to the corner of her mouth to dab at what looked like some raspberry filling. " 'Cause I'm feeling kind of shootie."

"Shootie?" Freddie whispered to me.

"And bangie," Rhonda added with a quick jump of her eyebrows.

Freddie buried his face in his hands. "We're all going to die."

Seconds boomed by as the two women faced off.

Suddenly Laurie fired a wild shot in the air and sprinted to the side.

She was getting away!

I jumped to my feet, and took off after her. She was running for the trees to the side of the berry. I was already losing her in the kilowatt glare. Suddenly, the black silhouette of a giant butterfly flew out of the brush feet away from Laurie.

"Mom?"

I skidded to a stop, floored by the sight. I had never seen something so fluttery look so enraged. But that didn't change the fact that Laurie had a gun.

"Mom!" I shouted. "No!"

She launched herself at Laurie, her silky caftan rippling around her body as she flew through the air. Her outstretched arms slapped around Laurie, tackling her to the ground.

I sprinted toward them just in time to hear, "No one! No one threatens my daughter!" She quickly straddled Laurie with strength I didn't know she had, pinning Laurie's arms with her knees. "Do you hear me?"

"Mom," I said, struggling to catch my breath. My eyes widened when I saw her hands wrapped around Laurie's neck. "It's okay. You got her. The police can handle this."

"I'm not sure she heard me," my mother growled back through gritted teeth.

"She did. She heard you," I said, placing my hands on her shoulders. "You can let go of her throat now."

"Wow," a new voice at my shoulder said. "I didn't think she had it in her."

My head twirled around. "Tweety?" This was getting ridiculous. "What the—"

"So the apple got it from the tree after all," Kit Kat added, waddling toward our little group.

"Where did you two come from?"

Kit Kat's eyes stayed focused on my mother, but she answered, "We came with your . . . what do you call them? The Omega Three . . . Six . . . or Nine sisters?" She jabbed her thumb back.

I looked to the forest. All the women . . . all the women

from the camp were filtering out of the trees. "What, is the entire town going to show up next? Whoa, Mom!" I had forgotten momentarily that my mother was still strangling Laurie. "Rhonda? Little help over here!"

My mother tilted her face around, her big eyes meeting mine. She blinked a few times. "I'm strangling her, aren't I?"

"Little bit."

My mother pulled her hands away from Laurie's throat. "I don't know what came over me," she said, taking a breath. "Although, in the wild, the mother is the most dangerous of animals."

"Uh-huh," I said, helping her get to her feet as Rhonda ran up and planted a foot on Laurie's abdomen.

"I think it was the realization that you were in actual danger," my mother continued, watching Rhonda lead Laurie away. She was jerking against her cuffs, but she seemed to sense it was over. "You see, I've been having a hard time believing this whole murder thing, but the women were having such fun. To be honest, I even wondered once or twice if you were making the whole thing up for attention, like when you were a kid."

"Attention?" My brow furrowed, hard.

"You know, like when you used to bite all those kids," she said, blinking her big eyes, "so that I'd spend more time with you?"

"Mom—"

Freddie suddenly stepped in front of me. "Ms. Bloom, may I say your caftan is lovely tonight, and the matching headband? Very Rambo-esque."

"Thank you, Freddie. It's so nice to see you. I—"

Freddie spun me away before my mother could finish. Two squad cars edged around Candace's truck, illuminating the happy crowd of women rushing toward us. Rhonda handed Laurie off to another officer.

Freddie and I were swept up by the ladies to gather around our hero.

"And that, my friends," Rhonda said, looping her thumbs around her gun belt, "is how you apprehend a murderer."

We all turned to watch the squad car's door slam, trapping Laurie inside.

"How did you know?" I asked.

"Well, I can't take the credit for that," Rhonda said. "Freddie here called 911." Freddie smiled and waved his phone in the air. "Once I got the call," Rhonda said, chest swelling to pop her badge forward, "I dropped my pie and, well, you know the rest."

I nodded.

"And once we saw Rhonda heading for the berry, we just knew you were in trouble," Susan Anderson said. The woman who cried every day now had happy tears in her eyes.

I suddenly remembered something. "But what about Tommy? We need to question Laurie!" I took a few quick steps toward the squad car. "He could still be alive! We need to help him!"

"Oh, he's alive all right," Grady called out, walking over, boxers now on. "I meant to tell you. He showed up at the police station looking for protection."

"From Laurie?"

"No. From the development company. He thought " Grady paused to flash a sideways look at Candace before lowering his voice. "He thought Candace and the development company were killing everyone to shut them up. He tried to stage his own suicide to throw them off his trail."

"But all that blood?"

"Yeah, he was trying to make it look legit and cut a little too deeply," he said, shaking his head. "He's at the hospital now with Harry, who is awake, by the way, and doing much better."

"I told you from day one Candace didn't do it," Rhonda said, turning on Grady. "But you were still investigating her, weren't you?"

Grady shrugged almost sheepishly.

"Some people's bosses," she whispered under her breath.

I smiled, looking around at everyone. "I don't even know how to begin to thank all of you."

"No need," Lydia said, planting her hands on her hips. "I think I speak for all of us, when I say this retreat was exactly what we needed. You see, I was starting to believe my ex that maybe I was boring. Now, I know that's the furthest thing from the truth. I owe you, *Dr.* Bloom."

I laughed weakly. "Lydia, my mother and I are really sorry if we somewhat intentionally gave you the wrong impression about what I do for a living. We—"

She held up a hand. "Your mother tells me she's hired a licensed professional starting next week. That's all I need to know. In fact, I think the less said the better."

"But really, I want you all to know how grateful I am for your help," I said, trying to meet everyone's eyes. "Rhonda, if you hadn't have shown up when you did . . ."

"No sense going there," Rhonda said, again hiking up her police belt. "It took us a while to find you guys. I'm just glad we made it in time." Rhonda turned to look at Grady, still half naked. "You should really keep your phone on you."

Grady smiled, and the women let out a collective sigh. He then trotted off in the direction of his clothes.

Freddie leaned in closer to me to whisper. "So what do you make of that whole streaking-the-festival business?"

"I . . . I have no idea what that was all about."

"Issues," Freddie said, nodding.

"Seriously, right?"

"But I think his heart, if not his ego, might be in the right place." Then Freddie smacked me on the shoulder.

"What?"

"Go to him," he said dreamily.

I furrowed my brow. "Weren't you the one who said we should stay away from each other?"

"Oh, you totally should. There's no way it's going to work out. But this here is a moment. I love moments."

I didn't need to be asked twice. I jogged over to Grady, who was lifting one foot into his pant leg. He stopped to look up at me.

I suddenly didn't know what to say. "So . . ."

"So," he replied.

"That, uh, turned out well."

"All things considered. I'd say so, *Dr.* Bloom."

"Yeah, it's an honorary title." I shoved my hands deep in my pockets and rocked back and forth on my heels. "So you ran into Mrs. McAdams."

"Uh-huh. She was the one who caught you too back then, right?"

"Yup."

"I thought she looked a little like she had seen a ghost. That's when I realized I probably hadn't thought this whole thing all the way through."

I looked away to squint into the headlights of a squad car. "Probably not."

We both paused for a beat.

Finally, I made a clicking sound with my tongue and said, "I think I might owe you an apol—"

Grady held up his hand. "I've been thinking about that thing you said about the dog going back to sniff the spot?"

I nodded.

"I think maybe you were on to something," Grady said, leaning toward me. "We don't seem too great at talking."

All sorts of squishy things were happening all over my body. I couldn't tear my eyes from his lips, moving quickly toward mine. Finally, I felt the heat from his breath—

"NO!"

Grady and I jerked back.

Candace stomped toward us like the maddest sunflower ever.

"This is not okay!"

Grady and I exchanged *uh-oh* glances.

"You two don't just get to kiss like it's some happy ending to the Erica and Grady story!"

"Candace," Grady began, "I really am sorry for—"

"For what?" she screamed. "For making me out to be an idiot?"

"Well, that's a little harsh. You're not an id—"

"Aw, you're worried about my self-esteem. How sweet." Her hands flailed above her head. "A second ago you thought I was a murderer!"

I cleared my throat. "Candace—"

"And you!" she said, turning on me with a wicked pointed finger. "I have been nothing but nice to you! All while you were being a total b—"

"Hey," I shouted before dropping my voice. "No need to swear."

"In fact, I have been nothing but kind to this entire town!" she said, turning to face everyone.

"I was on your side the entire time."

My jaw dropped as I spun to look at Freddie. "No you weren't!"

"Well, I was . . ." he said. "Right up until the end there."

Candace let out a scream of frustration.

"All I have done is care about this town! Worry about

how change would affect its citizens! I've been fighting my douche of a boss for weeks! And that!" she screamed, pointing at the back of the giant berry. "Do you know how many weeks I had to lobby for the company to pay for that? I even chipped in some of my own money."

"Aw, honey," Kit Kat said. "You shouldn't have done that."

Tweety nodded. "It's a little much."

"A little much," Candace said, shaking her head back and forth. "A little much," she repeated. "A little much?" she screamed. "You people suck! I was trying so hard to be nice! But you know what? You don't deserve nice!" She spun on her heel. "That's it!"

"Candace?" Grady called. "Where are you going?"

"I've had it!" she screamed. "I'm taking back my rasp-berry!"

We all exchanged confused glances as we watched her get in her truck and rev the engine.

Grady and I ran after her.

"Candace!" Grady waved his arms above his head for her to stop. She didn't cut the engine, but, after a moment, she unrolled the window. "You're not going to do anything crazy, are you?"

"Crazy? Me? Oh, that's rich," she said, gripping the wheel. "No, unlike every single one of you wack-jobs, I'm not crazy. I'm going to go to the transistor and turn off the power. It's costing me a fortune! You people can light up your own damn social!"

"Um, Candace," I said, stepping forward a little. "I'm not sure you should be driving. You seem a little upset."

"Do I, Erica? Do I seem a little upset?"

Suddenly the tires spun . . . in reverse. Candace's eyes widened in surprise as the truck launched backward.

Everyone screamed as the rear cab plowed into a set of

wood beams that anchored the giant raspberry to the ground.

Earsplitting cracks filled the air as wood splintered.

Then everything stopped.

The only sound that remained was the steady thrum of the still running engine.

"Candace!" Grady yelled, rushing forward. "Are you okay?"

Her pale face nodded from behind the windshield.

"Turn off the truck, and get out very slowly," he ordered.

Candace nodded again then followed his instructions. Once she was out, we rushed over to the rest of the group before turning back to see the damage. The truck had destroyed at least a third of the wood scaffolding.

"It's okay, right?" my mother asked in a whisper.

"I think so," Grady muttered. "It looks stable."

"I didn't mean . . . I mean . . ." Candace put her hand to her chest. "I didn't cut corners. It should be fine."

"It's okay," Freddie said. "We're good."

A deafening metallic *PING!* tore through the air.

A support wire snapped.

PING!

Then another.

The one side of the berry began to lean forward toward the festival tents.

Everyone screamed.

"The town!" Freddie yelled. "The berry is going to flatten the entire town!"

Chapter Twenty-four

"Okay, so I might have jumped the shark with the whole 'the berry's going to flatten the town!' thing," Freddie said, waving his hands in mock terror.

We sat on a dock at the town marina watching the sun come up. I looked over my shoulder at the giant berry, the very top corner bent in, just a touch.

"Nah, I really thought it was going to go too," I said, taking a sip of coffee from a paper cup.

"Leave it to Candace to nail the details," Freddie replied. "Did you notice she requested to give her statement at the station? Guess she didn't want to hang out."

"Yeah, I actually tried calling her about an hour ago to apologize. She's already blocked my number." I sighed. "It's too bad. I like her so much more for losing it like that."

"She blocked me too," Freddie said, staring out at the water. "But don't worry. I'll Facebook her."

I nodded.

"All things considered, though, we did an awesome job solving this murder," Freddie said. "I'm seriously thinking we should make a business out of this or something."

I scratched my forehead. "You know we didn't actually solve the murder, right?"

Freddie turned to look at me. "But it wouldn't have been solved without us."

"Huh, you're right," I said, splashing my toes in the water. "It's practically the same thing."

"Practically, exactly."

"So, I haven't even asked you how the book is going," I said, watching the sun break the horizon. "Have you written anything?"

"Not yet." Freddie stopped to take a sip. "But I've spent about five hours on the Internet looking up stuff, and I came across a formula to name private detectives. It works every time."

"Okay."

"First you pick a four-letter boy name, and then, for the last name, you pick a tool."

"Seriously?"

Freddie held up his fist. "Jack Trowel. Abel Saw. John Rake," he said, adding a finger with each name.

"Huh."

"You try it."

"Um, okay, Jeff . . . Hose."

Freddie's hand dropped, his expression a mixture of confusion and disgust. "Way to ruin it." He sighed and looked over his shoulder. "Uh-oh, here comes trouble."

I turned to see Grady walking down the main strip toward us.

"How is it possible for him to look that good after being up all night?" Freddie asked. "Sometimes I hate him."

"Me too."

"And sometimes you looove him," he said, bumping me with his shoulder.

"You think I should go over?"

"I've decided it's probably best to stay out of it."

I got to my feet, picking up my shoes in one hand.

"Oh! But I forgot to tell you," Freddie said. "You missed it, but Kit Kat and Tweety had a go at Grady when you were being questioned."

"Huh?"

"Oh, yeah, they were listing all of their crimes, trying to get him to arrest them."

"What?"

"Yeah, I heard Tweety, or it might have been Kit Kat, yelling 'Take me in, Sheriff! I've got a pocket full of dollar bills'! Then she chased him for a bit, trying to shove the money in his pants."

"Oh, that's fantastic."

"Yeah, the paper might have even gotten a picture," Freddie said happily. He then looked up at me, shielding his eyes with one hand. "So what are you going to say to him?"

"I don't know," I said, inhaling deeply. "Maybe I'll ask him if he wants to have coffee . . . maybe . . . maybe in Delaware."

A few hours later, my mother and I were standing on the porch with the last handful of women getting ready to leave for the airport. I closed my eyes and inhaled deeply. It was a perfect late-summer day. Hot, but not humid. Only a couple of cotton-ball clouds dotting the sky. Air heavy with the smell of cedar and maybe a hint of apple. Just perfect.

Susan Anderson came up beside me to take in the view. We watched some teenagers in the distance water-skiing. "I always wanted to try that."

I nodded. "You'll have to come back next year."

"Will you be here?"

"You never know. I've been thinking I should visit more." I was a little surprised to find that I really meant it.

She gently squeezed my arm. "Your mother would appreciate that."

I nodded then watched as she rolled her suitcase toward the porch steps.

Then a new voice spoke, grabbing my attention. "Now don't you let that sheriff get away." I turned to meet Maria Franelli's peacock-shadowed eyes. "Men like that don't just fall off the truck every day."

"We'll see," I said with a laugh. "It's complicated. I live in Chicago."

"Honey," she said. "I'd move to the moon for the chance to see that man naked."

My mother cleared her throat.

Maria cringed. "I'm kidding. I'm kidding." She turned to face my mom. "I no longer make any life decisions based solely on my relationships with men." She turned back to me and mouthed the words, *I'm lying. Right to the moon.* She then simulated a rocket taking off with her index finger.

I smiled and watched her follow Susan down the steps toward the gravel path.

Suddenly an arm linked through mine. Lydia Morgan.

"Lydia," I began, "I really would like to say sorry for what happened on the ropes course and—"

"Bup! I said no apologies. I had a wonderful time." She gave me a quick squeeze then walked toward the steps. After stepping down the first two, she turned back and gently wagged a finger at me. "And maybe you should consider taking some psychology classes. It doesn't take that long to get certified as a counselor in some fields. You might have a knack for it. I get a feeling about these things sometimes."

I scratched the side of my forehead. "Otter Lake does have a way of bringing out people's inner psychics."

My mother moved to stand beside me as we watched the women descend the log steps toward Red's pontoon. He was already moving up the stairs to give them a hand with their suitcases. Once he got them to the mainland, they'd meet up with a driving service my mom had hired to take them to the airport.

After a few minutes, I took another deep breath and said, "Mom, I have to go soon. I want to try to see Harry before I catch the bus." Grady had called with the news that Harry was allowed visitors. Apparently he was already asking about medicinal marijuana, so I was guessing things were pretty much back to normal. "But before I do, I would like to say something."

"Of course, dear," she replied, eyes still on the lake.

"And this may be hard for me, so don't say anything until I've finished."

I felt her snap her gaze over to my face, but I couldn't quite turn to look her in the eye just yet.

"I've realized something," I said, pausing to roll my jaw a few times. "I think . . . I think maybe I've had it all wrong about the women who come here." I stared out at the departing pontoon over the tips of the trees. "I never really stopped to think that when they come here . . . they are at one of the worst times in their lives. Divorce. Death. Serious stuff."

My mother made a noise of agreement, but, as promised, didn't say anything.

I shook my head. "Then they're gone. That's all we really see of them. They go back to their lives, probably just to pick up the pieces and move on."

I paused a moment, trying to collect my thoughts. I caught a glimpse of Caesar sleeping in a patch of sun at the far end of the porch. He almost looked . . . cute.

"My entire life, I never really thought about what

happens to them after they leave." I wrapped my arms around my torso, lightly shaking my head. "For the most part, they're probably just really normal, average people."

My mother cleared her throat. "I'm sorry to interrupt, dear, but I'm not sure I understand."

"I'll get there. Give me a second." I took another steadying breath. "I am more than who I was that night of the social standing on the stage with Betsy."

"Good. Yes."

"And so are they." I gestured toward the boat. "I could have treated them—"

"Honey, you've been under a lot of stress."

I waved that away. "And I realized something else. The women that were here at this last retreat . . . even though their personal lives were in chaos, they still wanted to help *me*." I moved my hand to my chest. "Even though I wasn't particularly nice to them."

I let the words hang in the air. I felt my mother go still.

"And I realized that was all because they wanted to help *you*." I turned to face my mother. "And . . . and that must be because you really helped them."

I saw a sparkle come to her eyes.

"You do something good here, Mom." I swallowed hard. "I'm sorry I didn't see it before."

My mother's thin frame started to tremble. Not quite in an about-to-cry sort of way. It was more like . . . excitement.

"Are you okay?" I asked carefully. She looked near ready to burst, but her lips were pinched shut. "You . . . you can say something now if you want."

My mother lunged forward and wrapped me in her arms. "I knew you were moving home!"

"Wait . . . what?" I asked through her mounds of hair.

"Oh, Erica, I'm so happy," she said in my ear. "I always

knew, if I was just patient, you'd understand . . . you'd get the call to uplift your fellow sisters."

I tried to pull back, but she had me in a vise grip. "How did you get *that* from . . . what is going on right now?"

"We can fix up your room if you like and—"

I blew a curl from my mouth. "Mom, I'm not moving home. I was thinking I could probably visit a little more. Maybe next long weekend. I've got some vacation time, and—"

"And you can help with the cooking now that Laurie's gone!"

"Seriously, Mom, slow d—"

"Think of the midnight swims and the sunrise meditations!"

"Mom—"

"And what do you think about our hosting a sweat lodge for a group of nudists? A really nice colony contacted me, and I thought—"

"Mom!"

Coming soon. . .

Don't miss the next novel in the delightful
Otter Lake mystery series

Pumpkin PICKING *With* MURDER

Available in September 2016
from St. Martin's Paperbacks